Rosy Thornton grew up near Ipswich and studied law at Cambridge. She stayed on to do a Ph.D. and has been a lecturer there ever since. Rosy lives in a village near Cambridge with her partner, their two daughters and a springer spaniel called Treacle.

MORE THAN
LOVE LETTERS

Rosy Thornton

headline
review

First published in 2006 by HEADLINE REVIEW
An imprint of HEADLINE PUBLISHING GROUP

First published in paperback in 2007 by HEADLINE REVIEW
An imprint of HEADLINE PUBLISHING GROUP

1

978 0 7553 3387 5

Typeset in AGaramond by Palimpsest Book Production Limited,
Grangemouth, Stirlingshire

Printed and bound in Great Britain by
Mackays of Chatham plc, Chatham, Kent

Headline's policy is to use papers that are natural, renewable and
recyclable products and made from wood grown in sustainable
forests. The logging and manufacturing processes are expected
to conform to the environmental regulations of the country of origin.

HEADLINE PUBLISHING GROUP
A division of Hachette Livre UK Ltd
338 Euston Road
London NW1 3BH

www.reviewbooks.co.uk
www.hodderheadline.com

ACKNOWLEDGEMENTS

My gratitude goes to my family and friends (both real and virtual) who read the book in draft and gave me the benefit of their reactions: Mum, Dad and Chris, Neelam Srivastava, Jo Cowley, Louise Fryer, Hilary Ely, Helen Gurden, Alison Priest, Sue and Dave Billingham, Anne-Marie Shiels, Diane Nowell, Charlotte Houldcroft and, especially, fellow Headline neophyte Phillipa Ashley. Thank you to Midge Gillies and Jim Kelly for their invaluable advice about the process. And to all the others who have merely had to listen to me banging on about it endlessly: I am truly sorry. I am also indebted to everyone in the C19 message-board community for their encouragement of my writing in the first place (blame them).

Particularly grateful thanks are due to my editor, Clare Foss, who has borne my shilly-shallying with the patience of a saint, and to my long-suffering agent, friend and part-time psychotherapist, Robert Dudley, who through his critical input transformed the text – not least by pointing out that in the first draft I had made the rookie error of forgetting to include a plot. And most of all to Mike, Fadela and Natalie, who have had to live with me all this time.

42 Gledhill Street
Ipswich
Suffolk IP3 2DA

Mr Richard Slater, MP
House of Commons
London SW1A 0AA

14 September 2004

Dear Mr Slater,

I am writing to you as my constituency MP to express my concern about VAT on sanitary protection. As you know, these essential goods have been subject to a lowered rate of 5 per cent VAT since January 2001, but in my view they should be zero-rated. Mr Singh in my local chemist's tells me that the special 5 per cent rate causes great accounting headaches for pharmacists. For me, the charging of any VAT on sanitary towels and tampons is an unarguable example of sex discrimination. It is also a hygiene issue.

Yours sincerely,
Margaret Hayton.

House of Commons
London SW1A 0AA

20 September 2004

Dear Ms Hayton,

Thank you for your letter of 14 September, raising an issue of concern. Your view has been noted, and I can assure you that I shall be looking into this matter in the near future.

Yours sincerely,
Richard Slater, MP.

42 Gledhill Street
Ipswich
Suffolk IP3 2DA

Mr Richard Slater, MP
House of Commons
London SW1A 0AA

28 November 2004

Dear Mr Slater,

I am writing to you as my constituency MP because I am dismayed about the British government's failure to take steps to implement the EU Emissions Trading Directive, which is to come into effect in most member states in January 2005. The government is planning instead, I understand, to increase allocations of carbon emissions to British power generation and other industries, placing in serious jeopardy our ability to meet Kyoto targets for cuts in greenhouse gas emissions by 2012. Do we want to be among those few European countries which are not keeping pace with staged reductions in emissions? (Us and the Greeks, basically.) It is the future of the planet that we are talking about here.

Yours sincerely,

Margaret Hayton.

House of Commons
London SW1A 0AA

4 December 2004

Dear Ms Hayton,

Thank you for your letter of 28 November, raising an issue of concern. Your view has been noted, and I can assure you that I shall be looking into this matter in the near future.

Yours sincerely,

Richard Slater, MP.

42 Gledhill Street
Ipswich
Suffolk IP3 2DA

Mr Richard Slater, MP
House of Commons
London SW1A 0AA

10 February 2005

Dear Mr Slater,

I am writing to you as my constituency MP to raise a matter of considerable local concern. The zip-wire in the park between Gledhill Street and Emery Street has been broken ever since I moved to Ipswich in September. Not only is this a considerable loss of amenity for the local children who use the park as their main play area, but the older children use the broken platforms from which the wire formerly ran as vantage points from which to 'bomb' the younger ones with twigs, sweet wrappers and other detritus. Only yesterday I had to comfort a small girl who was in tears as a result of such an attack. I hope steps may be taken as soon as possible either to mend the zip-wire or to remove the platforms. I wrote to the borough council about this back in October but have received no reply.

More dog waste bins in the park would also be a highly desirable improvement.

Yours sincerely,
Margaret Hayton.

House of Commons
London SW1A 0AA

16 February 2005

Dear Ms Hayton,

Thank you for your letter of 10 February, raising an issue of concern. Your view has been noted, and I can assure you that I shall be looking into this matter in the near future.

Yours sincerely,
Richard Slater, MP.

WITCH

Women of Ipswich Together Combating Homelessness

<u>Minutes of meeting</u> at Alison's house, 17 February 2005, 8 p.m.

<u>Present</u>: Alison, Ding, Emily, Pat, Pat, Persephone, Margaret

<u>Apologies for absence</u>: Susan

New member

We were pleased to welcome Margaret as a new member of the collective. Emily and Pat T. agreed to redraft the rota for emergency evening and weekend cover at Witch House to include Margaret's name. Alison agreed to go with Margaret on any call-outs for her first few times.

Witch House: current occupancy

Room 1: Carole

Room 2: Lauren

Room 3: [void]

Room 4: Joyce

Room 5: Helen

Referrals for room 3 were considered. The possibilities were (i) Moira, a 44-year-old who has been staying at the Women's Aid refuge since leaving her violent husband, but who finds the noisy child-dominated environment there affects her tinnitus badly, as well as her auditory hallucinations; and (ii) Nasreen, aged 18, newly arrived from Albania via Felixstowe, who has been referred through the Housing Advice Centre, and is currently sleeping on Pippa from Cyrenians's sofa. After some discussion it was decided to offer the room to Nasreen.

<u>News of residents</u>
Joyce is much better since Dr Gould changed her medication, and relationships in the house have been far easier as a result. There has been no repeat of the Coco Pops incident.

At the weekly house meeting, the main issue was still Carole's overuse of the washing machine, and her constant showering after other residents are in bed. Emily and Pat T. led a helpful discussion about the difficulties of living with obsessive-compulsive disorder. On the positive side, it was recognised that since Carole moved in there have been no more arguments about the state of the kitchen.

Mrs Roberston from number 27 has complained again about noisy male visitors late at night. Emily and Pat T. have spoken to Lauren once more about telling the boys to keep the noise down, and explained how vital it is for the future of the project that no money should change hands.

<u>News of former residents still receiving support</u>
We were pleased to hear that Marianne is out of rehab and working part-time at the chemist's.

Angie has gone back to her partner, now that he is out of prison, and they are trying to make another go of it. It was agreed that members of the collective should continue to visit on a weekly basis, provided this can be arranged at times when her partner is out of the house.

Finance

Lauren's housing benefit has finally come through, so there are no current rent arrears.

Ding has completed this year's application for the borough council grant and sent it off; she has also got the forms for the Lottery Fund application, although she reported that this is only available for capital grants or short-term revenue funding.

With her job going full-time and her mum being out of St Jude's and back home with her, Ding said that she wasn't sure whether she could continue to act as treasurer for much longer. Margaret will meet with Ding in the office on Saturday to hear about what the job involves, and may take on the role of treasurer from the beginning of the new financial year. Thanks were expressed to Margaret for this kind offer.

Any other business

We have all been invited to the Rape Crisis Centre social on the 25th; please bring a bottle and something for the pot-luck vegetarian buffet. (Any nut roasts should be carefully labelled, please, after what happened to Judy last year.)

Next week's meeting: 8 p.m., at Pat and Pat's house.

42 Gledhill Street
Ipswich

20 February 2005

Dear Gran,

It was so good to see you out of hospital and back home last week. How did the interview go with that woman (Kirsty, was it?) who you were seeing about being your home help? I do hope you find someone quickly – someone you can really get along with. I know you don't want just anyone coming in in the mornings to get you up, and seeing you in the old Little Mermaid pyjamas that you had when you were twelve. (Though that's me, not you – I don't suppose they had pyjamas for girls when you were twelve, did they?) But, you know, you do need to get someone soon, Gran. It must be very hard, with one side of your body not up to doing a lot, at least until the physiotherapy starts to kick in a bit. What a good thing the stroke affected your right-hand side – I mean, with you being left-handed like me. It's funny that, because Mum's not. It's something I must have got straight from you.

But it does mean you can write – and of course all the other things, like buttons and bras and spreading your Marmite. I always remember we had Marmite for tea at your house, making the toast in front of the fire, we never had it at home, no one except me liked it. I am sorry that this letter seems to keep going off in all directions, but when you said about writing rather than ringing, because of not getting to the phone so well, I thought I'd try to write just as if I was talking to you, and you know I don't think I've written a letter to family or friends for *years*, not since those awful production-line thank you letters Mum used to sit us down to write after Christmas when we were little. I guess you've had quite a few of those from me, down the years – wonder if you ever kept any of them? I'm sorry the letters were so soulless, but I do remember lots of the things you gave me, Gran. I've still got Killer-Eyes Ted here with me, sitting on the end of my bed – and the Jill pony books, it was you who started me on those, and I must have read them all about twenty times. And do you remember that funny puppet that was Little Red Riding Hood one way round and you turned it inside out and it was the wolf? I played with that non-stop, and I cried when I took it to school and Jackie Baker threw it on the roof of the infant toilets, and Mr Hughes wouldn't fetch it down with his ladder like he did all the footballs because he said I shouldn't have had it out in the playground in the first place.

My landlady (I suppose I should call her that, but it sounds so 1950s – really she's more like a normal housemate, even though she's miles older than me) is called Cora, and she likes to rent out the room because her husband Pete works away a lot on the oil rigs. He works three-month stints so I still haven't met him yet – I missed him at Christmas when I was at Mum and Dad's. I say Cora's older than me, but actually I've no idea how old she must be, maybe in her forties, maybe her fifties. I can never understand how people (usually older people) can seem to tell just how old other people are by looking at them. I mean, I know when people are young (student age or a little bit older, like me), and I can tell when they are old (it's the grey hair and wrinkles, isn't it, really?) but in that whole in-between zone, thirties and forties and fifties, well, I can never tell at all. Most of the other staff at school are in that middle zone. Except Karen (she's the person who helps in my class with Jack Caulfield, the blind boy I told you about), she's not much older than me. Oh, and Mrs Martin the deputy head, who's in the grey-and-wrinkles camp. And I honestly couldn't place the middlies to within ten or twenty years in most cases. Maybe it's because I never really look properly: they aren't young or old, they are just people. I guess it comes as you get older, spotting people that are younger or older than yourself. When you reach your age, Gran, do you lose the skill again, because everyone is just young?

Oh dear, I am worried now that Cora will walk over and see what I have written, about her age, I mean. She is writing a letter, too – we are sitting in the living room together, both writing away at our letters; it is very Jane Austen, I think. The lost art, and all that. She writes to Pete every week, never misses – I think it's rather sweet, at their age. Apparently it isn't always easy to get through to the rig on the phone, depends on the weather conditions in the North Sea or something.

Anyway, Cora seem very nice. There's a little Baby Belling in my room, and space to sit (mine's the front bedroom, the best one in the house, which is very kind of her and Pete), and at the beginning I used to do my baked potato or my pasta up there on my own, but I hated waking up to the smell of last night's onions, and it really seemed too much

trouble to cook just for one,
bread and honey for days on en
would disapprove of that, Gran!) An
in her kitchen doing the same thing. S
started to cook together most days. It was
first – she'd invite me down to share her suppe.
I'd do a return fixture upstairs. Now we always us
kitchen, whoever's turn it is to cook, because she's got
the little jars of herbs and spices and everything, and my
Baby Belling is under a slopy roof thing and right up
against the wardrobe door, so not the easiest to get to.

Oh dear, this letter has gone on a lot and I haven't really
told you anything yet! Well, work is going fine. We learned a
song about Louis Braille today (we've been doing about him
because of Jack); we're just finishing the class project on
spiders and starting one on Islam, and Daniel McNally hasn't
pulled down his own or anyone else's trousers for two weeks.
I've also joined a women's group. They meet every Thursday
evening, and they run a safe house for homeless women. They
seem like a really friendly bunch. Must go, I've promised I'll
take Cora's dog, Snuffy, out to the park. She's called after the
man who wrote the music for 'The West Wing' (which struck
me as odd, since Cora doesn't seem a very political person) –
the guy's name is W. G. Snuffy Walden, and apparently it
always made Cora and Pete laugh. Dreadful name for a
human being, Cora says, but an excellent one for a spaniel.

Lots of love,
Margaret.

42 Gledhill Street,
Ipswich

20 February 2005

Dearest Pete,

Well, I'm sitting in the old armchair that came from Aunt Alice when she died – I know how you always like to be able to picture me when I'm writing to you – and Snuffy is lying across my feet doing her impersonation of a draught-excluder – though I never saw a draught-excluder with its eyes tight shut and a yellow rubber duck still in its mouth.

Margaret is writing a letter too, in fact we are both sitting here scribbling away like it's a wet Sunday in a Jane Austen novel! It's her gran she's writing to. She had a stroke back just before Christmas, and has been in hospital all this time. Now she's home again, and getting by on her own, but she finds it stressful to try to get to the phone when it rings, and has told Margaret that she would rather have letters from her. I expect it's nicer anyway, when you're old and alone, to have a letter you can take out and re-read over and over, rather than a phone call which is over and done with once a week. I often get out your letters, Pete – I had a bundle of old ones out the other day, and it felt just as though you were here in the room with me.

You will like Margaret. She's fearfully earnest about things: she's just joined some homelessness group (all women they are) that runs a little hostel place near the town centre. She gets fired up about everything going – you should hear her sometimes in the mornings, she actually argues with the radio if John Humphrys has someone on she disagrees with. And she writes letters to her MP! I didn't know people still did that. I hardly know anything about him, though I've lived here for thirty years: that man Slater, you know, he's New Labour, and from what you read in the *Town Crier* he's too smooth for his own or anyone else's good. Maybe all this crusading passion is because Margaret's young; she's just in her first teaching job, so I guess she's twenty-three, maybe twenty-four. But even at that age I don't remember ever caring quite as much as she seems to! She's beautiful, too. I don't mean just pretty, I really do mean beautiful, it's the only word for it. I don't think I've ever described her to you, have I? She's tall, with curly almost-black hair, and big grey eyes with these little flecks of amber in them. And her skin – it's so white it's almost see-through. There's a word for it, I think it begins with a t, but I can't remember it. She has that gawky awkwardness of tall girls, completely unaware of her beauty. 'Coltish', I think would be the word for it – like Katy Carr before she fell out of the swing. (Sorry, Pete, I know you won't ever have read *What Katy Did*, but you know me and my books.) Anyway, Katy is too tomboyish an image for her, because of that astonishing skin.

Things have been pretty quiet in the bank this week – it was Dora's birthday, and she brought in cake for coffee break. Homemade it was, a proper old-fashioned Victoria sponge with raspberry jam and butter cream (real butter in it, too, none of your soft marge). I must admit I did enjoy my slice, but it made me sad to think she'd spent all the time making the cake for us – like she doesn't have enough on her plate, with her eldest back home after splitting from his wife, and Dave off work again with his bad back. She's the one who should be being spoiled on her birthday – and I bet she cooked a special tea at home, too. Oh, and the garden is starting to burst out all over the place, love: everything seems to be beginning to sprout these last few days. That forsythia we put in by the back fence – four years ago now, is it? I was trying to remember – is a riot of colour. I think it's come earlier this year, with the mild weather we've had, and that and the daffs really make a splash through the kitchen window.

Well, I'd better stop now, there's the supper to get on. I'm cooking for Margaret again. Chops, we're having. I did them for her once before and she really loved them; might do something for that pale complexion, too! All my love, Petey, and I miss you, as always.

Cora xxx

From: Margaret Hayton [margarethayton@yahoo.co.uk]
Sent: 22/2/05 22:07
To: Rebecca Prichard [becs444@btinternet.com]

Dear Becs,
You'd laugh at me. I've joined another of my groups that are going-to-change-the-world, as you always used to put it! It's homelessness *and* the great patriarchal conspiracy this time. It manages to combine all the aspects that you would send up most of both Women's

Action and the Homelessness Support Group, from college. They work as a collective (go on, sneer, you know you want to); two of them are paid workers and the rest are the voluntary support group, but they didn't bother to tell me which were which, and it didn't seem to matter. They meet every week in each other's houses. Last night Alison (who seems to be the sort of unofficial self-designated queen bee) served organic herbal tea without a trace of irony. There's a lesbian couple and they both appear to be called Pat. I suppose that can happen – it's not one of the difficulties of a gay lifestyle that had ever occurred to me before. Oh, and in fact, when I say I've joined the group, I also seem to have become treasurer. Not only did I make the mistake of revealing that I possess and know how to use a computer and spreadsheet package, but in a mad moment I actually uttered the fatal words, 'What does it involve?'

You'd also scoff – I've eaten pork chops three times without turning a hair! Cora, the woman whose house I'm living in, offered to cook a few weeks back, and I forgot to say anything (seems like everyone was veggie at college, or at least knew that I was, so it was never an issue) until it was too late and there it was, staring up at me from the plate, a big slab of no-messing, like-it-or-lump-it meat. Having eaten that and not said, of course, the next time I couldn't possibly tell her, or else she'd feel bad! What an idiot I am – I expect I'll have to swallow my principles (and a lump of dead pig) every Sunday evening from now on, until . . . Well, until I can afford a mortgage round here on my NQT main scale salary, which will be (does rapid calculation in head) oh that's right, never! I suppose up there you can pick up a three-bedroomed semi on your way back from Asda.

School is good: the head is on another planet but his deputy, Mrs Martin, seems quite sorted, and the rest of the staff are OK. There's a kid in my class, Jack, who's almost completely blind, so he comes with a full-time helper, Karen, which means always another body around the classroom. I've got Year 3s, which I think is my favourite stage. The Infant nuts and bolts are already in place – they've sounded out their phonetics, and they've learnt to count forwards in 2s, 5s and 10s and backwards in green bottles, speckled frogs and monkeys bouncing on the bed – and now they are just beginning to unfurl their Junior wings. They haven't yet absorbed the view that it's cool to be bored. The most feeble attempts at teacherly humour are still rewarded with gleeful delight, and everything is fresh and interesting, so that life resembles an endlessly rolling episode of 'Blue Peter'.

How are you getting on at that Ofsted-failing, sink-estate-fed place of yours? I don't see how you can ever take the mickey out of me again for my world-changing tendencies, after accepting that offer! Have you thought about hiring some personal protection? I know you've only got a Reception class, but I hear gun crime starts young on Moss Side!

And how is the delectable Phil, by the way? Are you still together?

Love,

Margaret x

From: Rebecca Prichard [becs444@btinternet.com]
Sent: 22/2/05 22:56
To: Margaret Hayton [margarethayton@yahoo.co.uk]

Hi Margaret, great to hear from you! I was beginning to think they didn't have the internet down there in Hicks-wich, sorry, I mean Ipswich! (Is it true that the streets are paved with sugar-beet?) And I knew it was no use trying to text you – I remember your views about mobiles irradiating the brain. I do like the sound of the two Pats, by the way – a couple both homosexual and homonymic.

The delectable Phil is history (which is strangely appropriate since he's got a post teaching it in Swindon). I guess the delicate bloom of our relationship may not have survived the distance between Manchester and Wiltshire, but in fact it had withered on the bough anyway before we'd even packed up and left college. It seems that Julie Biddulph also found him delectable – and so apparently did Letitia 'Tits' Carvaggio, just the once, when she was drunk at a post-exam party. Her outfit was really accentuating her name that night, as I recall; I went home early, and Phil always did have the willpower of a particularly suasible flea.

Since Phil there have been Aidan, Ben, and now my latest acquisition, Campbell (and no, before you say it, I've heard them all already – I am *not* working my way through the alphabet). Campbell is something of a toyboy, a third year Chem. Eng. student from UMIST. He's still here now, as a matter of fact. He has an essay to finish, which is why I happened to be checking my e-mails. He does such a cute little frowny thing when he's concentrating – makes me just want to bite his eyebrows!

But what about you, chuck? Any nice fresh-faced farmer boys on the horizon down there in Ipswich? Or are you still keeping up your vow of chastity? I seem to recall your being sworn off men, along with meat and overuse of the mobile, from some time in your second year, as being all equally injurious to brain, body or soul. You were practically married from the third week in college to your very own Mr Rochester (until it turned out he had that mad first wife locked in the attic), and for ever after that the cloistered nun! But I bet there are some Suffolk swains who can tempt you to leave the Order . . . ?

Big hugs,

Becs xx

PS. Incidentally, I am ignoring your taunts about the incomparable Brunswick Road Primary. I am not on a mission to save the socially excluded youth of tomorrow; I needed a job within striking distance of Dad's increasingly carcinomatose colon, and it was all I could get. But, since you ask, the kids are a blast. Four-year-olds are the same the world over. Teaching Reception is basically herding cats whether it's in Moss Side or Mayfair.

From: Margaret Hayton [margarethayton@yahoo.co.uk]
Sent: 22/2/05 23:05
To: Rebecca Prichard [becs444@btinternet.com]

Dear Becs,
I really am sorry about your dad, and for being so insensitive. Is it really that bad?

And you're not far wrong about Ipswich being a communications black spot. Cora doesn't even have a computer, and it's taken me until now to get broadband sorted out.

Sorry to hear about Phil, too (I'm sure there's a joke in there somewhere, continuing your metaphor, something about a flower of passion that wilts in Wilts: needs further work, I feel), but glad to hear you are keeping up the cracking pace that you set in college.

Night night. Sleep tight – or not.
Love,
Margaret xx

PS. I see you haven't forgotten the essay espièglerie game. (Do you remember I once informed Professor Sharkey that her own early work was 'haruspical'? And you swung some corkers past Fairbrother in Child Psych. – two 'proemials' and a 'fissiparous' in one assignment, as I recall.) I'll give you 5 for 'suasible' and 6 for 'homonymic'; 'carcinomatose' (if you haven't just made it up) is an 8.5.

WITCH
Women of Ipswich Together Combating Homelessness

<u>Minutes of meeting</u> at Pat and Pat's house, 24 February 2005, 8 p.m.

<u>Present</u>: Alison, Susan, Pat, Pat, Margaret, Ding, Emily, Persephone

<u>Apologies for absence</u>: None

Witch House: current occupancy
Room 1: Carole
Room 2: Lauren
Room 3: Nasreen
Room 4: Joyce
Room 5: Helen

News of residents
Nasreen moved in on Saturday. Unfortunately, Housing Benefit have informed her that as an asylum seeker she will

have no entitlement to any of the usual state benefits. She will receive a £35 weekly voucher for food, but nothing towards her rent.

Helen has been very distressed this week, and cutting up quite badly; she had to go into A&E for stitches on Sunday night (thanks to Alison for driving her there). Her GP has got her into some group therapy at the Young People's Psychiatric Unit, specifically for survivors of childhood sexual abuse.

Carole's application for move-on accommodation from Suffolk Churches Housing Association was unsuccessful, but they have suggested that she apply again the next time their lists are open.

Persephone has had a session with both Joyce and Helen to cleanse their auras. She is currently doing a course on Indian head massage, and suggested that several of the residents and ex-residents might benefit from this therapy.

<u>News of former residents still receiving support</u>
Marianne is doing well with her job at the chemist's, although Mr Singh is still keeping her mainly in the toiletries section.

<u>Finance</u>
This was Ding's last report as treasurer. There are currently no voids, and no rent arrears, except for Nasreen. Ding reported that since voids and bad debts have been so low this year, it should be possible to fund Nasreen's rent out of the 5 per cent voids allowance which is written into the budget, at least for the immediate future. This was agreed to.

It was decided to make the Lottery grant application for a new washer-drier. The old machine is now out of its extended warranty, and is not likely to last much longer (especially in the light of Carole's unsuccessful application for rehousing). It is already putting grey fluff on everyone's things.

Thanks were expressed to Ding for three years of excellent work as treasurer of WITCH – and to Margaret for taking on the job.

Any other business

Emily asked whether she could go on a welfare rights training day in April on understanding disability benefits. Ding confirmed that there was sufficient money left in the training budget to pay for this, and for any collective members who might also wish to attend. After some discussion, however, it was decided that the training budget was not appropriate to pay for Persephone's Indian head massage classes.

Next week's meeting: 8 p.m., at Persephone's house.

42 Gledhill Street
Ipswich
Suffolk IP2 3DA

Mrs Barbara McPherson
Director of Recreation and Amenities
Ipswich Borough Council

Civic House
Orwell Drive
Ipswich
Suffolk IP2 3QP

26 February 2005

Dear Mrs McPherson,

I am writing to you to raise my concern about the problem of dog-fouling in the small park between Gledhill Street and Emery Street. As you may know, there is at present only one bin provided in the park for dog waste, and it is a long way from the Emery Street entrance. Dog-owners who leave the park by that gate do not always bother to walk back and dispose of their dog's waste in the bin. At least one additional bin would, I am convinced, make a big difference. The park is used as a play area by many local children, and this form of pollution is not only unpleasant and a nuisance, it is a hygiene issue.

Yours sincerely,
Margaret Hayton.

The Hollies
East Markhurst

28 February 2005

Dear Margaret,

Thank you for your lovely long letter. You write such nice, chatty letters, it's almost like having you here with me. I've read it two or three times through, so I've really had my money's worth. I'm glad you and your landlady are

23

getting along, and that you've found these new ladies in the housing group to be friends with, too. I did worry about you at first, you know, all alone in a big new town like that. But you've always been good at making friends, right from a little girl, so I know I shouldn't have fretted. The very first day you started nursery school, I remember I went with Mum to meet you at three o'clock, and the first thing you said when you saw us was, 'I've got a new friend and she's called Horatio.' It took us three weeks to work out what her name really was – though your mum said Carnation wasn't much better than Horatio!

Your mum still phones me. But I'm using the frame to get about, and with the phone being in the hall, it takes me a while. So many times I seem to get there and the person rings off just before I pick up. I need to lean myself up against the frame, so I can free my good left hand to lift the receiver. Or if I do manage to answer, it will just be somebody selling something – as if I needed a conservatory at my time of life! Or life insurance – there's not a lot left to insure, I told the girl last time, but she didn't laugh, I suppose she was scared of being rude. I've told Mum to let it ring a nice long while if she calls. I suppose she's too busy to sit down and write a letter – most people are these days. There's always some Mothers' Union meeting, or choir practice, or the church magazine to get out, or just someone round at the vicarage needing tea and sympathy. It's a full-time job for her as well as your dad, I always think. I sometimes wonder how these lady vicars get on, because I can't see their husbands taking on all the parish jobs, somehow, can you?

Kirsty, the young lady who is coming in to help me, is really kind. She comes every day except Sunday, and she is supposed to get me up, help me wash and dress, and get my breakfast. I feel really guilty, because I've been so used to getting up early, seven o'clock prompt, ever since your grandad was alive, and of course in hospital they were always round with a cup of tea ever so early too. Well, Kirsty comes at nine o'clock, which is when she starts work, and that's fair enough, she has her own little ones to get up and fed and off to school first. But I feel so idle just sitting in bed until she comes, so sometimes I have a wash and a piece of toast before she arrives, and then hop back into bed when I hear the gate. Then I have to pretend to be hungry when she makes my breakfast later. (I can tell you, love, because I know you'd never say anything.)

There are lots of things I can manage one-handed, the kettle and the toaster, and saucepans – you'd be surprised what you can do when you have to. But tin openers are impossible, and peeling potatoes. Often I get Kirsty to peel me some veg for my tea when she's there in the morning, and she'll leave them in a plastic bag in the fridge. Or else I've started to buy those bags ready peeled and chopped from the chill section in the Co-op. There was a man on the television saying how bad they are for the environment – all that packaging and whatnot, and I thought to myself, I know someone who wouldn't approve, then. But I think you'll forgive your old one-armed gran, won't you? Anyway, as far as cooking tea goes, I often don't want so much these days – it's getting older, and not being able to get out and about to work up an appetite, I suppose. And having two breakfasts most days helps too!

I hope school is still going well. Do you still take the children out on nature rambles when the weather warms up? I used to love nature rambles more than anything when I was at school.

What's 'The West Wing', by the way? Is it something I should watch, do you think? Would I understand it? I am so grateful that you started me off watching 'Friends'. I used to really look forward to my Friday evenings, and I was so pleased when Rachel decided not to go to Paris in the end. She and Ross make such a lovely couple, don't they?

Love from your Gran xx

From: Margaret Hayton [margarethayton@yahoo.co.uk]
Sent: 1/3/05 02:49
To: Rebecca Prichard [becs444@btinternet.com]

Dear Becs,

I've just got back from my first call-out on the Witch House emergency rota, and I know we are meant to be hot on confidentiality, but you live miles away, and I've got to tell someone. It was Helen, she's one of the younger residents, nineteen I found out tonight, though I'd have guessed much younger to look at her, she's dead skinny and really sort of fragile-looking.

She sounded really weird on the phone, said she'd taken an overdose, so I just phoned Alison first (because she's said she'll go with me the first time or so) and then got straight on my bike. The house is only five minutes away.

When I got there Helen was just sitting on her bed, looking sort of dazed. She'd taken a lot of her anti-depressants, plus a few aspirin. She hadn't taken the whole bottle or anything – she'd been meaning to, she said, but then she'd changed her mind, and stopped and called me. She seemed really scared. I rang for an ambulance, but I hadn't any idea what to say to Helen, so I just held her hand and hoped Alison wouldn't be long. Then we heard Alison's car, and as soon as she got there she took charge. She was super-efficient, just as if this happened all the time (and from what Helen told me later, perhaps it does). She asked exactly what Helen had taken, how many and of what, and wrote it down, and put the bottles and packets in a bag. Then she took Helen into the bathroom and got the toothmug and made her drink about ten mugfuls of water, until she was copiously sick, clumps of undigested tablets all down the sink in this watery vomit. Then we got in the car – Alison phoned to cancel the ambulance, which still hadn't arrived – and we were at A&E within ten minutes of Alison's arrival on the scene. Blimey, I wouldn't want to be her kid's teacher at a parents' evening, if she had any kind of bone to pick!

Mind you, after all that prompt action, of course we then sat there waiting for forty minutes before we got to see a doctor. He gave Helen another emetic and she was sick again (he made her hold a stainless steel bowl, and she had to be sick there with everyone watching), but there was nothing more to come now, so I don't think it did any good. It seemed to me like he wanted to punish her for wasting his time with something that was her fault when he'd got all these other people waiting – I guess maybe he's met her before up there. But it's not her fault. She's depressed, she really is ill, just like all the others. Then he checked her pulse and blood pressure, and shone one of those little torch things into her eyes, and told her to see her GP in the morning for a check-over.

Alison drove us back to Witch House, and she had to leave, but I said I'd stay a bit, so Helen and I made a cup of tea and took it up to her room. Her stomach was really sore from all the vomiting, but weak and milky seemed OK. Anyway, she seemed to have sort of unfrozen, if you know what I mean, and she started talking, and I ended up staying until – well, what is it now? – quarter to three! Her dad abused her, it's horrible. Started when she was still at primary school, eight or nine she was, and it didn't stop until she finally got up her courage to leave, and came to Witch House, nearly two years ago. She just packed a few things, and got on the bus, and went to the CAB. They sent her to WITCH, and luckily there was a space straight away. She didn't speak to her parents for about six months, and when she finally got up courage to ring, her mum just pretended everything was normal, and asked how she was, and where she was living and stuff. She even goes round there for Sunday lunch sometimes now – her mum is always on at her to go – and no one ever asks her why she left, and she hasn't said anything, and they all pretend they are a normal happy family. Her dad's an orthodontist, and probably plays golf, and goes to church on Sundays. But it's eating Helen up, you can see. She says the mornings when she wakes up and can get up and shower without a huge effort of will are few and far between. She didn't say so much about – well, you know, the suicidal feelings and the self-harm, and of course I wasn't about to ask. And here am I, getting back on my bike and pedalling back to my normality, my pain-free, livable life. I know it's a cliché, Becs, but I literally *cannot imagine* what it's like to be Helen, I really can't.

Anyway, sorry to load all this on you – you'll open this in the morning, I expect, and what a cheery start to your day that will be! Hope your dad isn't too bad, by the way.

Love,

Margaret xx

From: Margaret Hayton [margarethayton@yahoo.co.uk]
Sent: 1/3/05 07:17
To: Rebecca Prichard [becs444@btinternet.com]

Dear Becs,

I'm really sorry about that e-mail last night. I guess I was all wound up, and just needed to tell someone. Just ignore me. I'm quite calm again this morning. And I didn't even ask how you are, or what's going on with you. How is Campbell? Still tucked up in your bed and sleeping like a baby?

No, I haven't found anyone round here to tempt me out of my nun's habit yet, nor even worth setting my wimple at, to be honest. The male staff at school are all either married or ancient or both, and as my main social life at the moment (apart from chatting to Cora over our still highly carnivorous suppers) is WITCH – and, well, to be honest, I'm not going to meet any men that way, except maybe the odd violent ex-husband, and perhaps a psychiatrist or two.

They are really a brilliant lot of women, though – if a little, um, motley. The two Pats I've told you about, and Alison, who is a kind of absolute monarch manqué of collective working ('*la commune, c'est moi*'). She's a medical research scientist in the daytime – probably gets the bacteria whipped into line in the petri dishes. Ding (yes, that really does seem to be her name – but of course one doesn't like to ask) comes over as a bit ditzy, but to be fair to her she kept the account books in the sort of good order that would make a Swiss military tattoo look slipshod. Susan is very quiet, about my age I think, and Emily is older, must be close to retirement I'd say, and she and Pat T. are the paid workers at the house. No one gets a surname, it's all first names except the Pats get to be Pat T. and Pat W. respectively, to avoid descent into complete chaos. But my favourite is Persephone. She's an unfeasibly tall Jamaican woman, invariably swathed in some flamboyant African print like a furled oriflamme around a flagpole, the effect sometimes even topped off by one of those turban thingummies, and she's into alternative everything. Her laugh could fell trees, and she laughs *a lot*. She came to Britain as a kid with her mum, two of just twelve passengers on a cargo ship which, serendipitously, was carrying bananas. It is the one disappointment of her life that in forty years no one in oh-so-polite Ipswich has ever asked her whether she came over on the you-know-what. Pat and Pat call her Percy. On Planet Pat everyone has to have a masculine abbreviation for their name. If they start calling me Gary, I swear I'm leaving the group.

So what's new with you, anyway?

Love,

Margaret x

From: Rebecca Prichard [becs444@btinternet.com]
Sent: 1/3/05 08:07
To: Margaret Hayton [margarethayton@yahoo.co.uk]

Hi Margaret, you poor thing, last night sounds quite a trauma. But this is where all your do-gooding gets you, you see. Whereas I was tucked up in bed by ten thirty. Sadly, not with Campbell, who turned out to prefer the role of sugar daddy to that of toyboy, and has cast me aside in favour of some sixteen-year-old schoolgirl in a gym slip. (Actually, I have no idea at all what a gym slip is, or was. It sounds scratchy and uncomfortable though, so I bloody well hope she *does* have to wear one!) I have now decided that in order to get over this devastating rejection I really am going to work my way through the alphabet, so am out clubbing tonight with my classroom assistant, Paula, on the lookout for someone suitably therapeutic by the name of Daniel or Dean or David . . .

Becs xxx

OK, 'oriflamme' is a 5, and 'serendipitously' is a grudging 4.5. But no points for 'motley', you can do better than that, hon. They sound like a harlequinade, at the very least.

From: Margaret Hayton [margarethayton@yahoo.co.uk]
Sent: 1/3/05 08:09
To: Rebecca Prichard [becs444@btinternet.com]

Dougal? Darwin? Dmitri? Dante? Dhruv? Dartagnan? Dionysus? Happy hunting!
  Margaret xx

42 Gledhill Street
Ipswich
Suffolk IP3 2DA

Mr Richard Slater, MP
House of Commons
London SW1A 0AA

5 March 2005

Dear Mr Slater,

I am writing to you again about the small park between Gledhill Street and Emery Street. Not only is the zip-wire still broken (see my letter of 10 February), but the problem of dog-fouling is getting worse. I myself regularly walk my housemate's springer spaniel in the park, always ensuring that I scoop up behind her and place the waste in the bin provided. Other dog-owners, however, are not so community-minded as myself, and the area is becoming quite unpleasant for the children to play in. I see it as a hygiene issue.

I am sure that the provision of another bin designated for dog waste, closer to the Emery Street gate, would help to resolve the problem. I have written to the borough council about the matter, but have received no reply.

Yours sincerely,

Margaret Hayton.

PS. I should be grateful if you could send me a proper answer to this letter, and not just another of your standard form replies. Do you even read your correspondence?

House of Commons
London SW1A 0AA

11 March 2005

Dear Ms Hayton,

Thank you for your letter of 5 March, raising an issue of concern. Your view has been noted, and I can assure you that I shall be looking into this matter in the near future.

Yours sincerely,

Richard Slater, MP.

From: Richard Slater [rpslater@hc.parliament.uk]
Sent: 12/3/05 14:28
To: Michael Carragan [mmcarragan@hc.parliament.uk]

Hi Michael,

How is life in the heady heights of the Home Office,

then? Do you have your own junior ministerial office with a shiny green junior ministerial telephone and a shiny pink junior ministerial secretary? Shall I come round and see? (Do they let us rank-and-file mortals inside there?)

Of course, as you know, the Ruler Of The World passed over me again in the latest reshuffle – all for standing by my principles and abstaining in the Iraq vote! It's all so unfair: it's not like I haven't put in the graft. I served my eight years on the borough council, five of them as chair of the Refuse Disposal Sub-Committee. I dutifully cut my teeth by standing for sodding Unwinnable South-East, lurking in the rain like a grinning moron in a shopping centre in Leatherhead ('Would you like to meet the Labour candidate, madam?' – 'No, not really.'). And I ran a tight campaign, though I say it myself: we'd got out every one of the 137 Labour promises by lunchtime on polling day. I got my golden prize: the nomination for good old Ipswich, and I even won the seat with an increased majority. I was young, I was bright, I was (if you'll excuse the expression) thrusting: universally tipped for high office. And then the ROTW had to have that bloody war! It's not like I haven't tried to make amends. I've been so far up the Whips' bottoms that I could see their Weetabix most days: volunteering for Standing Committees on every strand of red tape going, coming in for divisions on a Friday night when everyone else was either in the pub or on the train back to their nice warm wives and constituencies. Just how many more months in back bench purgatory do you think the ROTW has in mind for me before I am allowed to knock on the door again?

I know I should be concentrating on just being a Good Constituency MP, in the grand tradition of those down the years who've considered it an honour simply to serve their public. But, to be honest, what used to be the golden prize feels increasingly like the wooden spoon. Good God, it's all so trivial! It's all just mad old biddies with no life who write me endless letters about nothing at all. I've got a new one, by the way – Doris or Margaret or one of those old lady names – she writes around once a fortnight, or that's how it seems, about all and anything. It was dog-fouling last week – actually DOG-FOULING! I thought my days of dealing with broken paving slabs and dog mess were over when I left the borough council. I thought, in my innocence, that once I was in Parliament I might get to do something real, something that mattered! Is this really what I went into politics for?

Anyway, sorry for the long rant, Michael, but if you do get a chance to whisper my name in any ears in those elevated circles in which you now move, well, I'll owe you one, mate. Or even several.

Richard.

Richard Slater (Labour)
Member of Parliament for Ipswich

From: Michael Carragan
[mmcarragan@hc.parliament.uk]
Sent: 12/3/05 14:42
To: Richard Slater [rpslater@hc.parliament.uk)

Hello Richard, greetings from the Hallowed Halls. I have my fair share of constituency stalkers too, you know. There's one who has turned up at every one of my monthly surgeries since the day I was elected, with a tartan coat and an elderly Skye terrier, both of which smell of mothballs. Never yet found out what she's after – she always goes away before she's called in. And now here we have our own special breed of Home Office letter-writer, too. There's a file my predecessor kept marked 'LFN', which she explained means Letters From Nutters, and there are some real finds in there, believe me. One of them thinks she is the love-child of Peter Sellers, and writes twice a week to get him released from HMP Parkhurst, where she believes he has been incarcerated since 1980.

As for whispered words in ears, don't think for a moment that the ROTWeiler ever comes near these less-than-smoke-filled rooms. I'm in office 4B on the corridor that time forgot, so unless the ear of Mrs Cadwallader with the tea trolley serves your purpose, I don't think I can help.

You can buy me one (or several) anyway, and we'll

weep into them together. What about Tuesday night at 9.30? Call me.

Michael.

Michael Carragan (Labour)
Member of Parliament for West Bromwich West

42 Gledhill Street
Ipswich

13 March 2005

Darling Petey,

I'm writing this one at the kitchen table, with a cup of tea beside me, in that mug you gave me with the springer spaniel on it. I remember when you came home with it you said it looked just like Snuffy, and instead of saying thank you I said Snuffy's ears are longer – but you didn't seem to mind.

I'm in here because Margaret is in the sitting-room with one of the girls from that hostel of hers, Jasmin or Yasmin I think she said her name was, a very pretty-looking girl, black hair and almond eyes and skin the colour of really milky coffee. I think she's from one of those eastern European countries, one that used to be in Yugoslavia, or maybe was part of Russia before the wall came down. Anyway, the poor little thing doesn't speak very good English yet, I think she's only been over here a few weeks, and Margaret is kindly teaching her a bit of reading and writing, so I left them to it. Margaret was using some of her Biff and Chip books from school, so I don't know what the poor girl will make of them, all about magic adventures and a key that glows and makes you go small. She was showing very willing, though, and she laughed and said that Floppy (the dog in the books) looks like Snuffy, which made me warm to her, as you can imagine. I nearly said, Snuffy's ears are longer, and then it made me think of you, and how much I miss you, and I had to come in here and get a tissue.

I suppose it's a problem for adults learning to read another language, because most of the easy books are for kids. Sarah at the bank (you know, the young one, who's been off travelling round the world) said she used to teach English to foreign people. She had a special word for it – something like Teflon, though it can't be that, that's the non-stick on frying pans. Anyway, she has a story about teaching some Japanese businessmen using a fairy story book because it was all she had, and when she asked them if there were any questions, one man asked her to give him an everyday example of a situation where he would use the expression 'by the hair on my chinny chin chin'!

Mr Davies told us we're going to have another refit at the bank, starting in May. So it will be all plaster dust and working out of cardboard boxes again, with the electricity off half the time and the computers down. It only seems five minutes since the last one, although when I work it out I think it must be eight or nine years – that was when we got rid of the counter and the glass and went over to everyone having their personal banker and sitting in easy chairs. Now, apparently, Head Office says it has to be back to counters, with a complicated new set-up for queuing. Dora's Dave is back at work, but he's still not to do any heavy lifting. Dora says, well that won't make much difference then, not at home at any rate.

I'm looking out at the forsythia as I write, and there are a few tulips now among the daffs. And the flowers are coming out on the quince – they're so waxy and bright orangey-red, I always think they look like the artificial ones you'd get at the florist's. The grass is shooting up, too. Mrs Edgar next door cut hers last week, and so did number 44, so ours is the one letting down the row. Margaret said she would do it, but I can't let her do everything, she is so helpful already. I start to wonder if she ever does anything just for *her*.

Snuffy just walked in with her ball in her mouth, and one of her ears inside out. I was thinking again how funny it is that she never notices. And suddenly I could just *hear* you in here with me, doing your Snuffy voice, saying, 'That's funny, everything sounds loud in here. Who turned the volume up?' And then you'd get on the floor and flip her ear back to normal, and shake her head from side to side and call her cloth-ears. I know that Snuffy misses you too, and it makes me sad that I can't explain to her why you aren't here.

Well, bye-bye for now, Pete – I love you,
Cora xxx

IPSWICH BOROUGH COUNCIL

MRS BARBARA MCPHERSON, MA: DIRECTOR OF
RECREATION AND AMENITIES
Civic House, Orwell Drive, Ipswich IP2 3QP

Margaret Hayton
42 Gledhill Street
Ipswich IP3 2DA

14 March 2005

Dear Ms Hayton,

Thank you for your letter of 26 February, raising your concern about dog-fouling in the public park located between Gledhill Street and Emery Street. I am pleased to be able to inform you that the provision of hygienic dog-waste disposal facilities in this area is scheduled for reconsideration in 2010, as part of this department's phased ten-year review programme of litter and dog-waste disposal arrangements in the central and west Ipswich area. I trust that this answers your query satisfactorily.

Yours sincerely,
Barbara McPherson.

Ipswich Borough Council – Working for Your *Community*

From: Rebecca Prichard [becs444@btinternet.com]
Sent: 15/3/05 22:14
To: Margaret Hayton [margarethayton@yahoo.co.uk]

Hi Margaret,

Do you remember, one night during our first elective teaching practice, how we drew up our patent taxonomy of parents?

Well, at Brunswick Road we have an oversupply of NESSies (Non English Speaking Smileys). I know that these are, by tradition, mostly natives of east and south-east Asia, but at our place we have quite a number from the sub-continent, too. There is also no shortage of DYTTies, that volatile and vituperative species, a branch of the genus known popularly in the US as 'white trash'. I have encountered both the common female, with its distinctive alarm cry, 'Don't You Talk To My Child Like That', and the rarer male ('Don't You Talk To My Wife Like That'), which can be violent if wrongly handled.

My class boasts just one MLH (or Mile-High) mum — so-called, if you remember, for her reliance upon Mother's Little Helpers. This one is a classic specimen: one hip supporting a baby, the other itself supported upon a double buggy emitting stereo screaming, her eyes a glaze of chemical unconcern.

What we have not nearly enough of is your basic ABIEs (Always Brings In Egg-boxes).

How about your end?
Hugs,
Becs xx

From: Margaret Hayton [margarethayton@yahoo.co.uk]
Sent: 15/3/05 22:25
To: Rebecca Prichard [becs444@btinternet.com]

Dear Becs,

Like I would have forgotten!

St Edith's Primary, I am pleased to report, is positively awash with ABIEs. The egg-boxes are of course merely a cipher: it could be completed homework, reply slips, or old sheets for painting scenery. The ABIEs always man the tombola at the Christmas bazaar, they wield the spades for the new wildlife garden, they are first on the buzzers at PTA quiz nights. How on earth do you manage without them?

But I do have one DYTTy (female) – though I have so far avoided the calling in of her mate. And I also suffer the presence in small numbers of another species which I bet you are safe from in Moss Side. The dreaded FFF: brimming with class confidence and absolutely lacking in volume control, the infamous Four-by-Four Foghorn.

Love,

Margaret xx

('Vituperative': 2.5.)

WITCH
Women of Ipswich Together Combating Homelessness

<u>Extract from minutes of meeting</u> at Emily's house, 17 March 2005, 8 p.m.

<u>News of residents</u>
Helen took another overdose on Friday evening. Margaret went with her to A&E, and she was kept in overnight for observation, before being transferred to a psychiatric ward over the weekend, and discharged on Monday morning.

The residents at their weekly house meeting held the annual vote about whether to get a cat. Unanimous approval, as usual, was not achieved: Carole was concerned about the cleanliness aspect.

<u>News of former residents still receiving support</u>
Angie has left her husband and gone into the Women's Aid refuge. He has assaulted her a number of times, but she is reluctant to go to the police since this is a breach of his bail conditions, and she doesn't want him to go back to prison. Women's Aid are taking over supporting Angie for the present, but Emily and Pat T. will continue to liaise.

<u>Finance</u>
Margaret reported that there is a problem about our funding Nasreen's rent out of the voids allowance. Under current legislation, asylum seekers are not entitled to any recourse to public funds; she had spoken on the phone to a solicitor

she knows who works with a refugee centre in London, and it seems that if we use our own funds to support Nasreen's housing, this may place in jeopardy our core borough council grant funding. It was agreed that for the moment her rent could simply be treated as in arrears, while ways are found of fund-raising externally to cover it. Susan suggested holding a disco, but Alison pointed out that the likely profits would not go very far towards meeting £95 a week for the indefinite future. Alison agreed to help Margaret look into applications to relevant charities and grant-making trusts.

Any other business
The main downstairs living room, kitchen, and office areas are due for repainting, and Margaret reported that the maintenance budget should cover hiring a professional decorator. Pat and Pat recommended their friend Jo, who runs an all-women house maintenance company, Varnish 'n' Nails. It was agreed to approach them for a quote. Colours were discussed. Persephone favoured a warm ochre or orange, but magnolia was finally settled upon.

From: Richard Slater [rpslater@hc.parliament.uk]
Sent: 18/3/05 16:32
To: Michael Carragan [mmcarragan@hc.parliament.uk]

Hi Michael,
   Come on, mate, I have got to find a way of escaping from these stagnant back bench waters. All I need is a

very small rock to climb on to. Give me some ideas,
please! How can I win back the smiles of the Rottweiler?
What juicy bone should I toss in his direction? What's hot
at the moment in the Inner Circles? Help me out here.

In mounting desperation,
Richard.

Richard Slater (Labour)
Member of Parliament for Ipswich

From: Michael Carragan
[mmcarragan@hc.parliament.uk]
Sent: 18/3/05 16:50
To: Richard Slater [rpslater@hc.parliament.uk]

ASBOs, Richard, they are the thing. Yob culture in our
city centres on Friday and Saturday nights. The
unenviable task of our valiant boys in blue. The need
to arm them with greater powers, to make our streets
safe again for the law-abiding majority.

What you need is some kind of stunt. Get yourself
in the papers highlighting the problem in some way.
That will get you back under the eye of our glorious
leader.

Michael.

Michael Carragan (Labour),
Member of Parliament for West Bromwich West.

From: Richard Slater [rpslater@hc.parliament.uk]
Sent: 18/3/05 16:54
To: Michael Carragan [mmcarragan@hc.parliament.uk]

Thanks for the tip, Mike. I'll give it some thought. But don't you miss the days when we were in opposition and civil liberties were the thing?
  Richard.

Richard Slater (Labour)
Member of Parliament for Ipswich

> 42 Gledhill Street
> Ipswich

> 19 March 2005

Dear Gran,

I'm glad it's working out OK with Kirsty, and that you are managing to do a bit of cooking. Does Kirsty pick up your groceries, or can you get to the shops yourself now? As you see, I've sent you a mobile phone. I hope you won't think it's cheeky of me. It's only a basic one – I didn't think you'd want all the extra gadgets. There's no monthly charge, you just pay as you go. I've charged it up for you and put a card in with £30 of credit. That should keep you going for a bit, and then you can get a new card. They'll have them at the post office in East Markhurst. I expect you've read in the papers about the dangers of mobile phones, and they can definitely be a health hazard if you use them all the time. I'm always really careful to keep mine for emergencies, but I'm sure the occasional call won't do you any harm – I mean, you're not going to be chatting away on it all day, are you? I thought you could give Mum this number and then you can sit down comfortably and chat with her without needing to get out into the hall. But don't worry, I'll keep on writing to you, Gran! You can also arrange to block all those sales calls – there's a thing called the Telephone Preference Service. I'll sort it out for you next time I come over, if you want. I've just done it for us at home. Cora had stopped answering her phone at all in the early evenings. She said it was always someone trying to sell something, and I was worried she'd miss calls from her friends – not that she gets many. I think she's a bit of a loner really, sort of self-contained.

We get on ever so well, though. I suppose I've never exactly been gregarious, either. Anyway, you'd laugh – you remember how you always tease Dad about the state of his study, with more books visible than floor, let alone desk space? Well, Cora's house is a bit like that – books in heaps everywhere, including the kitchen and the loo. With the distinctive odour of the second-hand stall still clinging about them, they have long since exhausted the available shelf space, and are proofing every skirting board by at least one volume's thickness against mice. And a really eclectic mix she's got, too – everything from the Brontës to Mills and Boon. We have lots of the same favourites – like Lord Peter Wimsey, and *Frenchman's Creek*, and those Margaret Forster family histories (like the one with the old diary, you know, that I bought you for Christmas).

I've been feeling so grateful, recently, for us, for how things were when I was little, for how they still are. I mean, our family, Mum and Dad, and you, and Grandad when he was alive. It's seeing some of the women in the safe house I'm involved with now, the one I told you about. There's this girl Helen, just nineteen she is, and, well, her father abused her, and now she has terrible depression and has to take anti-depressant drugs, and she often feels suicidal or damages herself, cutting her arms and things. She called me out the other night (the support group have a telephone rota for emergencies), and when I got there one of the other residents let me in and said Helen was in her room, and she was just sitting on her bed, curled up in a kind of foetal position, eyes closed, hugging herself, and rocking slowly backwards and forwards. It took ten minutes before she could even speak to me at all. She hadn't taken anything, but she'd cut herself with a razor blade. Not deep cuts, I don't mean, not like when people slit their wrists, just a mass of scratches, all up her forearms, livid and raw and painful-looking. After a bit, once she could sort of let go a bit and uncoil herself, I got her to the office where the first aid stuff is, and helped her bind her arms up. I wondered if we should put something on the scratches, but she said no – she seemed to know all about what to do. But I think she was grateful to have me there, even if I wasn't much practical use. It's not that I was scared, Gran – it's not like she had tried to kill herself this time – but it's seeing another person in so much pain inside, and not being able to help.

Helen says she thinks she might be better going into the psychiatric hospital for a while. She's been in the house nearly two years, and she's very settled there. She is friendly with another resident called Lauren (though they are chalk and cheese! Lauren is ever so loud – she reminds me of my friend Becs from college, that you met at Mum and Dad's one time, do you remember? She'd just dyed a crimson streak in her hair and Dad said she looked like a badger in the sunset). Helen has also made friends with the new girl, Nasreen. Nasreen's English still isn't too good – she can't keep up with Lauren's sassy patter, but Helen never seems to mind taking the time to listen to what she's saying. Anyway, I know Helen really wants to stay, but the problem is Emily and Pat T. (they are the paid staff) only work Monday to Friday, and they finish at five o'clock, and even during the day they are often out at meetings or visiting the ex-residents that we still support. There's the phone rota in the evenings and at weekends, but it's not the same really. So we might say 'safe house' but of course it isn't; it doesn't have the cover to be really safe. I really think Helen might need a higher level of support. But I'm sure she thinks it will be a kind of defeat to have to go into hospital, an admission that she isn't coping.

I was thinking about what you said about nature rambles, and I thought how much I liked them too. When I was in the juniors I could have told you exactly which tree was a sycamore and an ash and a beech, but now I haven't a clue. I didn't even have a book that would tell me, I had to look them all up on the internet. Anyway, it wasn't in my lesson plan for the term but I decided to take my class out on Tuesday afternoon, since it was the last week of term – just round the school field, because you need parental permission letters in advance nowadays, and a formal risk assessment, to take them off site. I'd never realised how much variety there is, just in our own grounds – there were even some cowslips on the bank by the fence at the far end of the field. Then we got the pictures of all the different trees and plants and birds and insects that we'd seen on the smartboard, and they drew pictures of them and marked their identifying features. I hadn't seen them so engrossed since that doctor came in and showed them the human organs in jars. At least, they were engrossed until it turned out that Josh Cayley had an allergy to wild borage, and his fingers puffed up enormously where he'd been touching it, and he ran round the classroom saying he was Edward Sausagehands. We've also been doing that Islam project, you know, and yesterday I told them about how Muslims always keep their copy of the Koran on a high shelf, so you look up to it, and no other books can be higher than it is. Nicky Stefanopoulos said he's going to keep his football programmes on the top of his wardrobe from now on, and always wash his hand before he touches them.

We've been wondering about how to involve Jack Caulfield (the blind boy) in PE a bit more. He loves gymnastics, and swimming, but the problem is the team games – ball sports and things, you know. We played rounders last week, and of course he can't take a turn with the bat, and is no use at all as a short fielder. But we found he's surprisingly good at bowling. Point him the right direction, and after a couple of loose balls he quickly becomes very consistent at what Karen (who watches a lot of sport on TV) calls 'maintaining his length and line'. And you should see Jack run, Gran! He sprints full tilt across the school field, with that irrepressible imperative to expend energy that comes with being eight years old. Every now and then he'll trip, or hit someone, and go down full length, but more often than not he's fine. It's having the confidence to do it that is so hard to credit.

Well, look after yourself, won't you, Gran? Don't be trying to do *too* much yourself. Leave poor Kirsty something to do as well! And I'm really looking forward to seeing you at the weekend.

Lots of love,

Margaret x

From: Richard Slater [rpslater@hc.parliament.uk]
Sent: 24/3/05 16:06
To: Michael Carragan [mmcarragan@hc.parliament.uk]

Michael, hi. Are you going to be in London for Easter? Fancy a drink?

Richard.

Richard Slater (Labour)
Member of Parliament for Ipswich

From: Michael Carragan
[mmcarragan@hc.parliament.uk]
Sent: 24/3/05 16:30
To: Richard Slater [rpslater@hc.parliament.uk]

Sorry, mate, I'm going to my folks. Why don't you
bloody well go and see your mother?
 Michael.

 Michael Carragan (Labour)
 Member of Parliament for West Bromwich West

From: Richard Slater [rpslater@hc.parliament.uk]
Sent: 24/3/05 16:39
To: Michael Carragan [mmcarragan@hc.parliament.uk]

Hmm. Have a good Easter, anyway, Mike.
 Richard.

 Richard Slater (Labour)
 Member of Parliament for Ipswich

From: Rebecca Prichard [becs444@btinternet.com]
Sent: 24/3/05 22:02
To: Margaret Hayton [margarethayton@yahoo.co.uk]

Hi Margaret,

What are you doing for Easter? Going to your parents' place?

Becs xx

From: Margaret Hayton
[margarethayton@yahoo.co.uk]
Sent: 24/3/05 22:26
To: Rebecca Prichard [becs444@btinternet.com]

Dear Becs,

No, Easter is Dad's busiest day of the year, I'd only be in the way. Last year I went home on Good Friday, but was back in college by Saturday lunchtime. There were white lilies in the bath, elderly soprano voices piping 'Now the Green Blade Riseth' in questionable harmony from the dining room, and my bed was barely visible beneath sufficient Cadbury's mini-eggs to provision every Sunday School pupil in the home counties. This year I'm off to Gran's. You?

Margaret xx

From: Rebecca Prichard [becs444@btinternet.com]
Sent: 24/3/05 22:32
To: Margaret Hayton [margarethayton@yahoo.co.uk]

To Mum and Dad's as usual. I think we're all going to be home – me, Sam, and Emma with Tom and the children. Mum will probably have ordered a ten-kilo turkey. I swear the one we had at Christmas was really an emu.

Hugs,

Becs xxx

From: Richard Slater [rpslater@hc.parliament.uk]
Sent: 30/3/05 13:27
To: Michael Carragan [mmcarragan@hc.parliament.uk]

Hello Michael,

So, ASBOs it is. I called my mate Geoff Howard at the *Town Crier* and have fixed up for the two of us to accompany a pair of Suffolk Constabulary's finest (Kev and Ian) on their patrol of the town centre on Friday night. All I need now is a fine evening, a fair wind, and for the youth of Ipswich to do their worst.

Richard.

Richard Slater (Labour)
Member of Parliament for Ipswich

From: Michael Carragan
[mmcarragan@hc.parliament.uk]
Sent: 30/3/05 14:03
To: Richard Slater [rpslater@hc.parliament.uk]

I think you're in luck, Richard – Friday's forecast is for perfect binge-drinking weather.

While I've got you there – you're the expert on constituency cranks, aren't you? How do you manage to shake them off? In addition to my camphorous tartan shadow with the mutt, one of my long-standing serial letter-writers has joined the throng of regulars at my surgeries. It's a whole long story about a pelvic injury at work and problems with disability benefit and a refused insurance claim. Pretty sure he's an entrenched non-voter anyway, and there's no good publicity in malingerers with unromantic maladies, but he tends to hang around and complain about my inactivity on his behalf, and he has an unusually carrying voice. How do I get rid of him?
Michael.

Michael Carragan (Labour)
Member of Parliament for West Bromwich West

From: Richard Slater [rpslater@hc.parliament.uk]
Sent: 30/3/05 14:11
To: Michael Carragan [mmcarragan@hc.parliament.uk]

What you need to do is to create a filtering system. I
have my own honed to a fine degree of discrimination.
As we all know, being seen to be doing Good Works
in the constituency is essential to one's image – even
for you lucky sods who have one foot in higher
places – but you have to pick the right issues. You
sift through the mailbag and you select only those
correspondents whose problems promise any political
mileage. Good sob stories, which will earn you
Brownie points if you appear in the local rag with the
smiling beneficiary of your heroic efforts. Out go the
popular turn-offs (teenage mums who can't get a
council flat, cabbies who've lost their licence, and
anyone who's ever been in prison) and also the plain
boring (leylandii hedges, rising damp and the like).
Instead, you pick out the few that look sexy and
image-boosting, the kind of fights you want to see
yourself associated with, and you invite them to
attend your next surgery, giving an appointed hour
and venue.

Then (and this is the clever bit), you dodge all the
rest of the mob by moving your surgery around
without telling anyone. Anywhere will do, as long as
it's obscure enough to throw the surgery squatters off
the scent. Once mine used always to be held in the
Mandela Suite at the town hall, but now they are all
over the place: community centres, school halls, scout
huts. I fully expect to be holding court one of these
months in the gents at the back of a turf accountant

on the Woodbridge Road. You can present it as 'neighbourhood outreach', all perfectly laudable. Of course, my well-trained constituency staff do advertise the venue in the *Town Crier* each month, though I've never managed to spot it myself – the notice is probably nestling somewhere in the small ads, between litters of golden labrador puppies and second-hand cross trainers. Result? – nice quiet surgeries, devoid of the shifting cast of crazies and time-wasters who used to inhabit the waiting room, and peopled instead by a manageable number of grateful, non-abusive, media-friendly petitioners, rich fodder for my Richard-Slater-as-Model-Constituency-MP campaign. Works a treat.

Richard.

Richard Slater (Labour)
Member of Parliament for Ipswich

42 Gledhill Street
Ipswich
Suffolk IP3 2DA

The Today Programme
BBC Radio 4
Television Centre
Wood Lane
London W12 7RJ

31 March 2005

Dear Sir or Madam,

I am writing to question the balance of an interview which I heard on this morning's Today programme.

Your correspondent was talking to a British Jewish couple who had gone out to build a house on the West Bank as part of the wave of Israeli settlement there. Asked why they had chosen to do this, the husband spoke of the need for 'a safe home for the Jewish people'. This went wholly unchallenged by your interviewer. But the couple were from Folkestone. Wasn't that a safe enough home? The people of Kent and the surrounding counties are not exactly sworn to driving the Jewish population of Folkestone into the sea.

Yours faithfully,

Margaret Hayton.

PS. I think John Humphrys is to be congratulated – he does an excellent job.

From: Richard Slater
[richard.slater@btopenworld.com]
Sent: 2/4/05 00:31
To: Michael Carragan [mikecarragan@yahoo.com]

Hi Michael,

Well, I wouldn't say my publicity event this evening was the greatest runaway success. There were Kev and Ian in their reinforced helmets. There were the pubs, pouring out the lager. All that was needed was for the drunken loutery of Ipswich to do their bit. I wasn't asking for much: a little bespattering of the pavement with vomit, maybe someone urinating in the doorway of Next, perhaps a gentle jostle or the playful toss of a beer can or two in our direction.

But no! The pubs closed at the appointed hour, and their clientele, warmly befuddled and sporting affable smiles, swayed quietly away towards the bus stops and taxi ranks, where they formed orderly (if not indeed positively matey) queues, or else dispersed, in stumbling but benevolent twos and threes, towards cocoa and bed. Mindful of the date, I half expected twenty or so yobs with public disorder on their minds to jump out from behind Barclays bank and shout 'April fool'. Even Kev and Ian were apologetic (perhaps mistaking me for someone empowered to cut their Friday night overtime) and kept saying that it is not normally this quiet.

Finally, at around 11.45, a likely-looking gaggle of shaven-headed youths approached us, taking up the whole width of the pavement in a promisingly threatening manner, and announcing to the world in general in cacophonous baritones that Norwich City stood in grave danger of relegation. Upon seeing us, they began to make those piggy snorting noises so wittily directed by crowds at the police. Just as they drew level, one of them – a thickset and heavily tattooed young man – accosted Ian with a jut of the chin and the word 'Oi', and a broad arm began to rain blows upon Ian's shoulders and back. I was debating whether to intervene (the press being present, after all) or to follow my instinct and run like the wind, when it became clear that the bombardment which Ian was taking was in fact bestowed in a spirit of affection. It seems they had been at school together. It was when Ian produced a photo of his new baby, which was passed solemnly round the group of skinheads, that Geoff cut his losses and went home.

Any more bright ideas, Michael?

Richard.

PS. It wasn't a completely wasted evening, however. I did acquire a Suffolk Constabulary souvenir keyring, which is also a lighter. Unfortunately, being neither a smoker nor an arsonist, I am unlikely to get much use out of it.

From: Michael Carragan [mikecarragan@yahoo.com]
Sent: 2/4/05 09:57
To: Richard Slater [richard.slater@btopenworld.com]

Do the Suffolk Fire Service have a matching one with a water pistol to put out the fires?

Michael.

From: Richard Slater [richard.slater@btopenworld.com]
Sent: 2/4/05 10:24
To: Michael Carragan [mikecarragan@yahoo.com]

And the ambulance service do one with a tiny oxygen mask and burns blanket. I may collect the set.
   Richard.

WITCH
Women of Ipswich Together Combating Homelessness

                                           42 Gledhill Street
                                                     Ipswich
                                           Suffolk IP3 2DA

Mr Richard Slater, MP
House of Commons
London SW1A 0AA

                                                6 April 2005

Dear Mr Slater,
   As treasurer of WITCH I am writing to you, our constituency MP, about a matter of government policy which has recently had a direct impact upon our service provision, and about which we feel considerable dismay.
   You are probably aware that asylum seekers are not entitled to any recourse to state funds unless and until their application for leave to remain in the country is successful. This means that even a voluntary project such as Witch House cannot offer financial assistance to an asylum seeker

without putting our local authority grant at risk. In our view, this is an attack upon one of the most vulnerable groups of homeless people, and a serious impediment to a group such as ours in our aim to provide a service for those most in need of it. We are currently housing a young asylum seeker, and are having to fund-raise from charitable sources to meet the cost of her accommodation with us. If we cannot raise the sums required, she will lose her room and the support which we provide with it.

I am by this time fully aware that you do not consider correspondence from your constituents to be a high priority, but I urge you most strongly, please do not ignore the plight of this young woman and hundreds like her. I will soon be able to wallpaper my bedroom with your standard form letters. Or perhaps I will bundle them all up and post them to the Prime Minister to show him how much you care about your constituents' concerns.

Yours sincerely,
Margaret Hayton.

From: Michael Carragan
[mmcarragan@hc.parliament.uk]
Sent: 7/4/05 14:42
To: Richard Slater [rpslater@hc.parliament.uk]

Hi Richard,
So if ASBOs did not prove a fertile area, how

about PFI? It is rarely off the Rottweiler's lips.
  Michael.

Michael Carragan (Labour)
Member of Parliament for West Bromwich West

From: Richard Slater [rpslater@hc.parliament.uk]
Sent: 8/4/05 16:07
To: Michael Carragan [mmcarragan@hc.parliament.uk]

Michael, hi, and thanks for the suggestion. I've looked into it, and I am sorry to say that PFI has not so far exactly been a transformative influence upon health provision in Ipswich. No new hospital, not so much as a new ward. The sole achievement to date of private finance in the Suffolk Health Trust area is a small annexe to Ipswich General, providing an outpatients' service in prosthetics and orthotics. I am not quite sure whether posing with a wooden leg is exactly the publicity that is going to get me on to the shortlist for ministerial office, but I am past caring. I have fixed up to visit the new facility, with Geoff Howard of the *Crier* in tow again (plus a photographer) on 19 April.
  Tonight – you, me, beer?
  Richard.

Richard Slater (Labour)
Member of Parliament for Ipswich

House of Commons
London SW1A 0AA

11 April 2005

Dear Ms Hayton,

Thank you for your letter of 2 April, raising an issue of concern. May I suggest that you attend at my monthly constituency surgery, which will be held this Saturday, 16 April, in the Crawford & Phillips Memorial Hall, Felixstowe Road, Ipswich, between 9.30 a.m. and 12 noon. I hope that a 10.30 a.m. appointment will be convenient for you; if not, please phone the hall that morning on Ipswich 253440, and my secretary will fix an alternative time for you.

Yours sincerely,
Richard Slater, MP.

From: Richard Slater [rpslater@hc.parliament.uk]
Sent: 11/4/05 15:52
To: Michael Carragan [mmcarragan@hc.parliament.uk]

Hi Michael,

Oh, God, against all reason and judgement I have just agreed to meet one of my constituency stalkers on Saturday! It's that recent acquisition, Margaret, she of the canine faecal obsession. She meets none of the usual criteria to get through my screening process. Different issue every time, from the global to the trivial, all put with equal vehemence and with no apparent discrimination, and not one of them the least bit promising publicity-wise. (And I had been hoping to have a peaceful and potentially image-enhancing morning, too. I'd found a gem: the new landlord of a formerly rowdy drinkers' pub in the town centre – average age of punter sixteen and a half – who's had his application for an all-day licence turned down by the borough council. He's invested in a stack of high chairs and an imported Italian coffee machine the size of a Nissan Micra, and wants to create a family atmosphere and turn the place over to continental-style drinking. Now, there's one that presses all the right buttons – an absolute gift!)

But the trouble is, this Margaret person has got me running scared, actually threatening to tell the Rottweiler that I don't take constituents' letters seriously. I could do without that as things stand just now – I was just edging my way back to the door of the prime ministerial kennel and preparing to knock. So it sounds like she's not just an old biddy but a stroppy old biddy to boot. Or even possibly (since it appears that she's involved in that WITCH mob) a stroppy man-hating old biddy. Now trying to decide what to wear on Saturday: full body armour, or trainers for a quick getaway?

Richard.

Richard Slater (Labour)
Member of Parliament for Ipswich

From: Rebecca Prichard [becs444@btinternet.com]
Sent: 15/4/05 22:44
To: Margaret Hayton [margarethayton@yahoo.co.uk]

Hi, Margaret. So: latest instalment in my abecedarian love life. That night with Paula I did meet someone, but his name was Andrew and I've done A. He was pretty hot, though, and also fairly insistent, so I let him see me home in the taxi, but he didn't come in. I think he may have been put off when I kept asking if I could call him Drew.

But then I found him, right on my doorstep. Well, waiting outside my classroom at 3 p.m. every day, actually. Declan. He's the father of Zoe in my class – and before you say anything, yes, he is a *single* parent. (And the nearest thing I have to an ABIE.) Tall, with mussy dark hair that makes me want to fluffle it with my fingers, and to-die-for brown eyes. He's about the only dad that does the home-time pick-up, which is odd when he's one of the few who appear to be in gainful employment. He has one of those high-powered I-work-from-home-now kind of jobs, computers or consultancy or something, to fit round Zoe. Mind you, he can't be doing that well, or why would he still be living in Moss Side? We're still at a very early stage so I haven't asked exactly what he does, nor where Zoe's mum is. It's just been a couple of drinks. We haven't even been to bed yet (what, after two dates? What's going on, Becs, I hear you say, this is not like you), but obviously Zoe is a complication, and I have my reputation to worry about. I mean, I'm his daughter's teacher for Chrissakes!

So, what's with you? How was your Easter holiday? And what have your coven of (Ips)witches been up to?

Love and hugs,

Becs xxx

From: Margaret Hayton [margarethayton@yahoo.co.uk]
Sent: 15/4/05 23:32
To: Rebecca Prichard [becs444@btinternet.com]

Dear Becs,

Going out with a parent! Does the head know? Isn't it against paragraph 32(b) of the Primary Teachers' Penal Code? Up there with smoking within view of a minor, saying 'inches', or setting out a sum vertically before Key Stage Two? Punishable by public flogging at the wall-bars by the chair of governors? I suggest you locate Ed or Ethan immediately, to lead you back to the straight and narrow.

(By the way, I'm not sure you can have a lone male ABIE. They are normally female – or else come in pairs, dressed in matching rainwear.)

The main excitement here is that on Saturday I am going to meet my elusive MP, the slippery Mr Richard

Slater – he's invited me to his constituency surgery to talk
to him about asylum seekers. He holds it in some obscure
community hall – I'd always imagined these things
went on at the town hall, or the local Party HQ.
Anyway, I'm very glad of the opportunity: I really want
to convince him of how appalling it is that when
someone comes to this country thinking it will offer
her safety, and she's homeless, even a voluntary
organisation can't offer her support, if they are funded
by the state. It's just a nod towards the knee-jerk
xenophobes who think we're going to be swamped by
immigrants making bogus asylum claims and sponging
off social security – and what does it mean? People
like Nasreen (I don't think I mentioned her – she's an
Albanian girl living at Witch House), all on her own in
a strange country where she barely speaks the
language and certainly can't read a form, unable to
make use of the services she requires when she's
homeless and in need.

Trouble is, I'm sure he's not going to listen. He is
reputed to have been quite a lefty at one time, when
he was on the city council. Persephone says he
supported financing the Multi-cultural Centre, and
helped find the new premises for the Women's Aid
refuge after the old one was torched by someone's
ex-partner. But then, she says, he took being New
Labour so seriously in '97 that he freshly minted
himself. From what you read in the local press, he's
now so sensible that he makes a pair of lace-up Start-

Rites look like a walk on the wild side. He even abstained on the war in Iraq – I mean, he actually *abstained*! If he didn't agree with military intervention then why didn't he vote against like a decent human being? It's like saying, 'Hmm, should we violate international law and embark upon a war that will cost the lives of tens of thousands of Iraqis? Well, maybe not, but I don't really have much of a view one way or the other. Now, where were we, about those EU cabbage subsidies . . .'

Love,

Margaret xx

PS. 'Abecedarian' is a cool straight 8.

From: Rebecca Prichard [becs444@btinternet.com]
Sent: 15/4/05 23:34
To: Margaret Hayton [margarethayton@yahoo.co.uk]

If you nod towards a knee-jerk xenophobe (1.5 points), aren't you are in serious danger of getting clocked on the head? Sounds like you need to give *him* a good bashing about the brains with a copy of the Asylum and Immigration Act.

And *please* can I keep Declan? He's so pretty!

Becs xx

42 Gledhill Street
Ipswich

17 April 2005

Dearest Petey,

I feel like I've been busy recently, though I haven't exactly *done* much, to speak of. I suppose it's just that I don't seem to ever just sit and watch telly any more. Last night that Nasreen came round again, the girl I told you about from the hostel, for another session with Margaret and the Biff and Chip books. I made us all a pot of tea when they were finishing, and went and joined them in the sitting room. Nasreen has hers without any milk. Luckily she mentioned it before I'd done the cups, because I still always put the milk in first – do you remember how you always teased me about it when we first met, because you said it showed I was posh. What a joke! Mum and Dad were really proud when I got the job at the bank, but they'd still have laughed at the idea that a daughter of theirs could ever be posh. I just started doing it because then you can see better whether the tea has brewed enough, when you start to pour it in.

Anyway, we sat and chatted, and Nasreen is lovely. She's shy and her English is a bit shaky, but she has a really pretty smile. She always wears a scarf, but it's not one of those black ones that hide half your face, it doesn't even cover all her hair, she wears it back a bit on her forehead, and her hair all loose and escaping at the back. It's not even a special scarf, just an ordinary flowered one – I think Sarah at work has got one nearly the same, from

71

Debenhams in the sales after Christmas. And her hair is wonderful – so black it's almost purple or blue, and catching the light, so that it made me think of the word 'lustrous' out of one of my romances. I think she must put scent on it, because when I leaned over to pass her her tea I caught a waft of something sweet, like Turkish delight or cinnamon or that orange flower water Dora puts in her chocolate buns. Maybe there's no wonder that the men in the east think their women should cover up their hair, to keep that beauty all for themselves, I thought.

Well, then Nasreen started telling us why she'd left her country. It was me who asked her, I think Margaret had never liked to, but I suppose I was curious, why someone should leave their home and friends and come somewhere so different when she's so young (eighteen, she said). Snuffs went and sat next to her on the settee and put her head on her lap while she was talking. She always seems to pick up on it if someone is sad (you know what a comfort she's been to me without you here). It seems Nasreen had a boyfriend that her family didn't approve of. Gjergj, his name is apparently – she wrote it down for us because English people can never spell it – and I said, how funny, that's like my husband, his middle name is George, and that made her smile. Apparently it was because she is Muslim and he is a Christian. 'Albanian Orthodox' is what Margaret called it, I think – she seems to have been reading up on Nasreen's country. I'd never heard of it – I thought there was only Russian Orthodox and Greek Orthodox. Poor Nasreen must have been really scared. She says she thought her brothers would actually hurt her, or Gjergj, and that's why she ran away. Isn't it awful what families can do to one another, sometimes? And of course English families can be just as bad. There's another young girl in Margaret's hostel, really bad with her nerves she is, because her father abused her when she was little.

Me and Margaret have been swapping books. I've got her on to my old Nevil Shute novels, and she's lent me a book called *Ruth* – it made me think of your sister. But terribly sad, it is, it's about a girl who has a baby and she's not married and the man abandons her. It's by that Mrs Gaskell. (I wonder why she's always 'Mrs'? You never hear anyone saying 'Miss Austen', do you?) Funny that they never made us read Mrs Gaskell's books at school – it was always the male writers like Dickens and Thomas Hardy – well, apart from Jane Austen, but she was the only one. Margaret says she is named after someone in another one of Mrs Gaskell's books. Her dad chose it because it was his favourite story. She was talking about her name last night, in fact, how she has always hated it because she thinks it makes her sound old. I'd never really thought much about my name before – it's a pity really, because it means I never asked Mum and Dad about why they chose it, while they were alive. If you write it in capitals it looks rather like one of those things where the initials stand for something – an acronym, isn't it? – or the new name of something that used to be nationalised. But I like the way it has 'core' in it, like the heart of something. Because your name is at the heart of who you are, after all, isn't it? Your grandad was Peter, wasn't he? I can't remember how old you said you were when he died – about twelve, I think? I wonder if he was like you.

Margaret met the MP yesterday, at his 'surgery' as they call it – makes it sound like she's going to him with the flu. She wanted to talk to him about Nasreen, something about how she can't stay in the hostel because of being from abroad. I thought that was all illegal now, treating people differently because of where they're from, but apparently not. I asked her how it went, because she'd been full of nothing else all week beforehand, and she did say he is going to meet her again next week, and get her some answers, so I suppose she was fairly happy about it, but she had a sort of hazy look that she gets sometimes, so I decided not to ask her any more.

The rosemary alongside the path has come into flower this week. It looks a picture, and it's brought the bumble bees out of nowhere. It got me thinking about the year when Snuffy was a puppy, and she thought that all the springy plants, the rosemary and the hebes, were a game we'd put there specially for her. Do you remember how she used to take a run up and leap into the middle of the bushes as if they were a bouncy castle? You always knew when she'd been at it, because she'd come in smelling of rosemary, and then you'd go out and survey the damage, and poor Snuffs would creep under the kitchen table and look so guilty that you hadn't the heart to be cross with her. Most of the garden got flattened that summer – but it was only one year, because by the next spring she got too heavy to bounce and went straight through if she jumped on the plants. So then she got bored of it, and of course everything soon grew back to normal. You know, love, every time I call Snuffy in from the garden it reminds me of you, and how tickled I was when you came up with the name for her. Odd really, because we never even really watched 'The West Wing', did we? We just used to see the end credits before our Friday gardening programme. Mind you, you always preferred the ones on the BBC. But you used to tease me for looking less and less like Charlie Dimmock and more and more like Pippa Greenwood.

Dora at the bank has invited me to a do for her and Dave's thirtieth anniversary at the end of the month, at the social club at Dave's work. Nearly twenty years we've been friends now, me and Dora. I remember she took me under her wing on my very first day at the bank. 'We'll be Dora and Cora,' she said – and we still are! Anyway, this anniversary got me thinking about their twenty-fifth. Do you remember, Pete? They had it in that boat they've turned into a pub down at the docks, and you kept making jokes about having another tot of rum, and calling everyone 'me hearties' and 'landlubbers' until it drove me crazy and I went up on deck in a huff. But then when I was looking over the railings you came after me and put your arms round me from behind and took hold of my breasts and said 'Ahoy there', and that you'd found a chest of treasure, and suddenly it all seemed funny again, and I turned round and you kissed me.

I miss you, Petey. Love you for ever,

Cora xxx

From: Michael Carragan
[mmcarragan@hc.parliament.uk]
Sent: 18/4/05 15:47
To: Richard Slater [rpslater@hc.parliament.uk]

Richard, hi! Well, you'll be pleased to know I did my duty by you this morning. A rare appearance by the Rottweiler at a meeting on franchising of prison kitchen services. As I followed him out at the end, blending myself amongst the phalanx of special advisers by walking very quickly with my mobile phone adhered to one ear, I was able to slide seamlessly from the subject of privatised porridge to the question of when the Iraq vote refuseniks will be allowed out of gaol. I even managed to mention your name. He emitted a kind of small grunt as he outpaced me down the corridor, but there was no visible curl of the prime ministerial lip.

Speaking of slathering jaws, how did it go on Saturday with your ageing feminist tub-thumper?

Michael.

Michael Carragan (Labour)
Member of Parliament for West Bromwich West

From: Richard Slater [rpslater@hc.parliament.uk]
Sent: 18/4/05 16:19
To: Michael Carragan [mmcarragan@hc.parliament.uk]

Hello, Michael. Very grateful for the plug with ROTW. Fancy a drink tonight to analyse that grunt in more detail?

The gods of back bench servitude have smiled on me for once, in the matter of the tub-thumper. She was due at 10.30, and I stepped out into the lobby expecting something tweedy and sexagenarian, but the only non-empty chair (see how my venue-hopping works?) was occupied by a twenty-something vision in stone-washed denim and Polartec, with a cloud of dark ringlets and huge, serious eyes. Disbelieving, I even called her name, 'Margaret Hayton', addressing the light fittings non-committally. The vision rose, and came forward and held out its hand gravely, and I couldn't think of anything to say except 'Richard Slater' (which was unnecessary information), or anything to do except go on shaking her hand like a slightly senile vicar at a parish tea.

Turns out she is a junior school teacher. It was good to be forewarned – you wouldn't try to put anything over on someone who regularly stands up and faces thirty unescorted eight year olds. She talked some sense, too – and in an impassioned tone which was very hard to resist. Or at least, I found myself finding it so. It was all about the 1996 legislation – the Asylum and Immigration Act, you know, the one when asylum seekers lost the right to council housing and other state support. She has a solicitor friend who works with refugees who thinks that voluntary organisations may also be precluded from offering housing if they are grant-aided by national or local government. Is this your neck of the Home Office woods, by any chance? Might pick your brains about it later. I told her I would certainly be looking into it, and she gave this laugh, except it was a laugh which made me feel depressed. Not that she was laughing at me, it wasn't that, it was more sad and self-mocking, and it seemed to belong more to the old Margaret, the hard-bitten matron of my imagination, than to this fresh and clear-eyed creature. And before I knew what was happening I had taken hold of her hand again . . . and asked her to come back next Saturday! What was I thinking of? There's nothing glamorous about the arcane detail of borough council grant-making powers, and asylum seekers certainly aren't the darlings of the public's heart right now. What's more, I don't have another one of my ex-directory surgeries in Ipswich for another four weeks, and I had planned on spending next Saturday in London, conducting a stratigraphic survey of the layered deposits of paperwork on my desk, and maybe making time to check out that new second-hand bookshop in Goswell Road.

You can berate me for my stupidity tonight – how about meeting at 10 p.m. in the Lobby?
Richard.

Richard Slater (Labour)
Member of Parliament for Ipswich

From: Margaret Hayton
[margarethayton@yahoo.co.uk]
Sent: 18/4/05 22:10
To: Rebecca Prichard [becs444@btinternet.com]

Dear Becs,

How are Zoe and her dad, then? Has she asked Daddy what Miss Prichard is doing in the bathroom in her underwear yet? (I bet you're a bit nervous when it's her turn to 'Show and Tell' about her weekend.)

Well, I had my meeting with Mr Slater. In fact he told me to call him Richard, but it doesn't seem right calling your MP by his first name, somehow. Like calling someone's grandad Reginald, or when Dad's bishop asked me to call him Sid. Though he does seem more of a Richard than a Mr Slater, actually. He's not as old as he looks in the pictures in the paper, and he's got nice eyes.

When I got there I had to wait a bit, and there were rows of chairs like at the dentist, but no one there waiting except me. He came out of his office and called my name, and I got really embarrassed, you know how I always do if someone says my name in public. Not that it was exactly in public, there were only the two of us there, but you know what I mean. I hate – *hate* – my name. I always imagine people looking round, expecting to see a woman in her fifties, in a sensible raincoat – and I'm sure that was what he was thinking. People have aunts, and even great-aunts, called Margaret; I've never met anyone else our age cursed with the name. You can't shorten it either. Imagine being a Madge, that would be even worse (slatternly 1950s housewife with a fag in her mouth and curlers in her hair), or a Marge (cartoon character with yellow face and two-foot blue beehive). And my best friend from school had a border collie called Meg. That just leaves Maggie . . . and for me the only image that conjures up is documentary footage on TV from the 1980s, CND demos, or striking miners on picket lines, and that inevitable angry chanting: 'Maggie, Maggie, Maggie – out, out, out!' Still, I suppose it could have been worse – Dad didn't just like Elizabeth Gaskell, he was also into George Eliot and Thomas Hardy, so I might have ended up a Rosamond or a Bathsheba.

Sorry, I digress. Basically, he seemed interested (though I suspect Mr Richard Slater MP might be adept at seeming all sorts of things). He's going to meet with me again next Saturday and tell me what he's been able to find out. I think next time I'll wear my interview blouse, and those black trousers I had for graduation, instead of just jeans. I need to look more businesslike. Then he might take me more seriously, you know – not just think I'm some kind of kid.

I know it sounds corny, Becs – but wouldn't it be just amazing if I were really able to make a difference over this issue?

Love,

Margaret xx

From: Rebecca Prichard [becs444@btinternet.com]
Sent: 18/4/05 22:44
To: Margaret Hayton [margarethayton@yahoo.co.uk]

Hi Margaret,

First of all: Declan. I think he is gorgeous, and things are hotting up nicely. I care nothing for your contumely and vilipendency – it's water off a duck's back, chuck.

Second of all: this Richard bloke. Nice eyes, eh?

And third of all: names. At least Margaret Hale is a decent heroine. Virtuous, but feisty with it. My mum called me Rebecca after the Daphne du Maurier (or in fact more likely the Hitchcock). Having read the book, at age fifteen, I took her to task about naming me after someone who is so obnoxious, so faithless and philandering, that she ends up drowned for her trouble – and has an extremely questionable relationship with her housekeeper. It seems to have passed Mum by completely that Rebecca wasn't the name of the heroine. Come to think of it, she didn't have a name at all, did she, the second wife? Maybe I should change my name to /&%>, the schoolteacher formerly known as Becs.

Hugs,

Becs xx

From: Margaret Hayton [margarethayton@yahoo.co.uk]
Sent: 18/4/05 22:49
To: Rebecca Prichard [becs444@btinternet.com]

Dear /&%>,

'Contumely' and 'vilipendency' are both 7s, though I strongly suspect illegal use of the thesaurus. I've never dared use 'contumely' myself. I suspect it of perfidy – a noun in adverb's clothing.

Margaret xx

MP FALLS ON FEET

Ipswich MP Mr Richard Slater today fell on his feet during a visit to a new annexe at Ipswich General Hospital. The new department deals with artificial limbs, and Mr Slater was slightly injured when he tripped over a pair of prosthetic feet, knocking himself out on a consulting table and spraining a finger in his fall. But he was certainly in the right place, as Dr Clive Troman was immediately on hand to administer first aid. 'Normally I deal with amputees,' said Dr Troman, 'specialising mainly in hemipelvectomy patients. However, I have not forgotten my basic resuscitation techniques, and was able to employ them to good effect upon Mr Slater.'

Mr Slater commented: 'As I was coming round I heard Dr Troman saying that the forefinger was broken and would have to come off. It was a relief to discover that he was talking about a prosthetic hand which I had knocked to the floor, rather than my own!'

The Hollies
East Markhurst

19 April 2005

Dear Margaret,

I feel very modern with my mobile telephone. You'll have me 'texting' next – writing half the words in code like the youngsters do. I've seen them doing it on EastEnders. Thank you very much, my dear – you always were a thoughtful girl. Do you remember when you were little, about four I think, and your torch batteries kept running down, and Mum found out you were leaving it on in the toy box every night in case your dolls were afraid of the dark? And I was thinking last night about our golden wedding, up at the village hall, and how Grandad couldn't remember who anyone was, and got upset. You took him in the little side kitchen and made him a cup of tea and managed to calm him down, and he told me later he'd really enjoyed his day. It's funny how, even when his Alzheimer's was getting bad, he always seemed to remember you, love. Because, you know, sometimes he couldn't even remember who I was, and all he seemed able to recall was things from when he was a boy. That used to make me cry more than anything – married to me fifty years, and he would look at me as if I were a stranger and tell me that he wanted to go home.

I am sorry to hear about your friend, the one who wants to harm herself, and I'm sure that you *do* help her, love, even if you only sit with her sometimes when she's feeling low. And you needn't worry, I do know about child abuse. We never talked about it in my day, of course, but your generation didn't invent it, believe me. And I watch a lot of daytime television these days, remember. I know more about all sorts of things, sex included, than I ever did when your grandad was alive! I'm sorry she might have to go into hospital. But I don't think she needs to think of it as a 'defeat' as you call it. When I was a girl they didn't call it the psychiatric hospital, they called it the mental asylum –

a safe place for people who couldn't manage in the outside world. Maybe that's what your friend needs at the moment, a little bit of asylum.

Mrs Ashby at church was asking after you the other day, and she wanted to know whether you are 'courting'. Such a sweet old-fashioned expression, I thought – I haven't heard it since I was a girl. It's what my old mum would have said. Anyway, I told her I was much too polite ever to ask you! I know you haven't mentioned anyone 'special' since that nice boy in college, Mark wasn't it, the one who came to the vicarage for Christmas with us all one year? At one time it seemed like you never came to visit without him. He used to butter me up something rotten, bringing me sherry, and teasing me about being the 'merry widow'. But I'm guessing that's all ended long since. I hope he didn't break your heart, dear. I know what these charmers can be.

Kirsty is very kind. She does pick up my shopping, not that I get through a lot of things. I can walk to the post office myself now, but still find it hard to manage a carrier bag as well as the frame. She's a thoughtful girl, too. Yesterday she brought me in a lot of women's magazines that she had finished with, and she says she will pick up some library books for me next time she goes into Winchester. But you never know what they'll have, and it isn't easy for someone else to choose books for you, when they don't know what you like, or what you've already read. Still, maybe she'll get me reading something new, something she likes, and perhaps I'll like it too. I wouldn't want to be too narrowly stuck in my tastes just because I'm an old lady! I watched an episode of that 'West Wing' and quite enjoyed it. I wonder if it's really like that for politicians? It all seems such a muddle, somehow.

Take care of yourself, dear.

Love from Gran xxx

ST EDITH'S PRIMARY SCHOOL
St Edith's Lane, Ipswich IP3 5BJ

20 April 2005

Nativity Play

This is to inform parents that the Key Stage Two Nativity Play will take place at 2 p.m. on Tuesday 10 May. It has been decided after all to stage the production, which had to be cancelled in December due to an epidemic of diarrhoea and vomiting amongst the snowflakes.

Doors open at 1.30 p.m. and parents are advised to come early if they wish to get a good seat. May we remind you once again that flash photography is not allowed; this year we will not be using a real donkey, so there should be less risk to the fabric of the school hall, but nevertheless the flashes can be equally distracting for human cast members.

Mrs E. Martin
Deputy Head

YOUR LETTERS

Sir, I am writing to express my concern about the state of some of the cycle paths in Ipswich town centre, and in particular the problem of raised metalwork. There are numerous instances, usually where the road surface has been repaired, where gratings or manhole covers are set considerably above the level of the surrounding tarmac. A particularly bad example is in the contraflow cycle lane in Godolphin Street, close to the junction with Parkside Road. Cyclists are obliged either to risk riding over these obstacles, or swerving out of the cycle lane, both of which are very dangerous. Yesterday I saw an elderly gentleman wobble and almost fall off his bike while trying to circumnavigate a raised grating. I have written to the borough council about this matter on two occasions, but as yet have received no reply.

M. Hayton, 42 Gledhill Street, Ipswich.

WITCH
Women of Ipswich Together Combating Homelessness

<u>Extract from minutes of meeting</u> at Ding's house, 21 April 2005, 8 p.m.

<u>News of residents</u>
Helen has arranged to go into hospital over the weekend while Witch House is unstaffed. If it goes well, she may

decide to do this regularly for a while. Pat T. has ascertained that this will not affect her housing benefit.

Lauren has been given another warning about noise after Mrs Robertson from number 27 complained again; she claims that some boys poured a can of lager on to the primulas in her front window box after she came out and told them to keep quiet. It was agreed to invite Mrs Robertson to attend the next house meeting, to air her concerns.

Joyce has been trying to reduce the levels of her medication, but in the interests of other residents she has agreed to do it only by slow degrees and under Dr Gould's supervision.

Varnish 'n' Nails started work on the repainting of the downstairs this week. Carole has gone to stay with her sister until it is finished, because the dust is giving her nightmares.

News of former residents still receiving support
Marianne has unfortunately lost her job at the chemist's, after Mr Singh found she had been inhaling the aerosol deodorants. She has applied for a job at the newsagent's on Mawson Street.

Any other business
It was decided that we couldn't have the joint meeting with Women's Aid at Witch House next week because we've got the decorators in.

From: Margaret Hayton [margarethayton@yahoo.co.uk]
Sent: 23/4/05 22:13
To: Rebecca Prichard [becs444@btinternet.com]

Dear Becs,

I had my second meeting with Richard Slater today, and I think it went OK. It seemed to be a good idea, wearing my interview blouse, because this time he had his eyes fixed intently on my face the whole time, and seemed to be really listening to my arguments. And I know it's not like me to notice something like this, but I have to say he has a very nice throat. I think what drew my attention to it was that his Adam's apple kept bobbing up and down, like he was swallowing a lot. Maybe I was staring at it, because in fact he said that he had got a dry throat, and got himself some water, and I said, I hope you aren't getting a cold, because sometimes my throat feels dry and scratchy just before I go down with one. And then I thought, what am I doing, blathering to an MP about sore throats. He must think I am a complete idiot!

Anyway, he had spoken to colleagues at the Home Office – apparently he's pally with a junior minister there. It seems that what is supposed to happen is that asylum seekers who don't have relatives or friends over here to support them are all channelled into housing in 'reception zones' (which under this 'dispersal' policy they have can mean wherever they choose to send you, Glasgow or Birmingham or anywhere with no

housing shortage – in fact quite possibly Moss Side!).
Or else one of those awful accommodation centres –
you know, you've seen them on TV, I'm sure – usually
some bleak converted barracks or something. It would
be like being in prison! It's so unfair – Nasreen is happy
with us, and she gets the support of Emily and Pat T.,
plus I have been helping her with her reading, and
she's a really good influence on Lauren, one of the
other residents, who she's become friends with (sorry,
with whom she's become friends!).

But Richard says that although asylum seekers aren't
entitled to normal homeless persons' accommodation,
what we can do is persuade the borough council to
designate Witch House as being appropriate temporary
housing for Nasreen under the Immigration and Asylum
Act 1999, and then her rent will be paid by the Home
Office. It's a bit unusual, but he thinks it is allowed by
the regulations. I went straight round and told Nasreen.
Her English isn't up to the minutiae of immigration law,
but she was absolutely delighted to know she might be
able to stay with us until they make the decision on
her asylum application. In fact, she threw her arms
round my neck and hugged me. Mock all you wish, but
cycling home I found myself in tears.

Love,
Margaret xx

PS. How's your dad? You haven't mentioned him for
ages, and I'm never sure if I should ask.

From: Rebecca Prichard [becs444@btinternet.com]
Sent: 23/4/05 23:50
To: Margaret Hayton [margarethayton@yahoo.co.uk]

Hi there, Margaret! First it was nice eyes, now it's a nice throat. You want to watch out, my girl, your eyes seem to be moving downwards, and anyway, isn't looking lustfully upon a man against your anchoritic vows? But I'm very glad that you may have sorted things out for your friend Nasreen.

Speaking of lust, I just got back from Declan's. He asked me to stay over, and I *sooooo* wanted to, but you're not wrong about the ticklish problem of Zoe and bathrooms and underwear and difficult explanations. It's bad enough trying to relax and enjoy Declan's exceedingly attentive ministrations whilst suppressing the resultant noises of appreciation (and believe me, there is much to appreciate!). I'm scared of even breathing too rhythmically. Declan's flat is very small. Unlike his other assets . . . I really want to sleep all night with him and wake up with his body wrapped around me. So I know I'm in big trouble, because this isn't like me at all – normally I value my space in bed. I've always been a wham, bam, shut-the-door-on-your-way-out-and-I'll-call-you-tomorrow kind of girl. What is happening to me, Margaret?

As far as Dad is concerned, I think you can assume no news is good news. He's much the same. But

believe me, I shan't be shy about boring you with all
the ghastly details if he gets worse.

Big hugs,

Becs xxx

PS. If Zoe 'outs' me at school, and I am denied my
human rights by the Brunswick Road Governors, I
may be seeking asylum in Albania.

From: Margaret Hayton [margarethayton@yahoo.co.uk]
Sent: 23/4/05 22:55
To: Rebecca Prichard [becs444@btinternet.com]

Dear Becs,

It wasn't lust – purely an aesthetic observation. And
'anchoritic' is only a 5.5.

Margaret xx

From: Richard Slater [rpslater@hc.parliament.uk]
Sent: 25/4/05 14:14
To: Michael Carragan [mmcarragan@hc.parliament.uk]

Hi Michael,

Thanks for helping with that information about
housing for asylum seekers on Friday. I had my second
meeting with Margaret on Saturday, and she seemed
really happy with what you'd come up with for me.

May God and the National Women's Executive Committee forgive me, but she really does have the most breathtaking breasts. Last time she had on jeans and a fleece which didn't give more than a general impression of height and presumptive slender curves, but this time she was wearing a less than impregnable creamy blouse, with something lacy and insubstantial underneath. I found myself gulping somewhat in the manner of a concupiscent bullfrog. I tried hard to get a grip on myself by concentrating all my attention on her face, like someone who has been on one too many interpersonal skills courses. She'd got her hair scooped back from her face this time, in some kind of rather fetching clip arrangement, but wayward tendrils kept escaping at the sides. It is just one shade away from black, and her eyes, I decided after some very serious analysis, are not exactly hazel, more grey, but with little spangles of gold. And her skin is simply amazing – so white that it's nearly translucent, with a delta of tiny blue veins just visible near the corners of her eyes. But then, of course, my reprobate male imagination kept returning to other areas of blue-veined whiteness . . . And she is terribly sweet, too. She asked me if I was getting a cold, which I found obscurely touching. I had this strange feeling that she might actually offer to blow my nose, as if I were a dribbly child in her class.

Good grief, what am I getting into here, Mike? I don't have space in my life for a complication like this.

I can't just go out with her a few times, maybe a show, maybe bed, like with Laura last spring. Laura was a grown-up, we both knew what was what, nobody harboured any expectations and nobody created any. It's not just that Margaret is young. (Though she undeniably is. I haven't dared to ask her quite how young, but a qualified primary school teacher can't be less than, what, twenty-three can she?) It's that she's so . . . unspoilt, somehow. And I don't mean in the way you're thinking, you old hound! I mean all that idealistic fervour, those blazing principles, all undiluted and untarnished, and not yet sunk beneath a cushioning layer of cynicism. I can't take on all that – I don't want the responsibility. Let's have another drink soon, and you can remind me not to be such a crazed loon over a diaphanous blouse and a pair of earnest eyes.

Richard.

Richard Slater (Labour)
Member of Parliament for Ipswich

From: Rebecca Prichard [becs444@btinternet.com]
Sent: 27/4/05 22:06
To: Margaret Hayton [margarethayton@yahoo.co.uk]

Hi Margaret,

Out with Declan again tonight, or rather in with Declan. I'm still feeling self-conscious about the escape of any unstifled mid-coital vocalisations, so we have taken to selecting his noisiest video as background to our activities, just in case Zoe wakes up. *The Guns of Navarone* would perhaps not hitherto have been my chosen mood-inducer, but I have begun to find that I quite enjoy all the gunfire while Declan is storming my mountain fortress. I haven't even felt the need to imagine that he's Gregory Peck.

Brunswick Road Primary continues true to form. In Show and Tell today Jamie Turcott informed the class that his mum's throwing a party for his brother tonight, to celebrate his release from youth custody. Only Vrisha Chopra made the understandable assumption that this had anything to do with custard. Most of the class can barely tell you the days of the week, but they know that youth custody means prison for kids.

Becs xx

From: Margaret Hayton [margarethayton@yahoo.co.uk]
Sent: 27/4/05 22:32
To: Rebecca Prichard [becs444@btinternet.com]

Dear Becs,

St Edith's, by comparison, is not exactly life on the edge. In Circle Time yesterday Abby Bentham showed the class a pencil. Rainbow coloured, I'll

95

concede, and with a rubber on the end shaped like a daisy, but nevertheless *a pencil*. Why is it that all Year 3 girls, and none of the boys, share an obsession with stationery? Vicky Taylor in my class has pencil cases rather in the manner in which Imelda Marcos had shoes – beyond need, beyond reason. It makes me want to tell her that there are small Philippino children who would be grateful for just one plastic zip-up in which to keep their gel pens. I wonder what it is in the female genetic code which creates this overpowering drive towards the hoarding of notelets and envelopes. The male compulsion to run and kick a ball (or a stone, or an empty Coke can) I can understand. It may presumably be tracked back to some distant evolution from the hunting instinct. All those little boys who want to be Thierry Henry are really aspiring to be the supreme hunter, the one capable of dragging the most carcasses back to his encampment. But from what primal imperative does the collecting of neatly sharpened crayons derive?

By the way, if Declan's got the 1970s sequel, Mark made me watch it once and it's dire. Unless you want to be able to picture Declan as Harrison Ford.

Margaret xxx

42 Gledhill Street
Ipswich

29 April 2005

Dear Gran,

I'm glad you're using the mobile phone – Mum says she can chat to you a bit longer now when she calls. She says you've had a bit of a cold, too, so I'm sending you some echinacea to try. It isn't from the chemist, nothing strong, but it is meant to be very good. A friend of mine called Persephone, who's on the support group of our hostel, swears by it – apparently it boosts the body's own immune system, and helps you to fight off the infection.

I'm on my own here tonight – Cora has gone out to a wedding anniversary party for somebody at her work. It wasn't until she was getting ready that I realised, but I think it's the first time she's been out for an evening since I moved in last August. At least it means I've got a chance to sit down and write to you at last. I'm sorry it's been so long, and it's no excuse, I know, but I have had quite a busy time since I last wrote. I have had two meetings with my MP! Richard Slater, he's called, and he's in the Labour Party, and he seems quite helpful. He's got dark hair, and he's in that middle zone, you know, where I never know how old someone is. But I think he's probably near the younger end of it, because there aren't many lines on his face, except some crinkles round his eyes which make him look as though he might laugh a lot, though he was very serious with me.

The reason I met him was to talk about another girl in the hostel, called Nasreen, who is from Albania, and is seeking asylum in this country. Because she hasn't yet got permission to stay in Britain she isn't entitled to any housing benefit, and we were worried about how we could meet her rent. It looks as though Mr Slater may have found a way of getting round it, though, so we hope Nasreen will be able to carry on living in the house after all. I've been helping her with her English, especially reading and writing, and we've become quite close.

Hers is another harrowing story, though, Gran. Her family are Muslim, and from what I can make out they are fairly fundamentalist – even though all public religious worship is banned in Albania. It's supposed to be a secular state, apparently, and no one is allowed to attend a church or a mosque. I'm not sure 'fundamentalist' is quite the right word. I mean, Nasreen only wears a coloured scarf over her hair, not the formal hijab, and she talks about her mother going out to work, and Nasreen was still at college, and her dad was giving her driving lessons. But they are obviously quite extreme in some ways, because what happened was that Nasreen met a boy, Gjergj, and he's from a Christian background, and her father forbade her to go out with him. But they carried on seeing each other, meeting secretly after college, and then Nasreen's brothers found out (she has three older brothers), and they started to threaten her about it. She was quite determined not to give Gjergj up, and in the end two of her brothers caught her with him one day, kissing in the bus shelter. They dragged them apart and started slapping her face, so Gjergj rushed in to stop them, and then they turned on him, and she says they had him on the floor and were kicking him in the stomach and the head, and he was shouting at her to run, and so she did. She left that night, just packing a few clothes and a gold necklace which her grandmother gave her, which she sold to pay for her passage from Durrës to Felixstowe. She still doesn't even know if Gjergj is OK; she is too frightened to call him. She says it is because if her family knew she had been in touch with Gjergj they might kill him, or beat him again to try to discover where she is. They must do Shakespeare at school even in Albania, Gran, because after she had been telling me about it and her eyes were blurry with tears, she suddenly smiled and said 'like Romeo and Juliet'. I think she's incredibly brave.

Last night after the collective meeting we all went out for a drink, because it was Susan's birthday. It was good to get to talk, other than about the problems of the women in the hostel. Not that these women don't have problems of their own. One of them, Ding, has a mother with Alzheimer's living with her, and she worries about whether she's really safe to be left. The other day she put her Marks and Spencer meal for one in the spin dryer and microwaved the non-fast coloureds. The state of Ding's favourite blue silk shirt was bad enough after ten minutes on Defrost, but at least she didn't set the house on fire. Alison (she's the one who would be in charge if we weren't a collective) was telling us about her family. She's got three sons, and the middle one, Edward, has been diagnosed with a mild form of autism. Apparently he has always been 'difficult' – a bit uncommunicative and withdrawn, and given to furious tantrums. But the school just got him to a child psychologist, who referred him to a specialist. Alison being Alison, she's researched it all on the internet, and she's joined the local support group for parents of autistic kids. I expect she'll be organising them, too – she'll probably be chair by next month. Persephone, who's keen on alternative medicine and things, said that the Indian head massage she is learning can help with emotional problems and anger. It's all to do with getting the energy centres in the brain properly aligned, apparently. Alison said she could go over and try it on Edward, though I suspect she was only agreeing to be nice. Meanwhile Pat and Pat, who live together, were busy having an argument about whose mum they were due to visit for the bank holiday weekend. I am really getting very fond of all these people.

No, I'm not 'courting' at the moment, as Mrs Ashby puts it! I don't seem to meet any nice boys. I think it's hard once you aren't a student any more, and are out in the 'real world'. Not that I am exactly looking for someone. I've got lots of friends here now and plenty to fill my time, with being on the hostel support group. I haven't been out with anyone for quite a while actually, not since Mark. I know how much you all liked him – Mum and Dad as well as you, Gran. But it had to end, and it wasn't really his fault, not entirely. You see, we had been seeing each other at college, but he also had a girlfriend back home, someone he'd been seeing when they were both still at school, since they were fifteen. He had tried to end it with her when he met me, but it was difficult . . . She has problems, you see, mental health problems I mean, and whenever he tried to talk to her about breaking things off, she would get hysterical and clingy and go all to pieces, so somehow he could never quite bring himself to end it with her. I think he even worried what she might do, you know, if he really abandoned her. And of course I know he should have told me about her at the start, he knows that too, and he said he was sorry over and over. But when I found out about her, about the fact that he had been seeing her as well all that time, nearly two years it was, I just found I couldn't trust him any more. He said he would tell her it was over, if that's what I wanted, but I didn't want that either – how could I, Gran? How could I make the decision for him? How could I take the responsibility for doing that to this poor girl, when he hadn't been able to? Please don't say anything to Mum, though, will you? I have never told them, never told anyone about it really except my friend Becs, and now you.

Take care of that cold, anyway.

Lots of love,

Margaret x

METROPOLITAN POLICE

HOUSE OF COMMONS SPECIAL SECURITY SERVICE

House of Commons, London SW1A 0AA

<u>Incident Report: 29 April 2005</u>

At 10.15 a suspicious package was found in the House of Commons mail room, addressed to Mr Richard Slater, MP. The package consisted of a brown padded envelope, which was revealed by detection devices as appearing to contain a chemical substance, possibly in the form of small tablets. The package was sealed by the Chemical Response Unit and taken to the police laboratory, where analysis under controlled conditions revealed that the substance was exactly what an enclosed note claimed it to be, namely a herbal remedy, echinacea, sent to Mr Slater for his sore throat by a constituent.

Incident logged at 13.05 by Inspector R. D. Hampson, officer on duty.

From: Rebecca Prichard [becs444@btinternet.com]
Sent: 29/4/05 22:38
To: Margaret Hayton [margarethayton@yahoo.co.uk]

Hi Margaret,

I've got him here in my facinorous lair at last! Zoe is at her grandma's for the weekend, and I've got

Declan all to myself until Sunday morning when he picks her up – a whole day and, more importantly, two whole nights! He's in the shower now, or else I would not be frittering any of it away on the computer, believe me, but I was just dying to tell somebody, and I wasn't about to go bandying it around the staffroom at break. Nor can you exactly phone your mother and say, score, got my boyfriend tied down for two long nights of passion. Oh, Margaret, he's D-licious, D-lectable, D-stinctly D-sirable, and he's mine, all mine!

  Big hugs,

  Becs xx

From: Margaret Hayton [margarethayton@yahoo.co.uk]
Sent: 29/4/05 22:59
To: Rebecca Prichard [becs444@btinternet.com]

Dear Becs,

  Lucky you! Cora is out tonight, at a wedding anniversary bash which (and I tell you this only because it will satisfy your city-dwelling prejudices) is being held at the social club at the sugar factory. A club which, I kid you not, glories in the name of 'The Beet Goes On'. I suspect it may not exactly be 21 Piccadilly or Club V. So, with Cora out hitting the terpsichorean bacchanalia of the Ipswich club scene, my Friday night has consisted of sitting here writing a letter to my Gran. All I needed was a mug of cocoa and a plaid dressing gown and I would be a third-former at Mallory Towers. Or possibly I'm just in my convent again – do you picture contemplative Carmelites writing to their grandmothers?

Also, my head is itching. There has been an outbreak of head lice at school, apparently a much-anticipated annual event at St Edith's Primary when the weather grows warmer in the spring, much like hearing the first cuckoo. Or (so I am told, though it means nothing to me) like Ipswich's football team reaching the promotion play-offs. I guess we'll have to treat it as an occupational hazard, like coming home with three different cold bugs in the first week of term (at college they called it Fresher's Flu, remember?). Once the nits have arrived, the whole school is soon hopping with them, as a never-ending cycle of infection and reinfection is established. The girls are the worst, as they not only tend to have more hair, but also habitually congregate in gaggles with their heads bent close together. I'm fairly sure I haven't got them, but there is nothing like writing discreet notes to mothers in home-school journals all week to get your own scalp developing a sympathetic itch. Maybe I'll get some tea tree oil and douse myself anyway, if only to put a stop to all that imaginary scuttling that starts as soon as my head hits the pillow.

My sole consolation in this lonely and pest-ridden misery is W. G. Snuffy Walden. Have I mentioned her?

She is Cora's dog. She's actually on my knee at the moment, with her head on my typing arm, which does interfere somewhat with my mouse action. She has comedy ears, and when she pants (which is almost all the time) there is so much acreage of tongue that it is difficult to imagine how she eats or breathes when it's all inside. Her mouth also opens from an implausibly long way back in her head. Do you remember when we were small, there was an advert on TV (I remember it because it always made me laugh) for a toothbrush that had a bend in the handle, and it said you had to either use this toothbrush or else get a flip-top head? Well, Snuffy in panting mode is like the cartoon man with the flip-top head.

Oh, and I suppose you can have 6.5 for 'facinorous'.

Lots of love,

Margaret xx

From: Rebecca Prichard [becs444@btinternet.com]
Sent: 29/4/05 23:06
To: Margaret Hayton [margarethayton@yahoo.co.uk]

We don't have any nits in Moss Side – they've all moved out to nicer areas.

I'm not convinced that Greek scholars would allow the authenticity of your terpsichorean bacchanalia, but I'll give them a total of 13.

Becs xxx

42 Gledhill Street
Ipswich

Highways Department
Suffolk County Council
Shire Hall
King Street
Ipswich IP1 6JJ

30 April 2005

Dear Sir or Madam,

I am writing to you to bring to your attention the
non-functioning of a number of street lights in the
neighbourhood of Gledhill Street and Emery Street. Two
adjacent lights near the southern end of Emery Street,
next to the turning into St Matthew's Road, have been
out of order for over three months, and there are several
others in the vicinity which have not been working for
some time either.

These gaps in the street lighting are of particular
concern in view of the fact that the narrow pavements in
this part of the town are frequently dotted with wheelie
bins. Many of the houses lack any rear or side access and
therefore the bins have to be left out all week and not just
on the eve of a refuse collection. The bins being black,
they are very difficult to see when lying in the patches of
darkness created by broken street lamps. Only yesterday
my landlady, when out for a run without her spectacles,
was in collision with a wheelie bin thus concealed in
shadow.

I urge you to make it a priority to check and repair the

street lighting in this area of town, and thus to avert any further danger to short-sighted joggers and other members of the public.

Yours faithfully,

Margaret Hayton.

From: Michael Carragan [mmcarragan@hc.parliament.uk]
Sent: 2/5/05 11:23
To: Richard Slater [rpslater@hc.parliament.uk]

OK, not ASBOs, and not PFI – so what about ID cards? Get your upright and law-abiding mug put on a mocked-up identity card. Then you can stage your own arrest by those friends of yours in blue (Kev and Ian, was it?). As they are about to throw you into the back of the van, you produce your card, proving that you are not Billy 'Beet-face' Benson the notorious Stowmarket safe-cracker (or whoever tops the list of Suffolk's most wanted), but are in fact their democratically elected representative – thus demonstrating how the carrying of ID cards will protect the honest citizenry of Ipswich from the risk of being mistakenly apprehended.

Michael.

Michael Carragan (Labour)
Member of Parliament for West Bromwich West

From: Richard Slater [rpslater@hc.parliament.uk]
Sent: 2/5/05 11:42
To: Michael Carragan [mmcarragan@hc.parliament.uk]

No, Michael, enough! I would probably mislay the card, anyway, and end up serving a five stretch as Billy Beet-face. I have given up seeking the oxygen of publicity over causes in which I don't believe. I'm concentrating on constituency work from now on. I may be left with nothing but fresh air – but at least it will be less polluted!
    Richard.

Richard Slater (Labour)
Member of Parliament for Ipswich

42 Gledhill Street
Ipswich

4 May 2005

My darling Pete,

It's been quite exciting since I last wrote, love. Dora and Dave's 'do' was on Friday, and it was a lovely occasion. Dave made a sweet speech, but funny too, he quite made Dora blush with some of it, and there was a buffet – a beautiful spread it was, not just the usual cold pizza slices and dips but proper homemade vol-au-vents and quiches, and gorgeous puddings that you would have had to steer me away from if you'd been there. And then I felt guilty because I'd never thought to offer to help with the food, or even just to bring something, and it must have taken Dora half the week cooking and freezing in the evenings after work. There was dancing, not just a disco but live music, it was – some of Dave's workmates who have a tribute band called The Beet, and they played all those old ska numbers we used to love. Dave insisted on having me up on the floor (his bad back didn't seem to be getting in the way of his dance-floor moves), and I must admit I really enjoyed it. I can't remember the last time I danced! I hadn't heard some of those songs for years. Do you remember how you used to hum 'Mirror in the Bathroom' under your breath if you were waiting and I was taking too long getting ready to go out?

Today after work we had a big surprise. I answered the phone (I never just leave it ringing now, not since Margaret got that block on all the sales calls), and you'll never guess who it was. It was Margaret's MP (well, I suppose he's mine too, but you know what I mean). I called her, and she took the receiver, and she didn't seem able to say anything except 'yes' and 'OK' and 'thank you' a lot, especially 'thank you'. Then she put the phone down, and said in a dazed sort of voice, 'He's arranged another meeting, this time with the chair of the housing department as well,' and she was definitely a little bit pink. I've never seen so much colour in her cheeks – she is normally so pale. She seemed quite taken aback. I suppose it was being rung up at home by someone so important, someone from the government. And now she's going to meet this man from the council, too – she's quite the political wheeler-dealer these days, it seems!

Another thing: and this you really wouldn't believe, Pete, but Margaret has got me going out jogging with her! (Running, she calls it, I don't think they say jogging any more.) We just go round and round the little park at the end of the road, and she makes me do one more circuit each day. She says it's nicer with two, because you can chat and it takes your mind off the fact you are running, but actually Margaret chats and I just listen and grunt a bit – I don't have any puff left for talking. Yesterday we thought we'd take Snuffy along, kill two birds with one stone so to speak, but I don't think we'll be trying that again. She ran round with us for two circuits, sat at the gate and watched us with a puzzled look on her face for two more, and then the fifth time round she ran with us again, but just behind us, barking and jumping up to nip our bottoms every other stride! Poor old Snuffs – I think she thought I'd gone quite mad. She may be right, judging by the way my knees have been creaking this week when I get out of bed in the mornings.

Mrs Edgar from next door gave me some of her self-seeded foxgloves – she says they come up in her garden like weeds; they would take over if she let them. They also remind her of old Benjy, because he had that heart problem, you remember, when he got old, and she had to give him digitalis, she says, which is made out of foxgloves. She buried him among them, too. Anyway, I've found a few spaces, and they will add a bit of height and colour in the summer. When I was a girl I always liked to watch the bees crawling inside them, in Mum's garden at home.

I put on that album by The Beat tonight, Petey. I haven't had our old vinyl records out for ages – it was quite a little nostalgia session. I just played it quietly, after Margaret had gone up to her room. I wanted to be on my own – I suppose I didn't think it would be her kind of music, and I know it's silly of me but I didn't want her to hear 'Stand Down Margaret'! We really used to hate that name, didn't we? But she's so young, I don't suppose she thinks of that association . . . When it got to 'I Can't Get Used to Losing You' I missed you so much that I had to turn it off.

Love you always,

Cora xxx

From: Margaret Hayton [margarethayton@yahoo.co.uk]
Sent: 4/5/05 21:49
To: Rebecca Prichard [becs444@btinternet.com]

Dear Becs,

Guess what? He phoned me up tonight! Mr Slater – Richard, I mean. I hadn't expected him to do anything more about it after our last meeting, not after he'd already found out for us about getting designated as Nasreen's appropriate temporary accommodation. But he called me after work – he actually apologised for phoning me at home, said he'd got my number from Emily in the Witch House office, and he hoped that was all right. All right! I was just so impressed that he'd taken the trouble. He sounded different on the phone, Becs – younger. I think it was not being able to see the suit and tie, so that all you noticed was the hesitancy. Because now I come to think about it he always talks very hesitantly, not as if he's shy exactly, just doubtful. It's rather endearing really – and odd for a professional wordsmith like a politician, don't you think? Well, what he wanted to tell me was that he has fixed up a meeting for us – him as well as me, I mean – with the chair of the borough council's housing department, Mr Nicholls, on 16 May. He's made the appointment for 4 p.m., because he remembered that I teach in primary school, and said he thought I could be free by that time of day, which is very thoughtful of him. All I could think to say was thank you and that he needn't have bothered, but he just said that he thought Mr Nicholls (whom he calls Ted) would be more likely to agree to the designation with him there, so that he could see he was supporting us on this. I wasn't sure about him at first, so I'm glad to know that he really does care about ordinary people like Nasreen.

It has really cheered me up, because I had been a bit down in the dumps earlier. Last night I got another call from Helen in the hostel. Quite late it was – I had already gone to bed when she rang. She hadn't taken anything this time, nor cut herself, but she was pretty desperate. No tears – she doesn't seem to cry much, in fact, which surprised me at first because I'd always pictured people with depression crying all the time – she was sitting on her bed in her nightie, hugging her knees and rocking to and fro, and her face had this fixed, blank expression, with her eyes staring at nothing. It was difficult for her to speak at all, to begin with, she had to sort of unclamp her teeth – you could tell they had been set tight together. She just whispered, 'Hold me.' It was all she could say at first, and we sat together like that for what seemed like an hour, though I guess it was only about twenty minutes (I didn't like to look at my watch).

And then gradually she started to talk, about how at night-time she is afraid to go to sleep. It's like a fear of losing control, she says – she'll be in bed with her eyes closed and as soon as she feels herself drifting off panic seizes her and she wakes up with a jolt. It's so sad, because I adore that sensation – that delicious moment of slipping into unconsciousness and letting go, it's one of the best feelings in the world. But for Helen it is terrifying. She says it is because that's when her father used to come into her bedroom, in the night when she was asleep, and when she was a kid she used to think that if she could only stay awake it wouldn't happen, and then she started to get scared of going to sleep. I find it amazing that someone who is afraid of falling asleep should be capable of taking an overdose. But maybe it's because really it isn't the falling asleep that she's scared of, it's what follows, it's the waking up. Anyway, I stayed until she had dropped off, and then crept out. I left the light on. She'd asked me to, said she always sleeps that way. I don't even want to think about what demons the dark must hold for her.

Sorry, again, for the depressing rant. How are you? How are things with the unparagoned Declan?

Love,

Margaret xxx

From: Rebecca Prichard [becs444@btinternet.com]
Sent: 4/5/05 22:20
To: Margaret Hayton [margarethayton@yahoo.co.uk]

Don't ask, Margaret! We had such a great weekend, in bed and out (though mainly in, I must admit). At one point, at a moment of . . . well, let's just say, at an apogean moment, I found I was saying his name and then into my ravished and treacherous brain, all unbidden, came those words that you have to remember not to say without careful forethought, and I almost didn't remember not to say them. He was giving out really positive signals, too, about doing more things together, and he said that his brother is coming over the weekend after next, and I should come to dinner and meet him. And we all know that meeting a sibling is definitely on The Scale. Obviously nowhere near the top, with the heady heights of your own key, lending you his card and PIN or tea with the parents, but it's an established early rung, like letting you see him naked without breathing in and clenching. So of course I made all the right positive noises back, and it was all fixed up for Saturday night.

But then I saw him yesterday – we took Zoe to the multiplex after school so we could conduct our own discreet search for the Golden Ticket during *Charlie and the Chocolate Factory*. And when he was driving me home he happened to mention that his brother's name is Elliot! Mr E himself! Declan couldn't understand why I had suddenly gone cold on the idea of meeting him, and he turned equally frosty. By the time he pulled the car up at my flat, poor Zoe probably needed her thermals on, sat in there with the two of us.

I quite like 'unparagoned', though – have a 6 for it.

Hugs,

Becs xx

From: Margaret Hayton [margarethayton@yahoo.co.uk]
Sent: 4/5/05 22:28
To: Rebecca Prichard [becs444@btinternet.com]

Dear Becs,

Are you a woman or a . . . um, small pusillanimous mammal beginning with 'w'? If you feel the way your brain was telling you to tell him you do, then you can surely have dinner with Elliot without succumbing to his alphabetical attractions! Call Declan and fix it.

Your 'apogean' moment scores 5.5 – though I hope in real life it rated higher.

Margaret xxx

SLATER SLATES TAM-TAX

In a speech in the House of Commons yesterday, Ipswich MP Mr Richard Slater spoke out against the charging of VAT on tampons and sanitary towels. He has joined a group of mainly female back bench MPs in signing an Early Day Motion against VAT on these essential goods, which, he argues, casts an unfair tax burden on women, who already enjoy a smaller share of the nation's wealth. Mr Slater commented this morning: 'Women have enough to worry about every month with period pain and PMT, without having to pay a levy to the government as well. Indirect taxation already bleeds dry the poorer members of our society. We need to plug this particular drain upon women's income.' He was clearly embarrassed, however, by the actions of fellow campaigners who took Tampax from their handbags and flourished them behind him as he made his speech in the chamber. 'I understand why women wish to make the body political,' said a red-faced Mr Slater, 'but it doesn't have to mean reducing politics to the level of the body. Or at least not behind me with the television cameras rolling.'

The Hollies
East Markhurst

9 May 2005

Dear Margaret,

I just wanted to say thank you again for coming over at the weekend. It meant such a lot, and you were such a help. I really don't know what I would have done without you. I still can't think how it happened, though I've gone over and over it in my head. I wasn't doing anything foolish. I'd had my dinner, I'd finished the little bit of washing up, and was going to make myself a cup of tea. I was just reaching up to get the teapot down off the shelf, where it lives, you know, over the fridge. Maybe I hadn't quite got the frame standing square as I leaned on it, but as soon as I got hold of the pot I found myself off balance, and I suppose I couldn't manage to save myself by grabbing on to the frame because of the teapot in my hand, and then my legs went and the next thing I was on the kitchen floor. You will laugh at me, but the first thing I remember thinking was how glad I was that the teapot wasn't broken, because your grandad bought it for me when we went to Weston-super-Mare one year. He saw me admiring it in the shop and he nipped back later and got it without me knowing, and then gave it to me when we got back to the boarding house. Lying there, I didn't know the ankle was sprained to begin with, it was all such a shock, but I did know I couldn't manage to get myself up. I was so grateful to you then, love, for the mobile phone, which was in my cardigan pocket, so I could call Mrs Dorling from the corner, and of course she took one look and said I needed an ambulance. It was only when I got to the hospital that I realised I was still wearing my pinny.

I wasn't sure if I should phone you, when your mum couldn't come. I knew she wouldn't be able to really, not on a Saturday afternoon, she would never have got back for Sunday, and I know your dad starts with Early Communion at eight o'clock, and she has his breakfast to get for him first. It was Mum who suggested you, and with Kirsty already gone home and not due back until today, I couldn't think what else I could do. And I'm so glad I did call you, dear, even though it put you to such a lot of trouble, coming all that way on the train like that at the drop of a hat, when you are at school all week and probably have a hundred other jobs to get done at the weekends. They would have sent me home in an ambulance if you hadn't come to the hospital to escort me home on the bus, but I don't think I could have managed to get myself to bed on my own, nor to sort out my dinner on Sunday. And it's funny how taking a tumble like that shakes you up – not just the sprained ankle and the bumps and bruises, it gives your confidence a knock, too. Even today I keep thinking I'm going to go down again. Well, at least it might make me take more care!

When Kirsty came this morning, I asked her to go in the spare room and strip the bed, and I couldn't believe it when she said it was all stripped and the bedspread put back, and no sign of your dirty sheets. I couldn't understand it at all – it was Kirsty who said you must have taken them home with you to wash, you naughty girl. Kirsty could have put them in the machine for me, and I'm sure you are busy enough without extra laundry to do. Kirsty brought me two more library books this morning, too, which is terribly considerate of her. But to be honest I'm not sure they are my kind of thing. One has a picture of just the bottom half of a girl on the front cover, doing the hoovering in a miniskirt and stiletto heels, and she appears to have a half-empty wine bottle in one hand. I quite enjoyed one she brought me last week, but I find it such a distraction to be told in every chapter what shade of lipstick the heroine is wearing, and the name of the shop where she bought her blouse.

I'm feeling a bit tired tonight, so I'm sorry this isn't a longer letter, or a more interesting one. Oh, except I forgot to say to you when you were here, those tablets you sent me for my cold seemed to help a bit. It certainly cleared up quicker than they sometimes do. I'd never heard of that echinacea until a little while ago – Donna gave some to Josh on 'The West Wing' recently and I was wondering what it was. I cannot understand why those two don't get together – they would make such a lovely couple, don't you think? You are a treasure anyway, Margaret – I hope you know that.

Love from Gran xx

From: Margaret Hayton [margarethayton@yahoo.co.uk]
Sent: 10/5/05 22:26
To: Rebecca Prichard [becs444@btinternet.com]

Dear Becs,

In that parallel universe which is the Great British Primary School, we had our Nativity Play this afternoon. In the grand democratic tradition it was decreed that every child must take part. The complex troop manoeuvres involved in marshalling three hundred and eighty four to eleven year olds in numbered detachments on and off a stage measuring approximately two metres by four were carried out with awe-inspiring precision, according to a battle plan devised by Mrs Martin the deputy head.

My lot were mostly elves, attendant upon a somewhat unorthodox worshipper at the feet of the Christ-child in the form of Mother Christmas (played by an enormous, rotund girl of African-Caribbean heritage in Year 6). They looked very sweet, I must say, dressed in red and green, with their pixie hoods that we had made in class last week, and their rosy crimson cheeks. There was no need to apply make-up to most of them today, after my colleague Karen mistook acryllic modelling paint for the hypo-allergenic face colours before yesterday's dress rehearsal. The anomalous Momma Christmas and her little helpers were joined by the more traditional incongruity of forty tutu-wearing snowflakes on an arid Middle Eastern hillside, while a gesture towards multi-culturalism had Zach Goldberg (brother of David in my class) carrying a hanukkiah along with his shepherd's crook, and Deena Sachdeva appearing among the host of goodwill-bearing angels as the goddess Lakshmi, with a plastic lotus flower in her hair. The real show-stopper was a diminutive boy in Year 4 who played Herod with commanding vigour, his threat to slay all the first-born boy-children rendered only slightly less plausible by his swinging his feet back and forth on a cardboard throne several sizes too large for him.

Otherwise, not much to report here. I spent the weekend at my gran's – she's had a fall and sprained her ankle, to compound still being shaky and restricted in what she can do after her stroke. Oh, and Monday is when I'm going to see the borough's housing man with Richard Slater. What about you? Have you sorted it out with Declan, about meeting his brother?

Love,

Margaret xx

From: Rebecca Prichard [becs444@btinternet.com]
Sent: 10/5/05 22:53
To: Margaret Hayton [margarethayton@yahoo.co.uk]

Declan and I have kissed (and a lot more besides) and made up. Elliot is coming for dinner at Declan's on Saturday and I am going to join them.

We didn't have a Nativity Play, multi-cultural or otherwise, even at the regular season at Brunswick Road. It is too hard to get parents to come to anything. Except fund-raising bingo nights. And unfortunately those had to be stopped last term after the police were called in to quell a minor riot, triggered by an argument over a blue teddy bear the size of a St Bernard.

Merry Christmas,

Becs xxx

IPSWICH BOROUGH COUNCIL

MRS BARBARA MCPHERSON, MA: DIRECTOR OF
RECREATION AND AMENITIES

Civic House, Orwell Drive, Ipswich IP2 3QP

<u>Memo of meeting, Thursday 12 May 2005, 3.30 p.m.</u>

Mrs McPherson met Mr Richard Slater MP, at his request, to discuss repairs and improvements to play equipment and street furniture in and near the public park located between Gledhill Street and Emery Street. It was agreed that steps should be taken at the earliest possible opportunity to replace the zip-wire in the children's play area. After considerable discussion it was also decided that three additional hygienic dog-waste disposal facilities should be installed in the area, these to be situated (1) on the iron railings beside the Emery Street entrance, (2) on the lamp post outside the Gledhill Street entrance, and (3) on a free-standing wooden post to be installed close to the gravel path immediately south-west of the British Sugar gazebo (see highlighted map in file). It was further agreed that the installation of these units should be moved forward in the schedule from 2010, and be placed in the programme of works for winter 2005/06.

The meeting ended at 5.35 p.m.

Ipswich Borough Council – Working for Your *Community*

From: Richard Slater [rpslater@hc.parliament.uk]
Sent: 16/5/05 21:56
To: Michael Carragan [mmcarragon@hc.parliament.uk]

Michael, hi! I was hoping to catch you outside the chamber after the vote just now – where did you disappear to? I am a deranged and ever so slightly desperate man – I badly need someone to shake me out of it.

We had our meeting in Ipswich with the chair of housing today. Margaret arrived in a flurry of books and raincoat and glossy dark curls, with the aroma of poster paints still fresh upon her, and we went in together to see Ted Nicholls. He was more than willing to go along with the proposal of allowing Witch

House to be designated as appropriate statutory housing for Margaret's Albanian girl, thus providing me with an excellent opportunity for being bathed in gratitude from those wide, sincere grey eyes. As we came out I was about to suggest a celebratory drink, but suddenly I didn't want her to think I was the kind of dissolute parliamentarian who is in the habit of hitting the bar at 4.45 p.m. (yeah, I know, but save it, mate!) – and this was Ipswich not Westminster, so finding one open at that time of day might not have been easy anyway. So I just blurted out, 'Shall we go somewhere for a cup of tea?' as if I was her great-uncle Oswald come to take her out for her twelfth birthday. This piece of buffoonery was rewarded, surprisingly, by a smile, not pitying at all but so full of warmth you could have toasted muffins in its lambent glow. It was the first time I have seen her smile, really smile I mean, and it made me lose all the feeling in my knees – not a physiological effect I remember experiencing before, and one which makes it hard to do very much other than totter.

So totter I did, in the direction of the café at the Corn Exchange which was her suggested venue for our grand-avuncular tryst. The pavements were pretty crowded, by East Anglian standards, at that time of day, and as we walked side by side through the semi-throng it would have been the most natural thing in the world (according to a persistent voice in my head) to take hold of her hand, or at least to tuck a gently steering palm just beneath her elbow. Of course I didn't, but she did move very close to me a couple of times, to avoid on-coming pedestrians, so that there was light shoulder-bumping (she is tall, so we are almost of a height) and I could almost smell her hair. I even caught myself wishing it would rain so that she would have to lean in close under my umbrella – until I remembered that I don't possess an umbrella, and that I am not Jo's professor from *Good Wives*.

I poured, as any self-respecting great-uncle would. Some of what I had been hoping was girlish shyness but feared was deference, which had so far hung around her, evaporated into the steam as she hugged her cup close to her chin with both hands, and she began to talk. Really talk, quietly, but with a passion which set the air between us zinging, about the Albanian girl, Nasreen, and what she has come away from. I was mesmerised, not so much by what she was saying – although I genuinely did want to listen, and to understand and share her concern – but by the sheer ardour which trembled in her voice and shone from her eyes. I found myself considering their colour again – they really do repay careful study. They have a chameleon quality. Sometimes they seem the palest of greys, like the soft underneath of a tabby kitten, but in the café, through the steam from her teacup, they were pure, fathomless twilight.

My God, Mike, listen to me – see how far gone I am!
Anyway, I tell you this whole toe-curlingly embarrassing
tale in order to bring you some way towards understanding what I did next, idiot that I am. She was
leaning forward over the table in her earnest desire to
make me comprehend the extent of Nasreen's suffering
and valour, and her hair, which was loose and tumbling
like a curtain at one side of her face, looked in immi-
nent danger of falling in between me and one of those
spell-binding eyes. And before I even knew what
I was doing, I had reached out, and taken hold of a
thick curling strand, and was brushing it back from her
cheek in the direction of her ear – behind which, I
suppose (had I thought this through), I would have
tucked it.

The recoil was instant, and unmistakable. It wasn't
just surprise, or awkwardness, it was quite decided –
a door shutting in my face. She went on talking, but
her voice had slid into neutral, and her eyes dipped,
so that instead of that glorious full beam I was getting
half-lids (fringed, I have to say, with the densest
profusion of not-quite-black lashes). Suddenly I knew
she couldn't wait to get away from me.

And then it got worse. It was when she mentioned
Durrës, and I suddenly realised, Nasreen is from
Albania. I mean, she's not just an Albanian, she's an
Albanian Albanian. I'd always assumed she was from
Kosovo (I've no idea why) – but of course Albania is
on The List! So I had to break it to Margaret: that this

created a strong presumption that there could be no ground for an asylum claim, that Albania is deemed to be a 'safe' country. All her earlier passion returned then in a blaze of righteous anger, directed at a government (and by association, any elected member of the governing party) which was so blind as not to recognise other forms of oppression than political tyranny by the state. All I could do was sit and be buffeted by the blast, and watch the wreck of my pretensions crumbling before me.

Even so, I just wanted to stay and stare at her indignant, unattainable face until they threw us out on the pavement. I knew I couldn't, and I told her that I had to get back to London tonight for a division – and then hated myself because it sounded such a pompous line, me the big-shot politician, just when politicians were to her the lowest form of pond-life.

HELP!

Richard.

Richard Slater (Labour)
Member of Parliament for Ipswich

From: Michael Carragan
[mmcarragan@hc.parliament.uk]
Sent: 16/5/05 22:19
To: Richard Slater [rpslater@hc.parliament.uk]

And this is the madwoman who sent you the anthrax, right? You've certainly got it bad, Richard old son . . . Stay where you are. I've got a bottle of single malt and I'm coming straight over.

Michael.

Michael Carragan (Labour)
Member of Parliament for West Bromwich West

From: Margaret Hayton [margarethayton@yahoo.co.uk]
Sent: 16/5/05 22:36
To: Rebecca Prichard [becs444@btinternet.com]

Dear Becs,

I've got to tell you the latest about Nasreen's case. I'm so enraged about it I can hardly think about anything else! It all started off so well. You know we were meeting Mr Nicholls from the housing department? I mean Richard Slater and I, we were going to see him together. Well, the meeting went very smoothly – Mr Nicholls said he was happy for Nasreen to stay with us and receive her funding. Richard was brilliant – he seemed to know Mr Nicholls quite well and said all the right things. All I had to do was sit there and nod, really. And then when we came out Richard suggested we go and have a cup of tea, so sweet of him I thought, and also sort of businesslike. We went to the café at the Corn

Exchange, and it was funny walking through the streets with him – I mean, me, walking through Ipswich with the town's MP! I kept wondering if people recognised him, from the TV and the papers.

It was in the café that everything went wrong. The first thing was, I was telling Richard about Nasreen's situation, all about Gjergj, and her brothers' threats I mean, and suddenly he put his hand out and touched my hair. I suppose it must have been in his way or something. And it was awful because suddenly all I could think of was those head-lice, and how I still hadn't had a go at them with the tea tree oil, so of course I jerked my head backwards really sharply – I am sure he thought I was completely mad. And I couldn't rid myself of the creeping fear that maybe he had actually seen something moving in there, and that is why he was touching my hair, to try to flick it out, thinking it was a little spider or something. God, Becs, I can't tell you how mortifying it was! Up until that point, I think I could quite happily have sat there babbling on all evening, but now all I wanted was to be out of there in order to purge both my embarrassment and any uninvited insect life. I just couldn't meet his eye any more. I tried to cover up the embarrassment by telling him some more about Nasreen, but all at once he wasn't so much Richard, more Mr Slater MP again, and you could tell he was offended, because he went all sort of distant in his replies.

And then . . . well, I suppose I hadn't explained
things properly before, but he suddenly asked
if Nasreen is really from Albania, not a Kosovo
Albanian – and, oh, Becs, it's awful! It turns out that
Albania is on a statutory list of so-called 'safe'
countries which the Home Office keeps, and if you
are from a country on the list you have almost no
chance of being granted asylum, because you are
deemed not to be at risk of persecution. It's
completely crazy! Just because the Albanian
government isn't actually locking up dissidents, and
there is no civil war or genocide going on there,
Nasreen is presumed to be safe to go back, even
though her family are threatening to beat or kill her if
she ever sees Gjergj again, and quite possibly even
if she doesn't. It's as if there is only one kind of
oppression that counts, and that is oppression by the
state. But what about women's oppression? What
about dowry killings in India, a country which has
been judged to be 'safe' since January? (I looked up
all this stuff on the internet when I got home. First
thing I did, after I'd washed my hair with tea tree oil.)
Are those women safe? Is Nasreen really safe? It
makes me so angry!

I'm afraid I may have given Richard rather an
earful – you know what I'm like when I get going.
He seemed to take it quite well, but afterwards I
was left feeling vaguely uncomfortable – I mean, it's
hardly his fault how international human rights

instruments have defined entitlement to refugee status. And when he left, to go back to the House – he seems terribly dedicated – I remembered that I hadn't really properly said thank you to him for sorting out Nasreen's housing situation (even if it does turn out to be short-lived). I found myself wishing that he was still there so I could thank him and, rather more obscurely, that he would touch my hair again.

You were having dinner with D and E at the weekend, weren't you? What happened?

Love and hugs,

Margaret xx

From: Rebecca Prichard [becs444@btinternet.com]
Sent: 16/5/05 22:59
To: Margaret Hayton [margarethayton@yahoo.co.uk]

Hi, Margaret – what a bummer about Nasreen and this stupid rule about Albania. I'd like to see the Home Office official who made the list go and live in Albania and face a good going over.

Yes, Declan, Elliot and I all had dinner at Declan's flat on Saturday night. Declan did his signature dish of chicken vindaloo (well, actually, it's his only dish), and he thoughtfully provided me with a large bowl of yogurt to dilute the heat with, on account of my lacking the Y chromosome and therefore not particularly enjoying having the roof of my mouth napalmed. I should have seen the warning signs when Elliot asked Declan if there was any chilli pickle to go with it. Boys competing over curry heat endurance levels is the equivalent of rutting stags locking antlers over the hapless hind at the dinner table. I was breathing pure testosterone fumes. And indeed, when Elliot and I were washing up at the end of the night while Declan was checking on Zoe, he got quite unnecessarily close and flicked me playfully on the bum with the tea cloth. And the worst of it was, I quite liked that I could feel the heat of the vindaloo on his breath . . . But Declan is so great, he really is! I am a weak and wicked woman, and will be going straight to hell.

But, Margaret, hon, this whole Richard hair-touching thing – what was that all about? Because I'm really not sure it comes under the heading of expected behaviour from an MP towards a constituent, like shaking hands a lot, or kissing babies. *How* did he touch it exactly?

Big hugs,

Becs xx

From: Margaret Hayton [margarethayton@yahoo.co.uk]
Sent: 16/5/05 23:03
To: Rebecca Prichard [becs444@btinternet.com]

I don't know, he just reached out and touched it. Does

it matter? At least I am not teetering on the brink of the stygian abyss.

Margaret xxx

HANSARD HOUSE OF COMMONS DEBATES

Wednesday 18 May 2005

[Mr Speaker in the Chair]

Oral Answers to Questions

ENVIRONMENT, FOOD AND RURAL AFFAIRS

Climate Change

Mr Richard Slater (Ipswich) (Lab): First of all, may I say how delighted I am that the government has taken the necessary steps to implement the EU Emissions Trading Directive. Could the Secretary of State please comment upon the progress currently being made towards the renewable energy target of 10 per cent by 2010?

The Secretary of State for Environment, Food and Rural Affairs (Ms Sandra Harcourt): Substantial moves have already been made towards achievement of the 10 per cent target. By the end of 2005, for example, Britain will have over five hundred offshore windmills generating clean, renewable electricity. The government is leading the way by effecting changes on its own estate. The target (set in 2001) of 5 per cent renewable energy use by government departments by March 2003 has already been met, and good progress is being made towards achieving the target of 10 per cent by 2008.

Mr Slater: I thank my honourable friend for that reply. But is it likely that the national target of 10 per cent energy use from renewable sources by 2010 is going to be met?

Ms Harcourt: Um . . . I am pleased to report to the House that three government departments have so far set an excellent example by developing on-site Combined Heat and Power (or CHP) systems, to meet 100 per cent of their own space heating needs.

Mr Slater: Well, defra certainly generates plenty of hot air . . .

Ms Harcourt: A number of further inland sites for wind farms are also under consideration, subject to the necessary public consultations with local residents. Additional government funding is also being directed towards research into wave power and geo-thermal energy sources.

Mr Slater: I am delighted to hear about these initiatives, but aren't the results likely to be long term? Don't we need to be reducing our dependence upon fossil fuels rather more quickly if we are to meet our Kyoto obligations?

Mr Colin Harrison (Epsom) (Con): Didn't I read something about an alternative fuel oil made out of sugar-beet? Maybe the honourable member for Ipswich should be putting that in his car.

[Laughter]

Food Labelling

Mr Christopher Parker (Wolverhampton North) (Lab): Could the Secretary of State please comment upon stories in the press that under new EU regulations, all prepackaged pizzas (other than those made in Italy) are required to be labelled as dairy-topped tomato dough roundels?

WITCH
Women of Ipswich Together Combating Homelessness

<u>Extract from minutes of meeting</u> at Margaret's house, 19 May 2005, 8 p.m.

<u>News of residents</u>
There was a long discussion about Helen, who has been feeling increasingly desperate, and has suggested that she may need a full-time hospital admission for a while, rather

than the current arrangement of weekend respite stays. Margaret pointed out that it is bedtimes that are the worst, which is why she finds it difficult to cope in Witch House, given the staffing hours. Alison came up with a plan whereby members of the support group would, at least for a short trial period, provide more than the usual emergency telephone cover, and would take turns to go out to Witch House to sit with Helen for an hour each weekday evening at around 10.30 p.m., to help her get to sleep. This was agreed, and Alison volunteered to draw up a rota.

News of former residents still receiving support

We were sorry to hear that Marianne has lost her job at the newsagent's. When Mrs Bhandari noticed that her concentration had been dipping after breaks, Marianne admitted that she had been sniffing Tippex in the storeroom. Emily and Pat T. have been trying to find a place for her on another rehab scheme.

Any other business

Mrs Robertson from number 27 attended a house meeting last week, and afterwards Pat T. and Emily explained to her something about the project. She seemed a little mollified about noise and nuisance in the street, and has offered to lend Carole her dry foam carpet cleaner.

42 Gledhill Street
Ipswich

22 May 2005

Dearest Pete,

Another eventful week to report on here! First Margaret had that meeting with the MP and the man from the council as well, and I think that went OK, except that she then found out that poor Nasreen hasn't much hope of being allowed to stay in England, because of where she comes from. Apparently Albania isn't somewhere that we take refugees from any more. Poor Margaret took it very hard – she was talking about it half the evening, I don't think she could quite believe it. And it does seem very hard, to send the poor girl back into a situation like that, after she's had the courage to get away: she's sure to be punished for it, if she tries to go back home. Anyway, that was Monday, so on Tuesday I bought us both a nice piece of sirloin steak each for supper, as a cheer-up for Margaret (over ten pounds they cost me). I did chips and all the trimmings, grilled mushrooms and halved tomatoes – just the way you like it, Petey – and she seemed quite touched.

Then on Thursday Margaret's hostel support group had their meeting here. I gave them the sitting room, and came to sit and read in the kitchen, and then at half past nine I took them in some tea and a packet of Hobnobs, and stayed to chat a bit. They really do seem very nice ladies, and of course I had heard a lot about them all from Margaret. It felt as though I knew them already! Over the tea, one of them, Persephone (I think that's how you spell it, but you say it as if it ended with a y) was talking about starting some evening classes in herbalism, and you know me and all my herbs in the pots out the back, so I said that sounded interesting. And do you know, she's given me the details and we are going to start the classes together! I've sometimes thought about doing some classes, but I've never felt quite brave enough on my own somehow, and gardening does sound like my sort of thing, don't you think? It'll be every Tuesday at seven thirty.

On Wednesday, Mrs Edgar had been round with some more cuttings and bits and pieces for the garden. I said thank you very much, of course, but actually the beds are pretty full at the moment, everything's grown so much, so I wasn't sure where I'd find the gaps to put it all. But then after the meeting on Thursday, when Margaret's friends had all gone home, I suddenly had a brainwave, and I asked if there is a garden at the hostel. It turns out there is, not much more than a pocket handkerchief (I went to see it today), and it's very bare, nothing more than a patch of grass and some bits of overgrown ivy and other climbers on the fence. None of the women living in the house seem to know about gardens, and the staff don't have the time. It could certainly do with some brightening up, so I did a bit of digging over and put in some of Mrs Edgar's dogwood cuttings, and a few clumps of Michaelmas daisies. Nasreen came out to say hello and brought me a cup of tea, and she remembered to put in the milk, and another young woman, who introduced herself as Lauren, came and chatted to me. She seemed quite interested and even took a turn with the spade – though she'd got on the most unsuitable shoes, white with what we used to call kitten heels. I said I'd go back next weekend and dig in some compost, because the soil is ever so thin and sandy, and Lauren said she'd help me again, if I didn't mind, which was very nice of her.

I'm reading another one of Margaret's books. I finished the last one, *Ruth*, and it was so sad at the end it made me cry, so I asked if she had anything lighter. This one's by Anthony Trollope, and it's called *The Warden*. It's all about a Victorian vicar who is the warden of some almshouses. Margaret said it made her laugh because her father is a vicar, and it reminded her of the petty arguments that still go on today in church politics, but I think it's funny that she should have recommended it, because in a way her hostel is the modern equivalent of an almshouse, really.

Last week they started the refit at the bank. They've put up partitions which are supposed to keep the plaster dust away from where we are working, but it still finds its way through. We keep a J-cloth and some Mr Sheen handy all the time, but the computers still look as if they've been dusted with icing sugar, the way I do with my chocolate sponges sometimes. If you leave a cup of coffee standing for a while, it starts to look like one of those fancy cappuccinos they do in that new American place, Starbucks. It's ever so noisy, too – a bit of hardboard does nothing to keep out the banging. The drills are the worst. We either have to yell at the customers, or else wait for the gaps in the drilling and then speak really fast. I've got quite good at it now – during the loud bits I just smile at the customer and plan what I'm going to say when it goes quiet again. Mind you, I do get a few funny looks sometimes, if there's a particularly long spell of drilling.

The other big news is that on Friday Mr Slater, the MP, phoned up again to speak to Margaret. She didn't say much about it, afterwards, except that he wants her and Nasreen to go to London to meet a government human rights lawyer, and that he's going to meet them in Ipswich and travel down on the train with them, but it was lovely to see her looking hopeful again – her eyes were shining like I hadn't seen them shine all week.

With all my love, darling, and a big wet lick from Snuffy,

Cora xxx

From: Rebecca Prichard [becs444@btinternet.com]
Sent: 22/5/05 21:53
To: Margaret Hayton [margarethayton@yahoo.co.uk]

Hi! Oh God, Margaret, the gaping maw of eternal damnation is opening ever wider beneath my feet. I had a phone call on Friday night, quite late, after I had got back from Declan's . . . and it was Elliot. For a foot-soldier of Lucifer he doesn't half have a gorgeous voice. He said he was going to be over in Manchester again this weekend, and he knew Declan and Zoe were going to London to see Zoe's mum. (Did I tell you, turns out she is French, lives in Lyon, so if she's over here with work, as she is this weekend, Declan always takes the opportunity to let her see Zoe. They seem to get on well together still – it's all disgustingly adult and civilised.) So Elliot said, maybe he and I could meet for a drink. Which seemed perfectly reasonable. But it wasn't what he said, so much as the way he said it, as if having a drink was some kind of wickedly pleasurable intimate practice known only to handservants of the Dark Lord. I actually had to sit down to recover after he'd rung off. But by then it was too late – I appeared to have said yes. And only then did I wonder by what demonic craft he had obtained my number – because he sure as hell hadn't asked Declan!

Well, he was staying at the Mitre Hotel, and even I knew better than to agree to meet him in the bar there, so we agreed on a pub nearby, Saturday night, eight o'clock. I thought, public place, lots of people about, nice early hour, nowhere near bedtime, what can possibly be the harm? Oh, but never underestimate the wiles of the Archfiend, because of course what I had forgotten was that an early start meant more drinking time! After six or seven draughts from Beelzebub's accursed chalice (several of them doubles), I was in the hands of the Tempter. In the lift up to his hotel room, to be precise, with his hands doing exceedingly tempting things under my shirt, while he pressed me up against the carpeted wall, giving an ample demonstration of why he is known as the hornèd one. I made a last effort at saving my wretched soul and managed to tear myself away from him at the door to his room, and not go in to my certain perdition.

But I have sinned, and my fear is that I would sin again, and sin properly this time, if he only repeats the suggestion. He may be an emissary of the Evil One (and perhaps it goes with the territory) but, Margaret, he is hot, hot, hot!

As, coincidentally, am I. Something has gone wrong with the heating in my flat, so you can't have the hot water on without the central heating going full blast as well. I must get on to the landlords about it. (Unless, of course, it is the first Hadean flames beginning to lick around my ankles.)

Hugs,

Becs xxx

From: Margaret Hayton [margarethayton@yahoo.co.uk]
Sent: 22/5/05 22:38
To: Rebecca Prichard [becs444@btinternet.com]

Dear Becs,

Well, I'm not your confessor, what do you want me to say? But Declan trusts you. And Zoe trusts you even more, and when you have forgotten both of these men and moved on to Fabian or Guy, Zoe will still have a dad and an uncle who aren't speaking to each other, and a teacher who can't look her in the eye. Garlic is the thing. Garlic and a crucifix. (But maybe that's just vampires?) Or a chastity belt. You can borrow mine – I'm a vicar's daughter, remember, I've still got the one Daddy stitched me into when I was thirteen.

I had a phone call on Friday night, too – but in my case it was more like angel voices. It was Richard again – to tell me that he has fixed up a meeting in London for Nasreen and me, to talk to a human rights lawyer. Not someone from the Home Office, because there might be a conflict of interest there, but a woman at the Foreign Office, an expert on international law, who might be able to come up with some help on Nasreen's asylum case. He'd even remembered and made the appointment for the 31st, which is in half term. I asked if I could mention it to Caroline, you know, my friend from home who works at the refugee centre in Hounslow. I went to school with her – she was a couple of years older, but I knew her well because her mother was one of Dad's churchwardens. She came to stay with me one weekend in our first year, do you

143

remember? We thought she was very grown up and serious because she was at Oxford and reading Law and already doing her finals, and then she got drunk in the college bar and snogged Simon Shepperton. Well, she's a solicitor now, and knows quite a lot about asylum and refugee law, and Richard said of course, bring her along too. Nas and I are going to meet him in Ipswich and travel up on the train together – he said to meet by the statue of Sir Alf Ramsey, which is just on the way to the station.

I can hardly believe he's doing all this for Nasreen – it's so brilliant of him! I said thank you on the phone of course, but I just wanted him to be there, so that I could give him a hug.

Love,

Margaret xxx

FRANKIE'S

DOMESTIC PLUMBING AND HEATING SERVICES

114 Hume Park Road, Moss Side, Manchester M15 5TX

25 May 2005

Dear Miss Prichard

I have been instructed by your landlords, Fallowfield Properties Ltd, to carry out necessary repairs to the central heating system at Flat 4b, 85 Gainsborough Road, Moss Side. I will need to have access to the premises in order to carry out this work. I should therefore be grateful if you could contact me as soon as possible, so that we can arrange a date and time, at your convenience, when you will be able to be present to let me into the flat.

Yours sincerely,
Frankie Scott.

From: Michael Carragan
[mmcarragan@hc.parliament.uk]
Sent: 26/5/05 15:26
To: Richard Slater [rpslater@hc.parliament.uk]

I've been meaning to ask you, Richard – what on earth's going on? What has become of the celebrated Slater nose for picking the issues that cut the mustard? You've been well outside off-stump recently, mate.

First it was VAT on, er . . . ladies' sanitary items. (Bloody 'ell, I can't even sit through an advert for them myself. The merest glimpse of a laboratory bottle of blue liquid has me grabbing for the remote.) All that little fol-de-rol earned you was an unholy association with those harpies whose natural territory it is, and believe me when I say that they are not image-enhancing bedfellows – vociferous Iraq war objectors, to a woman. And then greenhouse gas emissions! Come on, Richard! Of course we're all committed to boosting renewables and meeting Tokyo targets on emissions – you know how hard it is to fault the Rottweiler's green credentials – but it isn't turning out to be that easy. So drawing public attention to the slow rate of progress is, well, frankly just plain rude. Like pointing out when your aunty's slip is showing, or your constituency chairman has got gravy on his tie. Take my word for it, that is not the road to Whitehall.

Michael.

Michael Carragan (Labour)
Member of Parliament for West Bromwich West

From: Richard Slater [rpslater@hc.parliament.uk]
Sent: 26/5/05 16:12
To: Michael Carragan [mmcarragan@hc.parliament.uk]

You are right of course, Michael, I have been straying most grievously from the path, and I must get back to some serious ducking for good-publicity apples. But in the last few weeks I find that I have been applying additional, and for me completely novel, criteria in the issue-selection process.

On a not wholly unrelated subject, I have arranged to meet Margaret and her asylum-seeking Albanian friend next Tuesday, and take them down to meet that human rights lawyer at the FO, Liz Thompson. Probably a fool's errand. But even if it's not exactly designed to win

me plaudits at No. 10, it might just temper the icy blast
of disapproval from another quarter.
Richard.

Richard Slater (Labour)
Member of Parliament for Ipswich

From: Michael Carragan
[mmcarragan@hc.parliament.uk]
Sent: 26/5/05 16:20
To: Richard Slater [rpslater@hc.parliament.uk]

Well, I suppose the odd diversion is harmless
enough – but for God's sake keep one eye on the
ball.
Michael.

Michael Carragan (Labour)
Member of Parliament for West Bromwich West

From: Margaret Hayton [margarethayton@yahoo.co.uk]
Sent: 27/5/05 19:05
To: Rebecca Prichard [becs444@btinternet.com]

Dear Becs,
Poor Cora was in such a flap tonight! She'd got
herself into something of a scrape at work. They are

147

having this refit in her bank – she was telling me about it the other night. Apparently there's a lot of noisy hammering and drilling, and it makes it very hard for them to make themselves heard when they are speaking to the customers. Cora has evolved this rather bizarre staccato delivery style, to get out what she needs to say in between the bursts of noise from the drills. She had me in stitches demonstrating it.

Well, today she said this customer came in, a young man whom she vaguely recognised as having been in a couple of times earlier in the week. Anyway, he came over to her and sat down (they don't have a counter, they each have their little area with comfy chairs), and instead of saying anything, he wordlessly handed her a note on a piece of paper. I suppose when you work in a bank you are always expecting to be robbed, so of course Cora immediately assumed that her worst fear had been realised, was far too scared to read the note, and just pressed the emergency button discreetly concealed in the arm of her chair. This activates a flashing light in the office of the branch manager, Mrs Davies, as well as sounding an alarm – not, unfortunately, at the bank but in the main headquarters of the Suffolk Constabulary.

Only then did Cora's eyes focus sufficiently for her to read what was written on the paper which the man had given her. Rather than 'Hand over all your cash, I've got a gun', it merely inquired politely, 'May I extend my overdraft limit to £250 please?' When a special

armed response unit arrived within minutes, Cora had
rather a lot of explaining to do. (Presumably hammered
out in quick bursts between the resumed drilling.)

  Margaret xx

From: Rebecca Prichard [becs444@btinternet.com]
Sent: 27/5/05 23:03
To: Margaret Hayton [margarethayton@yahoo.co.uk]

My bank don't like it when I try to extend my overdraft
either. But calling in armed police does sound like
rather an overreaction.

  Becs xxx

42 Gledhill Road
Ipswich

29 May 2005

Dear Gran,

  How are you getting on? How's the ankle? Mum said
that Kirsty has been coming in to do some extra hours over
these last few weekends, or otherwise I should have tried to
get over again myself, to help with your dinner and
anything else you might need doing. But I'll certainly come
next weekend, if that's all right, and I'll remember to bring
back those clean sheets. Can you put any weight on your
ankle yet? And have you been doing those stretches from
the sheet the physiotherapist gave you at the hospital? Or is
it still too painful?

I am packing up a few books to send you, while you are still not very mobile. They are just some old ones of mine which I enjoyed and I thought you might too, to provide some variation on what Kirsty brings you from the library. I expect you have already read all the classics that I've got, so I've chosen a few recent novels, mostly funny ones that I thought might cheer you up. The Kate Atkinson, especially, is a favourite of mine.

It's my half term holiday coming up this week. On Tuesday, I am going to London with Nasreen from the hostel and Richard Slater – the MP, you remember – to talk to a lawyer from the Foreign Office who might be able to help Nasreen with her claim to be able to stay in Britain. It's Mr Slater who fixed it all up. It is very good of him – he seems to be taking a genuine interest in Nasreen's case.

Nasreen came into school this week, on Wednesday, to talk to the children about her religion. We have been doing this project on Islam, you know, and there are hardly any Muslim kids in Year 3, only the doctor's twins in Mrs Allen's class, and it didn't seem right to put them on the spot. Nasreen went down really well. The children loved her, and they had lots of interesting questions – although David Goldberg did ask her whether she had ever known anyone who was a suicide bomber, which was a bit embarrassing. I found out quite a lot, too. Because they can't go out to a mosque, Nasreen's family just pray at home, or sometimes they get together with a few Muslim neighbours if it is a special festival or something. The men and boys pray in the sitting room and the women and girls pray in the hallway. It seems odd to observe this segregation even though it is just the family most of the time, but I suppose it is the tradition. I wondered if being asked about home would be upsetting for Nasreen, but actually she seemed pleased to be able to talk about it, quite proud in fact, and not sad at all.

Helen has been quite poorly, so for the past week or so we've all been taking turns going in to sit with her at bedtime, until she gets off to sleep. It's quite a commitment, but it's worked well so far: she hasn't taken an overdose, or even cut herself at all since last week. And it's only Monday to Friday, because she is still going into hospital over the weekends. On Wednesday evening I went into the hostel office to do the bank reconciliation, and I met Alison in there – she is one of the support group. She was on her way to sit with Helen, and meanwhile she was sorting out some problem for Lauren, another of the residents, talking to the social worker on the phone, and smoothing over whatever it was beautifully. Alison is so organised and super-confident, always completely on top of everything – I really wish I could be like that! Anyway, she offered to help with the bank stuff before she went up to Helen (Alison used to be treasurer when WITCH first started), and we got chatting, and she mentioned she had a hospital appointment the next day, and not very tactfully I said, 'Oh, what's wrong?' and she said, 'Nothing really, I'm pregnant.' And of course I had no idea what to say. I mean, normally you'd say 'Congratulations', at least to someone older and married, but there was something about the way she said it, and she's well into the middle zone, and she's got three big kids already, I think she said the youngest is in Year 5. So, because I couldn't think what else to say, I found myself asking her when it was, and if she'd like me to go with her, and she looked at me and said, 'Thank you, that would be great.'

Well, I wasn't sure what I was doing really, going along to hold the hand of somebody practically old enough to be my mother. But in the car on the way to the hospital Alison started talking, and she seemed to have thought it all through, very matter-of-fact she was, and she said she was going to ask for a termination. She hadn't intended the pregnancy, and she was talking about her kids. How the eldest boy, Robert, has got GCSEs next year, and how the autistic one, Edward, has been hell to live with just recently, and how disruptive it would be to have a baby in the house. She didn't mention her husband at all, so I didn't like to ask what he thought about it. Sitting in the waiting room at the maternity ward was awful. Everyone else seemed to be in couples, sitting holding hands and looking happy, and I thought how Alison had probably sat here before, with her husband, when she was expecting her other children, and wondered if she was thinking the same thing. It was actually quite funny, though, because they had told Alison to drink plenty of fluids beforehand and come with a full bladder, because of the scan, and then we had to wait a long time, and poor Alison was bursting, so we daren't even have a cup of tea from the machine.

Eventually they called her in, and she asked if I would go with her, and the woman doctor got her on a bed and put vaseline on her tummy and rubbed the scanner thing around a bit, looked at the screen, and hmmed to herself. Then she said, 'Wait here, I'm just going to fetch another doctor because I want a second opinion.' And we were left there for what seemed like ages, with Alison all cold and vaseliny and still dying for the loo. When she came back, with a male colleague, they both moved the scanner about and studied the screen, and then they nodded to each other, and the first doctor (the woman) said, 'There is an eight-week foetus there, Mrs Whiteley, but I'm afraid we can't find any heartbeat.' It was suddenly all just too much for Alison, after all that being brave and sensible and strong, and she just burst into tears. And the male doctor looked at her notes and said, 'But I thought you were planning on having a termination anyway?' as if to say, in that case what possible reason could she have for being emotional, she should be glad she'd been spared the difficulty! Well, I'm afraid I couldn't restrain myself then, Gran, even though I'm sure Alison just found it embarrassing. I had a real go at him. I actually asked him how he would feel if he'd just been told that his baby was dead inside him! And poor Alison now has to wait for a miscarriage, which can't be a very pleasant prospect.

I hope you don't mind my telling you all this, Gran, but I've been thinking about it a lot. There is one more cheerful thing to tell you, though. Cora decided to do some evening classes with Persephone, who is one of the women from the hostel support group, and the classes were on herbalism. I thought it was an odd choice, because Cora isn't usually interested in all those alternative therapies, in fact she goes to her GP and demands antibiotics if she gets so much as a cold. Well, it turned out that Cora thought herbalism meant how to *grow* herbs! I would love to have seen her face when she got there expecting gardening, and it was all these women talking about healing, and rediscovering the ancient lore of their grandmothers. (Not that you ever brewed up many herbal potions, at least not that I remember, Gran! A cup of tea and a hot water bottle was your usual prescription!)

Anyway, this letter is getting very long. I think I'd better stop there. But do look after yourself, and I hope your ankle is getting much better. I'll see you next Saturday.

Lots of love,

Margaret xxx

From: Margaret Hayton
[margarethayton@yahoo.co.uk]
Sent: 31/5/05 14:11
To: Rebecca Prichard [becs444@btinternet.com]

Dear Becs,

He didn't turn up – he sodding well didn't turn up!!! There were Nas and I, down by Sir Alf Ramsey as arranged – ten minutes early, even, because when I went round to the hostel to pick her up she was actually waiting outside the door for me, she was so excited about this meeting, and going to London, and everything. She had put such hopes on it, even though we'd all told her not to. She seemed certain this was going to be the solution to everything, that she would be able to stay in England, stay at Witch House. Well, he was supposed to be meeting us at 12.30, in order to catch the London train at 12.52, but it got to 12.45 and he still hadn't appeared, and we had to decide what to do. Nas wanted to go to the station and get the train anyway, but of course we didn't have the details of exactly who this human rights person at the Foreign Office is, nor any idea where to go to find her, so I tried to explain all this to Nas, but of course she got very upset – it was like all her hopes were evaporating before her eyes. How can he do this to her? So I took her back to the hostel, and came back here to try to call him and find out what on earth he was playing at. I had a real nightmare trying to find out his private number at the House of Commons, and when I eventually got hold of it, he wasn't answering his bloody phone.

Sorry to hit you with all this, Becs – but, God,

I hate men sometimes! And speaking of men . . .
how are things down there in the burning fiery
furnace?

Love,

Margaret xx

From: Rebecca Prichard [becs444@btinternet.com]
Sent: 31/5/05 14:45
To: Margaret Hayton [margarethayton@yahoo.co.uk]

Typical! He probably found he'd got some dreadfully
important meeting he had to go to – far more
important than Nasreen's whole future – about
mackerel quotas, or what buns to get in the House
of Commons tea room. Tell him he's a worm and
you'll be voting LibDem next time.

As to the fiery furnace, literal and metaphorical,
both problems have been solved in one fell swoop,
since you ask. My immortal soul is safe for the
moment. I decided you were right, about not coming
between the vindaloo brothers. And that you were
probably right before that too, about not dating a
parent. And then your unimpeachable and all-
pervading rightness was confirmed by the gods of
alphabetical providence, who sent me a sign. In the
form of the Adonis who came to mend my central
heating. Except he was not so much Adonis (I've
done A, as you know) as Frankie. I've ended it with

Declan, I'm not returning Elliot's calls, and I'm going out for a drink with Frankie tomorrow night.
   Big hugs,
   Becs xx

From: Margaret Hayton [margarethayton@yahoo.co.uk]
Sent: 31/5/05 14:49
To: Rebecca Prichard [becs444@btinternet.com]

Dear Becs,
   I despair of you, I really do. Even you cannot seriously have got it on with the plumber who came round to fix your pipes! Your life is descending into an imitation of a bad porno movie. And where is it all going to end? Are you finally going to settle down and get married to a guy named Zorba when you are fifty-eight?
   Love,
   Margaret xxx

Dear Margaret and every one,
   I just want to say I'm thanking you for every thing you doing for me. But now I'm going to London. Maybe I'm being safer in London, maybe I'm not being sent back home then.
   I missing you,
   Nasreen xx

From: Margaret Hayton [margarethayton@yahoo.co.uk]
Sent: 31/5/05 23:16
To: Rebecca Prichard [becs444@btinternet.com]

Dear Becs,

Oh, God, what am I going to do? It's just terrible, and I feel as if it's my fault! Except it isn't, it's bloody Richard Slater's fault – he should never have offered to help Nas, and got her hopes up, if he was going to ditch her like that, and leave her high and dry. Oh, Becs, it's just so awful, I hardly know how to tell you, but Cora's light was off when I got in, and I don't like to wake her, and I've just *got* to tell someone. I went round to the hostel at about ten o'clock – it was my turn to sit with Helen (we've got a rota going, you see), and afterwards I thought I'd just look in on Nas. But when I knocked on her door there was no reply, and what was odd was that the door wasn't quite closed, which was strange if she was asleep, so I just poked my head a little way round the door, just to check she was OK, because I had a sort of nasty feeling . . . And there was a note on the bed. Scribbled down on the back of an opened-out cardboard toothpaste packet. I suppose it was all she could find, probably from the bin. And it just said thanks and goodbye, and that she has gone to London! She seems to think that she will be safer there, that she won't get sent back to Albania if she is in London. But where can she go? She doesn't know anyone there –

she doesn't know anyone at all in England except us. I wondered if she'd got some crazy idea about trying to see that Foreign Office lawyer, because that's where we had been going to go today. Or maybe she just wants to 'disappear', like you hear about asylum seekers doing, and thinks it will be easier in London than in Ipswich, where there's always someone who knows someone who knows you . . . But it will be so dangerous – anyone could take advantage of her, she's so young, and she's got hardly any money and can't sign on, and her English still isn't very good. I don't want to call the police – that's the last thing she'd want, she'd be so scared if they came after her. And if she really does want to disappear, well, I don't really want to turn her in, do I? Oh, Becs, I feel I should go and look for her, but where would I even know where to start?

Love,

Margaret xx

From: Rebecca Prichard [becs444@btinternet.com]
Sent: 31/5/05 23:32
To: Margaret Hayton [margarethayton@yahoo.co.uk]

Margaret, I really am very sorry to hear about Nasreen and have no idea what to suggest. You must be really upset, hon. (In fact, I can tell by the state of your mixed metaphors. How can someone be both ditched and high and dry?) But don't worry, honestly. I'm sure London is not really the corrupting pit of iniquity you country bumpkins imagine it to be, and there are places she can go where they will help her. She managed to get out from Albania all right and made it to England by herself, so the girl must have a fair bit of gumption. She'll be OK, I'm certain of it. Maybe she'll try to contact your Richard bloke (though a fat lot of help he'll be, by the sound of it). Why don't you phone him in the morning?

Lots of love and hugs,

Becs xxx

From: Margaret Hayton [margarethayton@yahoo.co.uk]
Sent: 1/6/05 03:24
To: Rebecca Prichard [becs444@btinternet.com]

Oh, Becs, worse and worse. I woke up in the middle of the night with a lurching sensation in the pit of my stomach. It was something the head had said at school the other week about the 1970s, and it had suddenly come back to me in my sleep. I had this dreadful fear . . . well, it was more of a conviction really, but I had to make sure. So I got out of bed – it was nearly 3 a.m. – and I was too agitated even to get dressed, I just put on my fleece and wellies over my pyjamas like an escaped long-term psychiatric patient, and got my bike out and cycled off in the direction of the station. I went to the statue, where we'd waited for Richard. And it was just as I'd feared – it wasn't Sir Alf Ramsey. It was Sir Bobby Robson.

How was I to know, Becs? Dad was only interested in books, and for Mum sport began and ended with Torvill and Dean's gold medal-winning performance at the 1984 Winter Olympics. How was I supposed to be able to tell one bronze former England football manager from another? And what do they want to go and have two of them for, anyway? And how can I ever face Richard now? Because it's all my fault about Nasreen after all!

Love,

Margaret xxx

From: Rebecca Prichard [becs444@btinternet.com]
Sent: 1/6/05 08:23
To: Margaret Hayton [margarethayton@yahoo.co.uk]

I appreciate that now may not be the moment, my poor dear Margaret, to lambast you for your ignorance. I know almost nothing about football either, but (for future reference) Sir Alf is the tight-lipped sourface, and Sir Bob is the one who looks like a more enthusiastic version of somebody's grandad.

Becs xx

From: Richard Slater [rpslater@hc.parliament.uk]
Sent: 1/6/05 15:12
To: Michael Carragan [mmcarragan@hc.parliament.uk]

Hi Michael,

She never turned up! There I was, waiting by Sir Alf
as agreed – in fact I got there ten minutes early, I was
so determined not to keep them waiting. And that
despite spending a considerable time in W. H. Smith's
on my way down there, trying to choose between a
copy of the *New Internationalist* to read on the train
(which would say I was concerned, with a broad
outlook) and *Private Eye* (to show I don't take myself
or the administration too seriously). In the end I
bought both, just to be on the safe side. Well, we
were meant to be meeting at 12.30, so we could catch
the 12.52 train to Liverpool Street. When it got to
12.45 and they still hadn't arrived, I had to decide
what to do. My urge was to go and look for her, but
then I remembered that Liz Thompson would be
expecting us, and you know what these Foreign Office
types are like – alpha males of both genders! And of
course I am still trying not to blot my copybook, and
the Rottweiler always has his nose close to the
ground in the FO. So I had a long lonely train ride
back to London – though at least I had no shortage of
reading material.

I kept wondering why Margaret hadn't come. It
occurred to me that maybe the recollection of my

lunatic hair-grabbing antics had made her change her mind at the last minute. But she doesn't strike me as the nervous type – I would have imagined her as more likely to stand and face even an unwanted and slightly deranged predator than to take flight. And she seemed so dedicated to Nasreen. I just can't understand it, Mike.

I headed for my office, intending to call in and see if she had left a message for me, but only got as far as the doorstep, where I found the other lawyer (that solicitor friend of Margaret's from the refugee centre, Caroline she's called – another fearsomely forthright female) lying in wait for me. As we were already rather late, we headed straight round to Liz's chambers. (Why do the FO's lawyers insist upon calling their rooms 'chambers' as if they were Rumpole of the Bailey? All the other Government Legal Service people I've come across just have 'offices' like normal human beings.) Anyway, soon the two legal ladies were hard at it. The air was thick with acronyms, it was all CEDAW and UNHCR and ECRE, and they were bandying terms like 'gender-specific violence' and 'agents of persecution' and 'indirect state responsibility'. I must admit I had stopped trying to follow it all and was picturing Margaret's eyes the way they had looked in the Corn Exchange café, when suddenly they seemed to have cooked up between the two of them a brand new government policy directive. Exceptions for gender-based oppression, including intra-familial violence (or some such formula), even for women from countries on The List. Liz Thompson was going to take it up with her opposite number at your end today. I don't know who the poor sap is, but I do know I shouldn't want to be the one to stand in her way. When I left her chambers, she seemed to have the bit firmly between her teeth.

I wanted to ring Margaret straight away, but I didn't like to somehow. I didn't want to put pressure on her about whyever it was that she hadn't turned up at Sir Alf. But Liz said she'd phone me this afternoon and let me know what happened with the Home Office lawyer. If it's been agreed, then I am off to gift-wrap this important little piece of feminist policy reform, tie a big pink ribbon round it, write a gift tag falsely claiming it as all my own work, and lay it at Margaret's feet along with my poor trampled heart. Or at least, I am going to ring her up, anyway. Wish me luck!

Richard.

Richard Slater (Labour)
Member of Parliament for Ipswich

42 Gledhill Street
Ipswich

1 June 2005

Darling Petey,

Well, I'm on my own here tonight, so I thought I'd write to you with the latest news. Life is certainly more exciting since Margaret has been around! She appeared at breakfast looking dreadful – hair all over the place, under her eyes great dark circles, and in them a sort of feverish glitter. Nasreen has run away! She's gone to London, but no one knows exactly where. She left a note, which Margaret found last night, late, but it didn't give any clues about where she was planning to go. It seems to be something to do with that MP, Mr Slater. He was meant to be taking them both to London yesterday for a meeting – I think I told you about it – but he didn't turn up, and it seems that's what got Nasreen so upset. Margaret was cursing him yesterday at suppertime, I can tell you, though this morning when I mentioned him she went rather quiet and didn't say much at all. She seemed terribly upset, though. She didn't seem to know *what* to do, and even though I told her not to go blaming herself, I could see that was what she was thinking.

Then I had to go off to work, of course, although I hated leaving her alone. All day at the bank I kept imagining her, moping round the house by herself, because this week is her half term break. Anyway, as soon as I put my key in the lock tonight I could hear the phone ringing, so I rushed to pick it up, and it was Mr Slater, and he sounded excited, but also a bit worried, because he said he'd been calling and calling and hadn't got any reply, and did I know where Margaret was, because he really wanted to speak to her. I was opening my mouth to say I didn't know where she was, when my eye fell on a note, lying there just by the telephone. It was from Margaret, and it said that she has gone to London, too, to see if she can find Nasreen! Not a word about where she's going to look, or when she'll be back, or anything! So I read it to Mr Slater, and he said, what does she mean about Nasreen? So I explained to him about Nasreen running away, and about how upset Margaret was, and I nearly gave him a piece of my mind about agreeing to meet them yesterday and then not doing, but I bit it back, because it isn't really any of my business, is it? And it didn't seem right, really, to be rude to a Member of Parliament. Well, he went very quiet, in fact I actually wondered if he was still there, and then he suddenly just said 'thank you' as if he'd just remembered that *I* was there, and rang off.

I'm sitting right by the phone writing this. Snuffy won't settle down at all. She keeps cocking her ears and trotting to the front door every few minutes, as if she's expecting something, like maybe Margaret coming home. But she hasn't rung. I do hope she's all right – and Nasreen, too. It's getting late – I hope they're both somewhere safe! In fact I should be getting to bed myself, there's work in the morning, but I'm not sure I shall be able to sleep without knowing where Margaret is. Maybe I'll try some valerian tea. I've had some growing in the flower bed for years – I rather like those pale pink lacy flower heads – but on Tuesday at my evening class we learned about its healing properties, so I dug a plant up and cut up the root.

Apparently you just pour water on it from the kettle and the infusion helps you get off to sleep. Persephone was going to make some for Helen at the hostel. But I must say, Pete, it smells absolutely disgusting!

I'll write a longer letter next time. Love you for ever, Cora xxx

From: Richard Slater [richard.slater@btopenworld.com]
Sent: 2/6/05 01:08
To: Michael Carragan [mmcarragan@hc.parliament.uk]

Hi Michael,

Liz Thompson called at about four o'clock, and said that your people have OK'd the new asylum policy: a specific exception for gender-based violence. I got straight on the phone and rang Margaret's number. No reply, so I tried Witch House – the woman in the office there (at least I *think* it was a woman), Pat I think she said her name was, said Margaret hadn't been in. So I kept trying her home number. Every time it started ringing I played through in my head how her reaction would sound, how that sweet, serious voice would go all croaky with grateful emotion when I told her the good news . . . what a sad fool I am! In the end, the landlady, Cora, answered. She'd just got in from work, and Margaret still wasn't there. And then she found a note, and it was from Margaret, saying that she had gone to London to look for Nasreen. I couldn't understand what it was all about – Nasreen wasn't in London, how could she be, they had never turned up, never made it to the meeting . . . It just didn't make sense to me. But then Cora finally managed to impart the information in a way that my uncooperative brain would accept: Nasreen has run away. It seems as if she has come to London, gone into hiding, to avoid being sent back to Albania! Christ, what a mess, Mike – just when it looks like she'd have a good chance of being granted permanent leave to remain!

I rang off, and just sat there in a complete daze, picking up the phone and putting it down again several times, and twisting my mouse round and round abstractedly, until the cable cut off the blood supply to my left thumb and I had to carry out an emergency severance procedure using a novelty bottle opener given to me by the Suffolk Independent Brewers' Association. A modicum of feeling was beginning to be restored when there was a knock at the door, and suddenly there was Margaret, pale and distressed and lovely, standing in front of my desk as if summoned up by my unquiet subconscious. Well, I wasn't going to carry on sitting behind my desk if she was standing in front of it and, after a brief but brutal entanglement with an anglepoise lamp, I was round it and facing her, and she was pouring out her fears for Nasreen, and she seemed to be blaming it all (rather harshly, I felt) on herself, and (even more harshly) on Bobby Robson. God help me, what I wanted to do was to sweep her into my arms and clasp her to my manly bosom and pour words of soft comfort and consolation into her shell-like ear, as any red-blooded male would do. But I couldn't do it – the constant re-educative drip effect of our female comrades clearly has a lot to answer for, because I found I just couldn't take advantage of her unhappiness and vulnerability. Instead I just stood there lamely, offering platitudinous nothings about how I was sure everything would be all right. Even when she started crying and moved forward and actually laid her face on my chest, I rationed myself to a few impersonal pats on the shoulder. Plumbing new depths of inanity, I believe I may actually have uttered the words 'There, there'! How I wished I had been an unreconstructed Old Labour chauvinist so that I could have taken this blissful opportunity to do what I was longing to do – sink my hand into those dark ringlets and pull her head against my shoulder, and then bury my nose and mouth in the warm scent of her hair.

Anyway, you get the picture – I exercised unparalleled self-restraint. And when she had calmed down a bit, and my hormone levels had receded sufficiently to allow for the resumption of conscious thought, I suggested sitting down and making a list of places where we might try to look for Nasreen.

Margaret was adamant that we shouldn't call the police, because she thought it would frighten Nasreen, and I wasn't going to argue with her about it, at least for the moment. It was already past 5.30 p.m., so anywhere with office hours was going to be no help until the morning. We rang Caroline at the Hounslow refugee centre, and luckily she was still there. Although she knew nothing and had nothing much to suggest, Margaret seemed grateful to have been able to speak to her. Caroline's reassurances seemed to carry rather more weight than my own – but then perhaps she came up with a more persuasive argument for Nasreen's safety than 'There, there'. Since she almost certainly arrived either at Liverpool Street (if she came by train) or Victoria (if she took the bus), our best hope seemed to be that Nasreen would have approached an agency in one or other of those areas, so I made some calls, but with no success and, with increasing frequency, only to reach an out-of-hours message service. We then got in a taxi and actually went round to Centrepoint to talk to the staff there. Margaret produced a photo of Nasreen, which was very resourceful of her, and I suddenly realised that I didn't know what she looked like either, though I feel as if I know her, so it was odd to be peering at the face of a grinning stranger, surrounded by primary school children and looking about twelve herself. No luck there, anyway, but they suggested one or two other night shelters we might try, so we got back in the cab, and by the time we had drawn a blank at about five places it was getting late, and Margaret looked as though she had neither eaten nor slept for two days (which I suspect may well have been the case).

Making use of her weakened state, and the fact that I knew she would want to resume the search in the morning, I told her it would make sense to call it a day, and go back to my flat for sustenance and rest. The cabbie was a woman of the don't-try-anything-with-me-sonny type, and checked with Margaret whether that was what she wanted too, before obeying my directions. By this stage Margaret's usual pallor seemed to have intensified to something resembling a death mask in the street lights, and the driver looked at me as though she thought I might be concealing a chloroformed hanky somewhere about my person. Margaret nodded and attempted a smile, which seemed to do the trick, so an awkward situation explaining myself to the constabulary was averted, and twenty minutes later here we were.

Next came the mortifying discovery that the only things in my fridge were five bottles of Stella, a half-bottle of Soave which I filched from that party thrown at the DTI by the Italian trade delegation the other week, and a disconcertingly pliable carrot. Opening the bottle of Soave while I cooked seemed to strike rather too convivial a note, so I was obliged to contemplate the contents of the cupboard without the inspirational effects of any chemical stimulant. In the end, an antique tin of condensed mushroom soup and some dried pasta spirals were made to stand service as *gemelli ai porcini*, which she nevertheless consumed with touching gratitude.

I sat opposite her with my jacket on, as if we were a Select Committee and no motion had been put for dispensing with jacket and tie. I know it's a thoroughly disreputable habit of mine, but on days when I am not anticipating being seen in my shirtsleeves I only iron a strip four inches wide down the front of my shirt – just the bit that shows under my suit. It's all about gaining precious extra minutes under the duvet. So of course I didn't want to disrobe to reveal the rest of the garment, still shamefully wrinkled from its habitual place of storage (balled up in the bottom of the dryer). Somehow the stiff and increasingly sweaty discomfort of my outer garb suited my mood, mirroring with painful exactness my internal state of unrest.

Now she is in my bed, wearing only a free promotional T-shirt of mine, while I, having finally doffed jacket and tie and silently uncorked the Soave beneath the muffling concealment of a cushion, am now deadening my senses preparatory to a long lonely night in here on a two foot wide settee.

Richard.

From: Richard Slater [richard.slater@btopenworld.com]
Sent: 2/6/05 08:38
To: Michael Carragan [mmcarragan@hc.parliament.uk]

Michael, hello again. I trust you had a better night's sleep than I did. Every time I stirred – which was pretty often, believe me, with Margaret lying semi-clad on the other side of a piece of plasterboard – my left leg slipped down the gap between the back of the settee and the seat cushions, leading in every case to gradual loss of sensation, followed by pins and needles, and finally severe cramp. By six I had given up the uneven struggle and was up and dressed, my shirt ironed front and back, and was ploughing through the London Directory of Voluntary Organisations looking for places where a young Albanian girl with shaky English and no friends in the capital might possibly go to seek assistance.

At seven thirty Margaret appeared in the bedroom doorway, looking beautifully drowsy and dishevelled, and I stood up and dropped the directory to gaze at her. It was some minutes before I remembered to breathe, by which time the room was circling around me in a kind of stately gavotte. She was wearing nothing underneath my T-shirt, and it was a chilly morning for June, as her outline bore tangible testimony, and suddenly British Sugar's emblazoned claim that 'Nothing Tastes Sweeter' seemed to promise a new and tantalising truth.

I was by now quite decidedly gawking, and I told myself that I must say something – anything – at once, to dispel the impression of moon-faced idiocy. An offer of coffee would have fitted the bill perfectly: safe, and without emotional undertones. But I suddenly remembered that I still hadn't mentioned about my meeting with Liz, and the new policy initiative. It's just to cheer her up a bit, that's all, whispered a less than ingenuous voice in my head, and all at once I was telling her about how the asylum rules were to be modified to accord refugee status to women escaping domestic violence and sexual oppression. And her eyes, which had been inky as a storm-torn October night, melted into the pastel brume of a midsummer dawn, and the next thing I knew she had crossed over to where I stood and was hugging me. It seemed churlish not to put my arms round her and return the hug, so I did, and because her arms were lifted up to reach around my neck, there was distinct . . . well, perkiness, and jutting . . . followed by delicious pressing and flattening, and – oh God, Mike, it took me every ounce of will to disengage myself, turn her round and point her in the direction of the shower.

She says she must be back in Ipswich tonight to go to the WITCH meeting, so they can talk about what to do, and I said I'd go back with her on the train, but we've got most of the day to carry on the search. I've just rung the Albanian embassy and managed to get us an appointment for 10.30, because Mira in the Commons photcopying room is a friend of Lejla on the switchboard there. And now I'm off out to find milk and bread and a toothbrush for Margaret. (Would it be so very wicked to keep it afterwards and use it myself?)

Richard.

From: Michael Carragan
[mmcarragan@hc.parliament.uk]
Sent: 2/6/05 09:45
To: Richard Slater [richard.slater@btopenworld.com]

Richard – I have three pieces of advice for you, my friend.
1) Get a wireless mouse (that's assuming it is a new mouse you are needing, not a new thumb).
2) If you are planning on being gentlemanly again, get a wider settee. (Also handy for more ungentlemanly scenarios.)
3) The first moment that your feminist conscience allows you to consider her as no longer vulnerable, *tell her how you feel*. And then stop sending me these high-octane e-mails, especially before 10 a.m. Michael.

Michael Carragan (Labour)
Member of Parliament for West Bromwich West

WITCH
Women of Ipswich Together Combating Homelessness

<u>Extract from minutes of meeting</u> at Pat and Pat's house, 2 June 2005, 8 p.m.

<u>Present</u>: Alison, Ding, Susan, Pat, Pat, Persephone, Emily, Margaret. Also in attendance: Richard Slater (as observer).

News of residents
Margaret reported on Nasreen's disappearance, and what steps have been taken to try to find her. She and Richard have distributed copies of Nasreen's photo to over thirty night shelters, refugee organisations, multi-cultural centres and housing advice agencies in central London, although so far no information has been forthcoming. Margaret is still on half term, and will go back to London tomorrow to continue inquiries, assisted by Richard. It was decided that the police should still not be involved for the moment. It was also agreed that Nasreen's room should be held for her for the immediate future, and her rent funded out of the voids allowance.

The rota for supporting Helen is working well, and it was decided to continue it for another week at least.

We were happy to hear that, with Alison's help, Carole has found a job sterilising the apparatus at Alison's medical laboratory.

News of former residents still receiving support
Angie's husband assaulted her on Monday evening outside

the Women's Aid refuge. Angie is in hospital with broken ribs; her husband is back in prison.

Any other business
Margaret was asked to convey thanks to Cora, who has planted some petunias and busy lizzies to replace the primulas in Mrs Roberston's front window box. Cora also plans to stock the garden of Witch House with medicinal herbs.

From: Margaret Hayton [margarethayton@yahoo.co.uk]
Sent: 2/6/05 23:20
To: Rebecca Prichard [becs444@btinternet.com]

Dear Becs,

Well, it's been quite a few days – in fact, I can't believe it was only yesterday morning that I last e-mailed you! I just couldn't sit around here doing nothing, so I pocketed a photo of Nas that I took at school for the Islam display board, and caught the train to London. I had no idea where I was going to go or what I was going to do, and after I'd spent an unproductive hour and a half at Liverpool Street showing Nas's picture to people on newspaper stands and at sandwich kiosks, I was all out of ideas and feeling pretty desperate. So I got on the tube to Westminster and went to look for Richard's office. It had three names on the door, in fact, but he says one of them is an ancient Tory who is never there, and the other is a friend of his who has just moved to ministerial quarters at the Home Office, so he has the place mostly to himself. There was an awful lot of paper in there, but I wouldn't exactly say it looked organised, or as if any of it got dealt with very often. There also seemed to be a large number of rather peculiar knick-knacks dotted around the place, as though people are always bringing him things back from their holidays – including what looked like a large ceramic sugar-beet on his desk.

Well, for some reason, as soon as I got in there and he stood up and came towards me, all the worry about Nasreen, and about mixing up the statues and everything, suddenly got the better of me and I started crying like a baby. I dread to think what he must have thought of me! And in fact, you could tell he felt I was behaving like an embarrassing fool, because he patted me on the shoulder in a polite but dismissive sort of way – he couldn't back away fast enough. But he was fantastic, Becs. He suggested I ring Caroline, who was characteristically bracing, and then he took us round to some of the big night shelters in a taxi (I can't remember the last time I'd been in a cab!), and he even asked the driver to wait each time. It was pretty late by then, and I was just wondering about whether it would be better to try to find a cheap hotel, or to fork out the train fare to Ipswich and back again in the morning, when he kindly suggested that I stay over at his flat. It is quite central, near the Barbican, but tiny, and also full of heaps of paper and strange souvenirs. He made us something hot to eat – pasta, and it was even vegetarian, which just shows how thoughtful he is – and then he let me have his bedroom while he slept on the settee. I'm not used to such a big bed at Cora's, and it was all still unmade from where he'd been in it the night before, and I know it sounds weird, or else you're going to get completely the wrong idea, but there was a lingering masculine sort of smell about the pillow which I found oddly comforting, and I slept really well.

In the morning, though, I felt dreadful, thinking about me waking up in a comfortable safe bed, while Nas might be God knows where. I came out to look for Richard, and I think he must have sensed that I was down and needed a boost, because he told me what he hadn't liked to mention the night before, because the whole priority seemed to be just about finding Nas – he told me about what happened at his meeting with Caroline and the Foreign Office lawyer. And it's wonderful news, Becs – I could hardly believe it! Richard has persuaded the government to adopt a policy of granting refugee status to women at genuine risk of family violence or other gender-based oppression, even if it is not directly condoned by their state of origin, and even if they are from countries normally designated by the Home Office as being 'safe'. I found it completely overwhelming, the thought of what we had achieved – what Richard had achieved – for Nasreen, and for thousands of other women around the world who live in fear, of domestic beatings, of forced marriages, of 'honour' killings, of rape, abduction and sexual slavery. I just had to give him a hug, so I did, and he gave me a little comradely cuddle back, and then sent me off to have a shower. And in the shower I found myself reflecting upon how odd it was that he'd got his shirt and tie on again so early in the morning, all stiff and starchy where my arms were round his neck, and how he'd still had them on when I went to bed the night before, too. He'd even kept his jacket on although it was a warm evening – maybe Party rules don't permit MPs to appear in their shirtsleeves if a constituent is present! But it set me thinking how I've never seen him *without* his tie, and feeling just a little bit disappointed.

Anyway, he made us some really nice strong espresso in this Italian pot he's got, and we spent another busy day going round everywhere we could think of and showing people the photo of Nas. I asked Richard whether he didn't have other things he needed to be doing, at the House, but he said this was more important, and I really appreciated that. He even used his high-level contacts to get us an appointment at the Albanian embassy. Not that any of it did any good, but at least we tried. Richard said he wanted to be back in Ipswich tonight, so he came back on the train with me, and walked me back to Cora's. When I walked into the kitchen there was a dreadful fug, and none too pleasant a smell. She was boiling up yarrow and elderflower in the deep-fat fryer, apparently with the intention of putting the resultant virulent-looking green gloop in her bath 'to stimulate the system'. I'm not quite sure whether she meant her own system, or if its invigorating properties are directed at the waste water pipes.

I was just going to go and get out my bike to go to Pat and Pat's for the WITCH meeting when the doorbell rang and it was Richard again, asking if he could give me a lift, so of course I said why didn't he come along to help me tell everyone about our search for Nasreen. So he did – and he even dropped me off home afterwards. Cora came out to the door when I was saying goodbye, I guess she had heard the car, and she asked Richard in politely for a cup of tea, but it didn't seem a very good idea. She looked anxious. Even under the orange of the street lights I could see that her skin had gone a slightly greenish colour, and there was a faint aroma of the compost heap rising from underneath her dressing gown. I thought I'd better get her inside and sort her out.

But how is Frankie? Have you engaged in any expansion coupling yet? Has he let you tinker with his ballcock and free his hopper head, or given your

downpipes a good rodding? In fact, just help
yourself from the whole rich panoply of plumbing
pantagruelism.

Love,

Margaret xxx

From: Rebecca Prichard [becs444@btinternet.com]
Sent: 2/6/05 23:33
To: Margaret Hayton [margarethayton@yahoo.co.uk]

Hi Margaret! I'm sorry you've drawn a blank on
finding Nasreen. But what is going on with you and
Richard? Sniffing his bedclothes, picturing him
without his tie? I think you may have been out of
the market for so long that you've forgotten how to
recognise the symptoms. All right, so your mind
has been on other things, and I know he's old
enough . . . well, old enough to be your MP, but
really, chuck, wake up and smell the rich roast
Italian espresso!

As for Frankie, well, he's certainly very handy with
his toolbox. I might even consider letting him connect
up my ring-seal, and that's not normally something I
enjoy. 'Pantagruelism' is worth a 7.5.

Hugs,

Becs xxx

From: Richard Slater [richard.slater@btopenworld.com]
Sent: 3/6/05 22:41
To: Michael Carragan [mikecarragan@yahoo.com]

Hi Mike,

I took her back to Ipswich last night for her meeting, even went along to the coven with her to hold her hand (though sadly only figuratively). They were surprisingly warm and welcoming, or perhaps merely distracted from their man-eating habits by concern for the missing member of the pack. If things turned nasty I was planning to whip out the talisman of my recent achievement in feminist policy reform, but in the end it wasn't necessary, nor did it seem quite appropriate. I drove her home, leaving her in the hands of her landlady, whose skin tones resemble those of Morticia Addams. (I wonder if she has some rare disease.)

I picked her up first thing this morning, and we resumed our quest. I had borrowed the photo of Nasreen overnight and run off some copies of a 'Missing' poster on my printer at the Ipswich flat, and today we went back to a lot of the same places as yesterday, putting up the posters, and talking to people again. We even had lunch *à deux* in a little Albanian restaurant in Soho, rendered ever so slightly less *intime* by Margaret cross-examining all the waitresses over the bean soup and *fërgesë me piperka*. When it got to about six o'clock, just when I was hoping she might stay over with me again, she suddenly announced that she was going to see her grandmother in Hampshire, and would I drop her at the station. It turned out that the voluminous rucksack she had been lugging about all day (resolutely refusing my chivalrous offers of assistance) contained a large number of paperback novels, and whole set of clean sheets as well as a sleeping bag. I wondered whether they don't have their own bedding in Hampshire, or whether her grandmother lives some kind of spartan nomadic existence, without such fripperies, but thought it unwise to inquire too closely. I took her to Waterloo, gave her a peck on the cheek, and trudged off home.

I am a very bad person, though, Michael, because I found myself wishing that Nasreen would stay missing, so that I could spend every day just like today, walking around London, or sitting on the bus or Tube, with Margaret by my side, walking with her purposeful step, or gazing out with the crusading gleam in her eyes, engaged in our common undertaking. But she has a grandmother to visit, and school starts again on Monday, so of course it is all nonsense. So I am just going to drink the rest of this bottle of Laphroaig and replay this one day over again, except this time I will hold her hand while we walk along, and at the Waterloo ticket barrier it won't be her cheek I am kissing.

Richard.

From: Richard Slater [rpslater@hc.parliament.uk]
Sent: 6/6/05 16:27
To: Michael Carragan [mmcarragan@hc.parliament.uk]

Hi Michael,

Sorry about the slightly drunken and maundering e-mail on Friday night. Everything seems shinier and leafier and generally more birdsong-filled today. Because you are looking at (well, you will be, when I buy you a beer tonight) the brand-newest Assistant Under-Secretary in the Department of Culture, Media and Sport! OK, I know what you are going to say about me and culture – probably some 'out of my element' gag involving cats and synchronised swimming, or maybe something tried and trusted, about distinguishing my arts from my elbow, ha ha. But you can't deny my appreciation of media and sport. I combine them regularly, in fact, in the form of the football pages of the *Ipswich Town Crier*. And I don't care anyway, Mike – it's a job! At last, a little piece of recognition for all my horny-handed toil, my first small step towards high office. And indeed, it seems that it's going to be a very high office – a sort of glorified attic boxroom on the ninth floor of that ministerial concrete block in Cockspur Street, commanding a vertiginous view of the DTI car park.

The Rottweiler phoned me just after eleven this morning, and said would I come down to the Lobby. I duly went down and stood about hopefully. At length I was summoned into The Presence by a tap on the shoulder from an unelected 25-year-old henchperson in a sharp suit, who led me into a convenient alcove to receive the good news. When I'd imagined this moment, I suppose I'd always pictured a call to No. 10, so it was a little disconcerting just to be pulled behind the nearest pillar. It made me feel a bit like a cheap hooker – except that their paymasters are probably not accompanied throughout by a gaggle of special advisers talking in a stentorian manner into their mobiles.

It seems that word of my part in the change in asylum rules reached the prime ministerial ear, and that it proved timely in a number of respects. It won him favour with the women's lobby, and with the Asian women's lobby. It pleased the new President of the European Commission, who is hot on human trafficking issues, and to whom it has been sold as a blow against sexual enslavement worldwide. And at the same time it gave him the distance he happened to be looking for between HM Government and certain British Islamic groups, who regard the new rules as an unwarranted attack upon Muslim cultural practices. Apparently it has got right up the noses of a couple of West Midlands imams whom the Rottweiler was particularly hoping to annoy. All of which concatenation of circumstances adds up to the Iraq vote being quite forgotten, and me putting in an order for some new calling cards. (Funny how in the end it wasn't one of the hand-picked issues that did the trick, but something you could never have predicted at all.)

I'd really like to share my good fortune with Margaret, but with Nasreen still missing, I don't know . . . I don't want it to look as though I am contentedly enjoying the political side-benefits of the situation that led to her friend's misery. Even though, of course, that is exactly what I am doing! Oh, dear.

Richard.

PS. Do books count as culture? I read books.

Richard Slater (Labour)
Member of Parliament for Ipswich

From: Michael Carragan
[mmcarragan@hc.parliament.uk]
Sent: 6/6/05 16:58
To: Richard Slater [richard.slater@btopenworld.com]

I see my advice goes unheeded, as usual. Call me about that beer.
Michael.

Michael Carragan (Labour),
Member of Parliament for West Bromwich West.

Rosy Thornton

ST EDITH'S PRIMARY SCHOOL
St Edith's Lane, Ipswich IP3 5BJ
7 June 2005

<u>Summer Term Newsletter</u>
Hello everyone, and welcome back from half term, as we enter the final straight of this school year. I hope that you and your families managed to take advantage safely of the beautiful weather last week.

<u>Sun Precautions</u>
This brings me on to the first important notice of this newsletter. With warmer weather on the way, will parents please note that ALL children must be provided with a sun hat, a small water bottle (named, please!) and a tube of sunblock cream of at least factor 40. I am afraid that any children not suitably equipped will not be allowed outside at playtime if there is less than 85 per cent cloud cover.

<u>Sports Day</u>
Sports day will be held on Monday 11 July. Please ensure that your child has a sun hat, sunblock cream and plenty of water (see above). I am sorry to have to tell you that there will be no parents' race this year; following last year's unfortunate incident, the school's insurers have informed us that they can no longer undertake to cover the risks involved. Apologies to those mums who I know have been in training for this event since Easter.

Visit by M.P.

Ipswich's Member of Parliament Mr Richard Slater, who has just this week been appointed to a ministerial position in the Department of Culture, Media and Sport, is to visit the school and meet Year 3 pupils on Wednesday 15 June. We are grateful to Miss Hayton for fixing up this prestigious visit.

Suffolk Book Day

To celebrate Suffolk Book Day on Friday 24 June, pupils are invited, as last year, to come to school dressed as a favourite character from a book. Parents are asked for a voluntary contribution (we suggest that a minimum of 50p would be appropriate) towards the purchase of books, half for our own school library and half for our twin school in Kenya. Please encourage your children to use their imagination. Last year we had eighty-two Harry Potters.

Forthcoming Trips

We are pleased to say that British Sugar have kindly agreed to arrange for pupils from Years 5 and 6 to tour the factory again, to learn about the amazing journey of the sugar-beet as it is transformed into the sugar on your table. The infants, as last year, will be visiting the Lower Maysley Maize Maze. Please could parents equip their children with a brightly coloured (named) hat, and notify the class teacher in advance of any allergies to cereal crops.

End of Term Disco

This will be held on Thursday 21 July. Would parents,

especially of Year 5 and 6 girls, please ensure that their children are appropriately dressed. Underwear and body glitter are not an acceptable alternative to clothing.

Mrs E. Martin
Deputy Head

From: Margaret Hayton
[margarethayton@yahoo.co.uk]
Sent: 10/6/05 22:23
To: Rebecca Prichard [becs444@btinternet.com]

Dear Becs,

I had another day tramping round London last Friday, putting up 'Missing' posters that Richard had made. He came everywhere with me, took all day off to help, and he even took me to Waterloo to get the train to Gran's. At the barrier he started trying to apologise for the fact that we had discovered nothing, as if it was his fault, so I cut him off, maybe a bit abruptly, because he went quiet and was sort of staring at me, and then he leaned forward and brushed his lips on my cheek, all dry and soft. And I know it's stupid of me, Becs, but I couldn't help wishing that he would kiss me properly. Maybe it was something to do with him finally not wearing a tie. But mainly, I suppose, it's been so long since Mark, and a girl likes to feel . . . Well, if it goes on too long I always start to think that it's me. At home, I always put it down to the vicar's daughter thing: it took me until I was fifteen to even get properly groped in a pub car park! But I've never mentioned Dad to Richard, so he can't know, can he? I mean, you can't tell, can you? It's not like there's the faint aroma of ecclesiasticism hanging about me, or something? Or maybe it's because I'm a Margaret and Margarets are fundamentally unsnoggable.

Gran was cheerful, but I can tell her ankle is worse than she's letting on. She was in the sitting room and she'd built a kind of nest around herself, with heaps of books and magazines, and the TV listings by her elbow, and I don't think she moves from there all day. Cora had made me some gunge to take Gran out of Lord knows what agglomeration of garden greenery – she is really taking this herbalism thing seriously – and I offered to rub some on her ankle for her, but she just told me to leave it on the table. Wise woman. I did get her up and walking around a bit on Sunday, and I helped her with her physio exercises, but I don't think she bothers with them much by herself – the leaflet was right at the bottom of a pile of library books. I'd really like to speak to Kirsty about getting Gran moving a bit, but I hate to talk about her behind her back, as if she's a child.

We had a tremendous staff meeting on Tuesday, Becs, you'd have treasured it. Planning for the school trips. We took Years 3 and 4 round a rare breeds farm back in October, so we have nothing on this term for our lot, but the older juniors are going to tour the sugar works, which in this part of the world is referred to in hushed tones, much in the manner in which pilgrims might speak of the shrine at Walsingham. There is a certain amount of tasting of the product, in its various syrupy and solid states, permitted by the factory management, and the main topic of debate was how to set precise limits upon this aspect of the visit. By all accounts, last year's party behaved like so many Augustus Gloops. The infants are going round a maize maze. With no money, apparently, in actually growing useful things to eat (I have never been able to fathom the parallel economic universe which is agricultural subsidy), there is one of these approximately every five miles up the A12 and A140 during the summer months. There was a very long and serious discussion about how to prevent the little loves from getting lost (which I have to say did strike me somewhat as losing sight of the object of the exercise). It seems that one girl in Reception got separated from the herd last year, and only emerged, weeping in the consoling arms of the staff search party, at 5.15 p.m. when all her companions were back on the coach and into the fifteenth verse of 'One Man Went to Mow'. Her name, by divine coincidence, was Ruth. I don't know why it should have been this which did it, but suddenly I could no longer restrain the giggles that had been threatening to break loose from the off – but by the bemused looks I received, none of the rest of the St Edith's staff can have been nourished upon biblical texts with their porridge like I was at the vicarage.

Last night the WITCH crew all decamped to the pub after the meeting, and I discovered that Alison's husband has moved out. By mutual agreement, she said – though I wonder if that can ever be really true. Is the end of a relationship really something about which there can ever be a meeting of minds, when the loss of that common ground is usually part of the problem? All I know is that I'd be a wreck if I were Alison, left on her own with three boys, including Edward who is autistic and quite a handful, by all accounts. But she actually said it is a relief. She realises that she has been protecting her husband from the worst of Edward's behaviour, and at the same time trying to shield the boys from her husband's frequent over-reactions, and she is fed up with being caught in the middle. Her only worry seemed to be how she will manage the mortgage by herself.

The rest of the group didn't seem all that surprised to hear about the split-up. And it is true, now I come to think about it, that I have never once heard Alison mention her husband. I found out his name for the first time when she told me he had gone. (Derek. Never a name which bodes well. There are no good Dereks in any books – or indeed any Dereks at all, that I can recall.) Of course, there can be a bit of a thing in women's groups about not mentioning husbands or boyfriends overmuch, not wanting to seem to be joined at the hip. Do you remember Celia Jones at college, who used to bring that boyfriend of hers from home into every other sentence, and how it used to have the rest of Women's Action gritting their teeth and shuffling their Doc Martens in aggravation? But in WITCH, Susan talks about her boyfriend sometimes, and even Persephone refers to her ex now and again (though mainly, I must admit, to cast aspersions upon either his sexual prowess or his oral hygiene. And bad-mouthing men always goes down OK in a women's group). I've never been keen on women who constantly go on about their marvellous husbands, even when they are in a professional situation. It can come over as irrelevant and jarring, even self-belittling, as if they are not independent, whole people in their own right. But for a married person like Alison *never* to mention Derek's name, when she had talked quite a lot about her sons, well, I suppose I did wonder . . . I mean, Cora's married, and she talks about Pete. He just crops up, in the normal way of things. When I first moved in, in fact, she talked about little else – though with Cora I never found it irritating, more sad than anything. And people at school tell the occasional funny story in the staffroom, or their partners come up in conversation, you know, when they tell you what they did at the weekend. Mrs Martin the deputy head, for example, has a husband who is a conjuror. Having ready access to all the kids' dates of birth, she keeps him well supplied with bookings for children's parties – a flagrant misuse of corporate opportunity, ripe for referral to the Office of Fair Trading. Mind you, he hasn't been getting quite so many gigs since he produced a fluffy white rabbit out of Timothy Burgess's mother's piano stool too soon after the death of his beloved Thumper, reducing Timothy to howling inconsolability and transforming the rest of his birthday celebration into a wake.

But sorry, I'm rambling appallingly as usual. There is still no news of Nasreen. I'm going to go to London again at the weekend. We're going to try putting up some of the posters round the Tube stations. Richard has kindly said I can stay at his flat again on Saturday night. But tell me about Frankie. I trust he's got your system flowing freely?

Love,

Margaret xx

From: Rebecca Prichard [becs444@btinternet.com]
Sent: 10/6/05 22:45
To: Margaret Hayton [margarethayton@yahoo.co.uk]

Margaret, hi. Don't talk to me about staff meetings. Some of the old guard here could quibble for England. Last week there was a sweepstake among the younger staff after we saw the agenda. At 14 minutes, my pick was hopelessly short of the 26 and a half minutes spent discussing where to route the ducting for the new smartboard in the ICT room.

About Frankie: it turns out that he really does seem to believe that his life is a cheap porn movie, and I am not prepared to appear only in every third scene. So I have told him to take his plunger and get out.

I have looked up your Richard on the House of Commons website, by the way. He's not bad at all – I don't know what you are waiting for! I tell you, when things start to turn sour between me and Quentin or Quincy, you'd better watch out, hon!

Love and hugs,
Becs xx

Flat 6
14 Charterhouse Square
London EC1 9BL

12 June 2005

Dear Margaret,

I loved this weekend. I have felt more . . . useful, more engaged, more purposeful, more alive, these days that I have spent with you in London, even though our search hasn't yet produced any results, than I have felt since my early days in politics, when it still seemed like one individual could make a difference, just by caring enough.

You looked so beautiful in your too-big shirt and your old combat trousers, like something fragile and exotic that the florist has just casually wrapped up in old newspaper. We must have visited nearly every Tube station in central London, and you would have carried on all evening, but your eyes looked unnaturally bright and there were bluish smudges appearing beneath your lower lashes. I wanted to take my thumbs and softly brush all the worry and fatigue away from your eyelids. I hailed a taxi and took you home, and this time I had remembered to shop, and there was salad as well as pasta, and it did not seem so inappropriate to open the wine.

You were too tired and drained to talk, so I suggested you choose a video from the shelf, and you said, 'What's *Gregory's Girl*?' I went to see it when it came out, in the summer of 1981, with Ellie Shaw; you told me you were not born then. Not born – and I was old enough to be feeling up Ellie in the darkened cinema! That blazing summer, when discontent spilled over into rioting in every major British city. Even Ipswich's half-heartedly disaffected youth managed their own token skirmish. In that crucible, in the burning hatred of Thatcher and all that she stood for, my political convictions were forged. You were not born; your formative years had none of that bitterness and entrenched division and sharp-edged certainty. And yet you have such passion, for the things in which you believe.

We watched Bill Forsyth's gentle, aching comedy

together, and I explained to you how everyone mistakenly thinks that it is Dee Hepburn who is Gregory's girl, whereas in fact it is Clare Grogan. You were sitting on the floor, leaning back against the settee beside me, so that I could look at the cascading curls of your hair, and the tender stretch of white skin where the slope of your neck disappeared into the collar of your shirt, as often as at the screen, or oftener. And when Gregory lay on his back in the park next to Clare Grogan at last, and taught her to dance lying down, I wanted to be lying next to you, and learning the first slow cadences of our own dance together.

Of course, I cannot send you this letter, Margaret. It is going straight in the government issue shredder. But I think I am falling in love with you.

Richard.

IPSWICH TOWN CRIER   TUESDAY 14 JUNE 2005

BINS TO GET BINS

Ipswich Borough Council's Refuse Collection and Recycling Service yesterday launched their latest safety scheme – to put Day-Glo spectacles on all our wheelie bins!

'It is all about being seen,' said Director of Waste Collection and Disposal, Mr Paul Marston. 'With the wheelie bins being black, they are not easy to see during the hours of darkness, and they constitute a potential hazard to pedestrians.' The borough council are to issue every household in the town with a fluorescent yellow sticker to attach to their bin to make it easier to spot. 'The glasses motif was chosen to symbolise the concept of visibility,' explained Mr Marston, himself sporting a pair of varifocals in eye-catching blue frames.

It seems that the scheme was devised in response to intervention by Ipswich MP and new ministerial appointee Mr Richard Slater, acting upon complaints from concerned – or myopic – constituents. Mr Slater (who, as a member of the borough council from 1989 to 1997, served as chair of the Refuse Disposal Sub-Committee) was yesterday unavailable for comment.

42 Gledhill Street
Ipswich

15 June 2005

Dear Gran,

How have you been this week? It was great to see you last weekend. I'm just sorry it couldn't have been for longer. I hope you are doing your exercises – maybe Kirsty would help you with them, if you asked her?

Last weekend I went to London again, to carry on trying to trace Nasreen, like I told you. Richard spent all day Saturday, and half of Sunday, helping me put up the posters. It's so frustrating to think that now, thanks to the change to the asylum rules, she would be safe to come back to Ipswich, to the hostel, and not be sent back home, but she doesn't know, and we have no way of getting hold of her to tell her. I do hope that wherever she is, Gran, she is safe, and has found friends she can rely on. On Saturday night I stayed at Richard's flat. He cooked us a lovely vegetarian supper, and we watched an old video, some 1980s thing. It seemed a bit dated to me to be honest, and a lot of it was about football, so not really my thing, as you know. But it was set in a school, so some of the jokes about the staff and kids had me laughing with recognition. And it did have a rather quirky, sweet ending – which surprised me, because I wouldn't have had Richard down as an old romantic at all!

Today he came into school to meet my class. Of course it was very nice of him to take the time, and setting it up won me some serious Brownie points with the head. It fitted in well as part of their Citizenship programme (which is not at all what you would imagine, Gran; it's mostly about picking up litter and going to the dentist regularly). I was a bit taken aback when a photographer from the *Town Crier* turned up as well, but to be fair Richard seemed embarrassed about it, too. In fact he apologised to me about it at least fifteen times, until I started to feel sorry for the photographer. Anyway, he's promised me some prints for the display boards, so it was quite useful that he came.

I have a feeling that Richard is not very used to children. He opened with a few words about his job, which he delivered as though reading a prepared ministerial statement. Then Chloë Watson asked him if he had met the Queen, and he said no, at which juncture half of the girls lost interest. Josh Cayley asked him in a slightly belligerent tone what it is he actually does, and Richard replied that he helps to make laws. Simon Aldridge said, 'Like a sheriff?' and Josh drawled 'I am the law' like in a western, so then all the boys started giggling and Richard began to look slightly panicky. Then there was an unfortunate *faux pas* concerning our blind kid, Jack Caulfield. It happened to be Jack who asked whether MPs have to dress up smartly for work, and Richard laughingly gave what he hoped was the disarmingly self-deprecating reply, 'What does it look like?' Richard winced when I explained the reason for the general merriment which greeted this, but soldiered gamely on. Abby Bentham said that her dad says all the government do is take his money in taxes, so Richard started to explain how they use the money to provide schools and hospitals, and Nicky Stefanopoulos said, 'Oh, are you a doctor, then?' and he said, 'Er, no,' and looked hugely relieved when I said that was all there was time for and thank you for coming. By then I was wishing I'd had the foresight to plant a couple of sensible questions beforehand. I'm sure Bryony Cooke would have asked him about the woolsack with every semblance of breathless fascination, if I'd promised her she could sit on the end in assembly for a week. Even when he was leaving Richard was far from comfortable – it's the first time I've ever heard anyone say 'thank you for your time' to a bunch of eight year olds! I really thought he might shake them each individually by the hand, or give them all his card. But later, when the photographer had gone and I was in the classroom clearing up, I looked out into the playground and saw him in goal, while Josh and Nicky took shots at him, and he seemed to be doing OK.

I took Richard out for a thank you meal later (though in the end he insisted on paying half, which rather defeated the object). I suggested a little Italian place in the town centre, because he seems keen on pasta – in fact I'd just got back when I began this letter. I don't know if it was talking to the kids earlier that made him think of it, or what, but he came over all reminiscent about his childhood. It was rather touching, I thought.

Last night I was round at the hostel sitting with Helen again. She didn't want to talk, but she has an old Scrabble board from when she was a kid, and she suggested we have a game. I stayed until gone 1 a.m.; we must have played about ten games, sitting together on her bed, and it seemed to really take her mind off things. She says that when she is very depressed she cannot concentrate enough to read a book, it's just too demanding, and her own troubles keep intruding and squeezing out the story. But TV or the radio don't absorb her enough to take up her thoughts and drive out the pain. Scrabble seems to be perfect – it requires exactly the right amount of mechanical concentration to keep her brain occupied and leave no room for the bad feelings. Or at least not on the surface, for that short while.

I'll pack up some more books to post to you at the

weekend, to replace the ones I brought home with me this time. I'm only paying back the tiniest sliver of a vast debt, Gran. This week I've been reading *The Voyage of the Dawn Treader* to my class, and it reminded me of when you read it to me, at bedtimes, that week I came to stay when I was seven. Mum had had her hysterectomy, and Dad was between curates. There's something about C. S. Lewis's prose that still gets me every time, just like it did that first time. Not just the old familiar hairs-on-the-back-of-the-neck thing, but actually a physical vibration in my stomach muscles, a thrumming, like the resonanace of recognising something loved but half forgotten, or like the beginnings of laughter. Is it just getting older, or why is it that the books I encounter as an adult never have the power to do that to me?

Oh, and don't forget those exercises, will you?

Lots of love,

Margaret xx

From: Richard Slater [rpslater@hc.parliament.uk]
Sent: 16/6/05 15:12
To: Michael Carragan [mmcaragan@hc.parliament.uk]

Michael, I am a madman, a dolt, an addle-pate, a bedlamite – and growing worse by the day. Not only did I yesterday brave the scornful ravages of an entire classful of eight-year-old inquisitors for the sake of one of Margaret's smiles (and why on earth didn't she warn me that one of them was blind?), but then, having allowed her to take me out for dinner, I began prattling to her about guinea pigs. I don't know how it came upon me, Mike, I honestly don't. She was so relaxed and confident with that ruthless mob of small hatchet-wielders, and yet once we were alone in the restaurant she was suddenly watchful, and filled with quick tension, so that I found myself speaking softly and making no abrupt movements, as though in the presence of some nervous woodland creature. Maybe it was this mental image which set me off thinking about Napoleon, even though I swear I had forgotten all about him for years. But whatever the reason, there was no excuse for blabbering about him to another adult human being.

Even the name is embarrassing enough! Other children called their pets Toffee or Smudge, but I had to name a tortoiseshell guinea pig after a French military dictator – evidently even at the age of seven I felt stirrings towards power and statesmanship. Anyway, before I knew it I was pouring out to Margaret the entirety of Napoleon's less than imperial history. How he was fed almost exclusively on a diet of beet sugar, for example. It was one of the side-effects of growing up in Ipswich in the shadow of the sugar works. We lived close to a low railway bridge, under which the beet lorries had to pass on their way to the factory. They always approached the bridge piled high with beet in a jauntily bouffant manner, and emerged trimmed to a short back and sides, leaving piles of spilled sugar-beet at the foot of the bridge for me to collect in my bicycle saddlebags. I can see Napoleon now, looking up at me in cavian ecstasy, with the syrupy juice dribbling down his bearded chin. However, this seductively unsuitable diet quickly cost him both his waistline and all his teeth, and for four years, having lost the ability to do other than suck his food, he lived exclusively on Readybrek and well-boiled vegetable peelings. Until I went to stay with my Aunty Sylvia, who would have no truck with rodents with special dietary requirements. Napoleon was packed off in a cardboard box to live at the house of my friend Leon, where he was dead within the month.

Margaret, not unnaturally, greeted this whole sorry tale with a look in those beautiful, untamable eyes which can only be described as pitying. Her relief was manifest when the time came to argue about the bill.

The restorative effect of beer and your steadying conversation is urgently required.

Richard.

Richard Slater (Labour)
Member of Parliament for Ipswich

WITCH
Women of Ipswich Together Combating Homelessness

Extract from minutes of meeting at Persephone's house, 16

June 2005, 8 p.m.

New member

We were delighted to welcome Della Robertson from number 27, as a new member of the collective. Pat T. and Emily will redraft the evening/weekend cover rota, and the rota for sitting with Helen, to include Della's name. Alison agreed to go with Della on any emergency call-outs for her first few times.

News of residents

Helen has had a difficult week, even with the members of the collective continuing to come in in the evenings. She has cut up twice during the night, on one occasion needing to go to A&E for stitching. Helen feels that if things go on as they are, she may need to seek a full-time hospital admission, rather than just weekend respite admissions as at present.

Carole is greatly enjoying her job at the medical laboratory. Alison said that her supervisor reported that the test tubes have never been cleaner.

Any other business

Pat and Pat announced that they will be having a civil partnership ceremony on 21 December, the first day that the new legislation comes into force. Everyone is invited to attend. They had brought along a bottle of asti spumante to celebrate their announcement.

MANCHESTER ECHO   FRIDAY 17 JUNE 2005

WOMEN SEEKING MEN

Gareth? Greg? Grant? Graeme?
Lady of letters (23) seeks G
to pull her strings. Contact
Becs on 0905 213 2130
voicebox 66094.

From: Margaret Hayton [margarethayton@yahoo.co.uk]
Sent: 22/6/05 23:57
To: Rebecca Prichard [becs444@btinternet.com]

Dear Becs,

My evening has been a typical mixture of tragedy
and farce. St Edith's is holding its annual jamboree to
mark Suffolk Book Day on Friday. Without the least
hint of irony, literacy hour has been cancelled in
favour of the mass painting of scenes from Hans
Christian Andersen and the brothers Grimm. And the
kids and staff all have to dress up as a favourite
literary character for charity. Of course I was going to
go as Minerva McGonagall – after all she was the
heroine and role model for three-quarters of the girls
on the B.Ed. at college. All I would have needed is
some round glasses and that academic gown that
Gran insisted on buying me for graduation.

(Everyone else just got them from Moss Bros, but I think Gran had this idea that it would somehow come in useful in a primary school. Can't think when, unless it's when we're doing clay.) But the deputy head made such a fuss about how everyone came as characters from Harry Potter last year, and we mustn't feed the head's already worrying Albus Dumbledore delusions. And there was this video I watched at Richard's – *Gregory's Girl*, it was called, an '80s thing – and there's a little recurrent motif in it where a kid is wandering the corridors of his school in a huge penguin outfit. For some reason this stuck with me, and I thought, why don't I go for something a bit more challenging, do the thing properly? I mean, what is being a primary school teacher all about? This term I've been reading *The Twits* to my class, so I thought, I know, I'll go as the Roly-Poly Bird!

I bought some scarlet tights (15 denier was all I could get, so they'll be straight in holes), and I thought I'd wear those red shoes that I bought at college for that dressy party that Sara Bhattacharjee had in the second year, and then I never wore again because I can't walk in heels and they make me self-conscious about my height. I got some chicken wire – Cora had a roll of it because she puts it over her seedlings to keep off next-door-but-one's cat – and I bought a big bag of multi-coloured feathers from a craft and sewing shop in town. Then tonight I have been busy with newspaper and flour-and-water, papier-mâchéing like crazy and sticking on feathers. The beak I cut and pasted from a cereal packet, covered with yellow crepe paper. My room now resembles a parrot enclosure after a suicide bomb attack by a militant macaw. If one of the parrots had been reading the *Guardian*.

Then I pedalled off to Witch House to see Helen because it was my turn on the rota. She was in a bad way. Even in this warm weather she always wears a long-sleeved top, normally, because of all the scars on her arms, but tonight she was wearing a sleeveless T-shirt. She had been to see her mum. She has never been able to talk to her about how she's been feeling – I don't think she has even mentioned the hospital – but she thought if she went in a short-sleeved shirt her mum would have to say something. She didn't, of course: all she did was ask Helen why she doesn't move back home. So now Helen is all messed up again. She had been jabbing a pencil into her thigh, leaving quite deep marks; she'd punctured the skin in places and I was worried it might get infected or give her blood-poisoning or something, but she'd disinfected it herself and said it would be OK. I stayed until she was asleep as usual, but I am afraid she'll wake up later and hurt herself again. I really think soon she may have to go into hospital full-time for a while. She just isn't safe with us.

How are you, anyway? How's your dad?

Love,

Margaret xx

From: Rebecca Prichard [becs444@btinternet.com]
Sent: 23/6/05 08:16
To: Margaret Hayton [margarethayton@yahoo.co.uk]

Hi Margaret. Dad's actually not great at the moment, since you ask. He started a new lot of chemo two weeks ago, and it's leaving him pretty weak. His blood count was low at the weekend so they gave him a transfusion which perked him up a bit, but he's also very nauseous all the time. Mum has a hell of a job trying to get him to eat. She says it's like when she was pregnant. He doesn't fancy anything except soup, but whenever he has an empty stomach he feels sick, so she has him on a cream cracker, every hour, on the hour. The GP mentioned ginger tea, but you can imagine what my dad would say about anything herbal. He thinks tea is only tea if it's PG Tips, brewed to a deep orange, and has at least two sugars in it. Maybe your Cora has some suggestions for something Mum could slip in his Heinz cream of tomato. I've been trying to pop over about twice a week. It's hard for Em with the kids, and it being such a haul from Middlesbrough, and Sam's only just done his exams and is still finishing his dissertation, so there's only me really at the moment.

Meanwhile – don't mock! – my alphabetical compulsion has reduced me to the risible ignomiy of placing an ad in the Singles section of the local rag. Velvet tones on the voicebox announced themselves as belonging to Gil, which didn't seem a very promising name until I remembered Gilbert Blyth in the 'Anne' books. I met him as arranged last night, at a quiet pub outside the city centre, and encountered extremely promising velvet brown eyes to match the velvet voice. Sadly also a velvet scarf – but I have to assume, given the unambiguous nature of my ad, that I am none the less a member of his gender of preference. He displayed a broad range of conversational resources, covering film, music, world affairs, and the best methods of house-training a kitten. I hope that the kitten is real, and not an invented ploy for finding a way to an imagined kitten-loving soft spot in my girlish heart. I am informed that one should disbelieve 40 per cent of what blind dates tell you in their ads – I wonder if it is true of first meetings, too? I am now curious as to whether the comprehensiveness of his conversational aptitude reflects wide-ranging skills in other areas, too. I hope to find out soon – we have a second date scheduled for Friday night.

Big hugs,

Becs xxx

WITCH
Women of Ipswich Together Combating Homelessness

Extract from minutes of meeting at Susan's house, 23 June 2005, 8 p.m.

<u>News of residents</u>

Helen was today admitted into psychiatric hospital on a full-time basis as a voluntary patient. She was reluctant to take this step, but felt that it was the only way she could be safe. Margaret reported that housing benefit will continue to meet Helen's rent at Witch House for the first four weeks, after which the position will be reviewed.

Emily and Pat T. reported that they are a little concerned about Carole. She keeps staying very late at the medical lab, and the other residents say she even went in at the weekend, just to sterilise the test tubes one more time.

From: Richard Slater
[richard.slater@btopenworld.com]
Sent: 24/6/05 17:48
To: Michael Carragan [mikecarragan@yahoo.com]

Hi Michael,

Margaret phoned me this afternoon. I was over by the window when it rang. There's this pigeon, you see, it spends all day sitting on a small ledge just above the window of my new office, ceaselessly making this rather smug pigeon noise. Always three little self-satisfied notes, rising slightly in pitch, the third one a shade longer than the first two. It was reminding me of something, and after three days of it (I've had the window open non-stop, it's been so hot, so the audibility has been excellent) I finally realised what it was. It is

Paul Daniels, saying 'ho ho ho' in that irritating way he has. So of course, it had to be stopped. I was leaning out a short way and trying to poke the pigeon's feet with an inflatable tulip given to me by the Suffolk branch of the Anglo-Dutch Bulb Growers' Association.

Anyway, the phone went, as I have mentioned, but I decided to let it go through to the answerphone, because the tulip was too short by just a tantalising inch or so, and the pigeon was still insulting my intelligence with infuriating bonhomie from the ledge. After the beep, of course, came Margaret's voice, beginning to tell me that she was sorry I wasn't there and really sounding as though she meant it. The inflatable tulip drifted balletically down nine floors as I shot across the room, grabbing for the receiver, and in the process managing to knock flying the ceramic sugar-beet (you know, the one from the twinning of the Ipswich sugar works with the factory in Minsk, that I keep my paper clips in). So I was on the floor among the shards, for some reason trying to pick up all the paper clips, and Margaret was talking, and I couldn't take in what she was saying at first. She seemed very agitated. One of the young women in the hostel, someone called Lauren, had called Margaret on her mobile at school, to say that one of the girls she knows who works at King's Cross had told her that there has been a young Albanian working the area for the past two weeks, a new girl, long dark hair, about Nasreen's age. Of course Margaret had to come to London at once, to see if it really is her. She had come straight to the station from school and just caught the 3.20, and was calling me from the train, expecting to arrive at Liverpool Street at 4.35. I said I'd meet her there, grabbed my jacket and ran.

I was at Liverpool Street before her, and saw her as soon as she got down from the train. What I noticed first was the look of strained excitement on her face. I could read it all: the hope that her friend might be found, that she was alive and safe, the fear of what degradations she might have been led into by her desperation. Only then did I take in what she was wearing. Three-inch heels, bright red tights, and above mid-thigh an extravaganza of brilliant plumage which made her look like a rare visitor from the tropical rainforest. In her hands was what appeared to be the severed head of a giant chicken. My dry mouth refused to form either the words of comfort and shared hope for Nasreen's safety, or the obvious question about her apparel, which rose with equal speed in my mind, because (it shames me to admit) I was temporarily deprived of breath by the sight of the considerable and captivating length of Margaret's legs, clad only in sheer scarlet nylon. She caught the direction of my dumbfounded gaze, and offered a hasty and less than coherent explanation involving a fictional fowl. But her mind, at least, was set firmly upon the task in hand, and we were soon on the Circle Line and heading for King's Cross.

The presence of a bloke in a suit and tie, however, did nothing to further Margaret's inquiries. Once it was speedily deduced that I was not a customer, the only possibility remaining seemed to be that I was a plain-clothed arm of law enforcement, and there was in consequence a perhaps understandable reluctance to talk while I was in attendance. Reluctantly I left Margaret to carry on speaking to the girls alone, coming back here with a view to getting the car and picking her up later on, around seven o'clock.

God, Mike, I can't stand to think of that poor kid, escaping in fear of her life only to end up resorting to that existence down there. But even so, I really hope we're going to find her there.

Richard.

From: Margaret Hayton [margarethayton@yahoo.co.uk]
Sent: 24/6/05 23:41
To: Rebecca Prichard [becs444@btinternet.com]

Dear Becs,

I'm sending this from Richard's flat in London. He's gone to bed – I insisted it was my turn to have the settee – and I asked if I could check my e-mail on his computer.

It's been such an up and down day, Becs, I feel quite wrung out. We really thought we might have found Nasreen, but in the end it all came to nothing and we are back at square one. It was Lauren at the hostel who started it off – she called me at school to say that she had heard about a new Albanian girl working the streets at King's Cross. Lauren was a runaway in London for a while, and she knows some of the women down there. I suppose she may have worked there herself at one time, but of course I've never asked. Anyway, naturally I dashed straight to the train as soon as I'd packed up at school. There was no time to go home and change out of my Roly-Poly Bird costume, so I just took the head off, flattened out the body a bit so it looked less obviously bird-shaped, and stripped away the lower portion which had made walking difficult. I suppose I looked a complete madwoman – why couldn't I just have dressed up as Mrs Twit? – but to be honest all I could think about was getting to London and finding Nas. I called Richard from the train, and he came to help, but after a bit I decided the girls might talk more freely to a woman on her own, so he took off, promising to come back later to pick me up.

I talked to about a dozen women altogether before I tracked down the Albanian girl they had been talking about. It wasn't her. This one was called Rrezja, nineteen years old, and actually a Kosovo Albanian, from Pristina. She was only thirteen during the conflict there. She lost both her parents: her father (she believes, although she can never be sure) to a mass grave, courtesy of the Serbian security forces, and then her mother in the NATO bombardment, which also destroyed the family home. She spent a year in a refugee camp, she told me, and then lived in derelict buildings, or stayed in boyfriends' flats, until at sixteen she came to England with another girl in the back of a truck. 'To try to make a better life,' she said, and she still hopes to make enough money to get a flat and then look for a proper job. But she had bruises on her face and a split lip, and when I asked her where she is sleeping at the moment, she just shrugged. It's so horrible, Becs – I can't bear to think that Nas might be living that way. Some of the girls should clearly still be at school, but one of them, Rita, looked about Cora's age under the thick mask of make-up, though she was as skinny as a teenager (I suppose that will be drugs). I really don't know which is sadder.

At seven o'clock as arranged, Richard came slowly by in his car, looking out for me. When I saw him I stepped forward, and he wound down the window, but then I guess he saw I had been crying and in a moment he had pulled over and got out, and had me in his arms, hugging me tight. It was so good to see him, and to be taken back to his safe, clean flat, and my safe, clean life. He made us supper (pasta again, it seems to be his thing) and we talked for a long time. Well, mainly I talked and he listened, which he is very good at, and he even held my hand for a while, and after a lot of talking I calmed down a bit and things didn't seem quite so bleak. Richard said some things then. He spun me this whole picture of where Nas might be – washing dishes in the basement kitchen of some cheap and cheerful restaurant, and then swigging beer afterwards and laughing with the waitresses until late into the night. Coke, you mean, I said, because she is Muslim and doesn't drink, and he said, Diet Coke, you mean, because she's eighteen and female so she probably thinks her bum is too big. We laughed at that, and then he made up the settee for me with his far-too-big kingsize duvet, gave me a kiss on the tip of my nose, and went off to bed.

And tonight was your second date with Gil, wasn't it? I wonder how that went. And whether you are going over to your mum and dad's at the weekend.

I know I ought to be thinking about Nasreen, but instead I keep finding myself thinking about Richard. About how secure and comfortable it felt to be in his arms, on the pavement at King's Cross. About how he had one hand on the back of my neck, pulling my head in against his chest, just under his chin. And how I felt his fingers shift a little, until his thumb was running along just below the line of my jaw, as though he was going to lift my head up towards him. And how I wanted him to, I wanted him to lift my chin, and lower his mouth to mine, and kiss away all that fear and desolation. Oh God, Becs – I think I am falling in love with him.

Love,

Margaret xx

From: Rebecca Prichard [becs444@btinternet.com]
Sent: 25/6/05 09:34
To: Margaret Hayton [margarethayton@yahoo.co.uk]

Hi Margaret! Really sorry it wasn't her.

Gil (of the velvet eyes and scarf), it transpires, is a velvet kisser, too. Third date tomorrow night – hope to have opportunity to verify existence of kitten. As for Richard: it's the weekend, you're all cosied up in his flat – what is there possibly to stand in your way?

Just off out to get the papers, then over to see Mum and Dad.

Hugs,

Becs xxx

THE DAILY TRUMPET   SATURDAY 25 JUNE 2005

EXCLUSIVE

THE MINISTER
AND THE HOOKER

SLATER CAUGHT IN KERB-CRAWL SHAME

Richard Slater MP, recently appointed junior minister in the Department of Culture, Media and Sport, was last night caught on camera by the *Daily Trumpet*'s photographer as he picked up a prostitute in the notorious King's Cross area of London.

As commuters headed home for the weekend, Slater (41) was spotted in his car, crawling the kerbs outside King's Cross station, on the look-out for a girl to join him in a little of his own brand of SPORT, unaware that a representative of the MEDIA was on his tail. Theatregoers were already heading for the West End when the minister was sampling a seedier side of London CULTURE.

Our photographer snapped these incriminating pictures of Slater as he sprang from his car and accosted an exotically dressed working girl, publicly embracing her before ushering her to his waiting vehicle and driving off. Our photographs clearly show the dusky-haired beauty in some distress as she enters the minister's French-made blue Renault Mégane. (Evidently British-built cars are not good enough for Mr Slater and his sordid assignations.)

Despite being tipped for political stardom since he entered Parliament in 1997, Slater has been bypassed in numerous reshuffles, especially following his failure to support the government over the Iraq war. He has spoken in Parliament about the need to crack down on vice rings which exploit vulnerable women, and was recently instrumental in securing a change in asylum rules aimed partly at protecting girls victimised by the international sex slave trade. Ironically, it is this policy initiative which is thought to have earned Slater his recent promotion to the front bench. Now it seems that he takes a more than professional interest in the welfare of these girls!

The *Daily Trumpet* says: We have had ENOUGH of this Government's moralistic cant and hypocrisy! We have had ENOUGH of sleaze and spin. Caught red-handed in a red-light district, we say Richard Slater MUST GO!

More pictures, pages 2, 3, 5 and 7. Comment, page 6.

Flat 6
14 Charterhouse Square,
London EC1 9BL

The Prime Minister
10 Downing Street
London SW1A 2AA

25 June 2005

Dear Tim,

You will of course have seen this morning's *Daily Trumpet*, and I would like at once to take the opportunity of offering my sincere apologies for any embarrassment caused to yourself, the Party and the Government by my unguarded conduct. I am very sensible of the honour you have done me by entrusting me with ministerial office, and I am therefore particularly sorry to be the subject of such a scandal so soon after my appointment.

I do have an explanation for my actions which I trust will persuade you that I have been guilty of nothing worse than a reprehensible lack of circumspection. This explanation I would hope to give you on Monday, if you can spare the time to see me. If, having heard it, however, you feel that no explanation is likely to satisfy the people of Ipswich, or the country at large, or that only my departure from the Government will be sufficient to put a halt to the adverse publicity and prurient media interest which will naturally be attracted by this unfortunate event (not least to the other person involved), then I shall be ready with a letter tendering my immediate resignation.

Yours ever,

Richard.

From: Michael Carragan
[mmcarragan@hc.parliament.uk]
Sent: 27/6/05 11:49
To: Richard Slater [rpslater@hc.parliament.uk]

Hello, Richard. Well, at least you finally made the nationals: front page, above the fold! But where on earth have you been all weekend? I have been calling your number at both the London and the Ipswich flat, as well as at your office. I heard on the grapevine (coincidentally, over a pint in the Grapevine) that you are attempting to cling on to your perch at CM&S. I'm very glad to hear it. I would have hated you to have the distinction of possibly the shortest ever front bench career in the long, inglorious history of parliamentary peccadilloes.

I surmise from the spectacular vermilion legs which were spread before me alongside Saturday's cornflakes that it was the famous Margaret. (I think, if anything, the description in your e-mail may have underplayed them.) So, unless you have been seriously misleading me about the nature of her occupation, you are not in fact guilty as charged. So I'm sure you're right to try to brazen it out. But do you think the Rottweiler will back you? He might believe your explanation, but I fear that attracting bad press is actually a worse sin in his book than the mere solicitation of young women for sex.

By the way, you have featured large in the LFN postbag today (or rather the E-mails From Nutters inbox). Six correspondents have suggested ways in which the Government might deal with people such as you, all of which would almost certainly involve breach of Britain's international legal obligations concerning cruel and unusual punishments. There was also one from a lady in Slough who, having studied your picture in the *Trumpet*, is convinced that Richard Slater is an alias for Dennis Smith, a convicted sex offender currently serving his community service order in the gardens of her Day Centre. If you are indeed Dennis, I have to inform you that being within five hundred metres of King's Cross station is a breach of the terms of a suspended sentence which you received in 2003.

Get in touch, mate – I'm sure you need me to buy you a few stiff drinks.

Michael.

Michael Carragan (Labour),
Member of Parliament for West Bromwich West.

The Hollies
East Markhurst

27 June 2005

Dear Margaret,

What a lovely surprise to see you at the weekend, and it was nice to meet Richard, too. I could hardly believe it when you rang me and said you were actually on the way over, though of course you are always welcome, and you never need to ask first, I'm sure you know that, dear. You are no trouble, in fact quite the opposite – it was like having two full-time attendants! You really spoilt me, especially that delicious supper the two of you cooked up on Saturday evening – with a starter and everything. It was like eating out in a restaurant! And it was sweet of Richard to think of getting the candles when you did the shopping (though in fact I had some in the drawer that I keep for power cuts, but of course I wasn't going to tell him that). He reminds me a little bit of Mark, the way he was flattering and teasing me, but perhaps that's the wrong thing to say to you. I'm sure he's very different in lots of ways too.

You did look funny when you arrived, in those jeans of Richard's you had borrowed – what a strange girl you are, coming away without any proper clothes to put on. The legs weren't too long, with you being so tall, but even with his belt they were falling off you. It's those slender hips of yours. You are lucky you didn't inherit my ample behind, because your mum has got it as well, though I shouldn't say so, and in fact she was quite slim until she had you. I'd forgotten all about those old dresses of mine, too, until you asked about them when we were looking at the photo album after supper. All those old cotton prints – I bet some of them hadn't seen the light of day since about 1960! You don't need to bring it back, you know, the one you wore, I'll never wear those things again. Just throw it away if you don't want to keep it yourself. Oh, and could you tell Richard, thank you again for noticing that damp patch while he was up in the loft getting down the box. I've had a plumber out this morning. There was a slight leak in the hot water tank, but they've fixed it now.

Thank you for the outing on Sunday, too. It was so nice to be driven out, and that Renault of Richard's is very comfortable. I hadn't been to the New Forest for a long while, and fancy you remembering that spot where we used to go and play Pooh sticks when you were a little girl! We played it there, your grandad and I, when Mum was little, too. It's funny how sometimes the memories seem to compress themselves, when you get older. I was thinking of one particular picnic, and remembering you there as a toddler, sitting down backwards with a bump on the buttered buns, and then when I pictured your little frock all buttery, I suddenly realised it must have been your mum and not you at all. I wonder if you will ever go and play Pooh sticks there with your own children one day – I like to think that you might.

My ankle seems a little better this morning. Last night when I was going to bed I finally did try some of that smelly ointment that your landlady made, and it tingled a bit, but later I felt the stiffness might be a bit less. I will definitely try it again tonight.

I hope you won't mind my saying this, Margaret, but I really don't know what to tell Mrs Ashby at church now, if she asks whether you are courting. I may be an old pensioner, but I did notice the way he looks at you, dear, and just once or twice I thought you were looking at him the same way, though never both of you at the same time. Please forgive me if I say that I think Richard is a very nice man. (Listen to me, I sound like Aunt Gardiner writing to Elizabeth Bennet about how much she likes

Mr Darcy!) But I do think you would make a lovely couple.

Love from your Gran xx

From: Rebecca Prichard [becs444@btinternet.com]
Sent: 27/6/05 21:32
To: Margaret Hayton [margarethayton@yahoo.co.uk]

Hi Margaret, where on earth have you been all weekend? I've been calling, but Cora said you weren't there and was really cagey about where you'd gone and when you'd be back. And your mobile was switched off – though that's not so unusual – so I just got the inevitable voicemail message. All very mysterious, very cloak-and-dagger . . . But I suppose you are in hiding from those gannets in the tabloid press. I couldn't believe it when I saw it – how could they think that? Or how could they write it, anyway (or write it without checking their facts) – because actually you can see it was an easy mistake to make. That really was quite a spectacular outfit, you know, babe! I hardly dare to ask what they thought about it at school. It's not the done thing, usually, for primary school staff to be caught moonlighting as good-time girls – it's not exactly going to endear you to the moral majority on the PTA, is it? I know starting salaries aren't great, but even at Brunswick Road very few of us have resorted to selling ourselves on the streets. But joking apart, Margaret, really I can't imagine what a nightmare it must have been for you. How can those bastards just trample on people's lives like that?

My little problems pale in comparison, but things have come to an end with Gil. We had a good time last night, and it ended with a taxi back to his place. It turned out the kitten was for real – but Gil wasn't. He was in the kitchen making coffee and the kitten jumped up on to a side table in the sitting room, where my eye fell upon his mail. All clearly addressed to Mr W. Thurston. W! Upon close questioning he admitted to being not so much Gil as Bill, or just possibly, at a pinch, Will. I was out of there. If a man is prepared to lie about the initial letter of his name to get into your knickers, then where does that leave trust?

I'm seriously thinking of giving up men for a bit. You and me both, perhaps? Unless Richard takes more kindly than I imagine most men would to your tarnishing his shiny new job (which, do you think he is going to be able to hang on to, by the way?). Maybe we can set up our own exclusive Order and indulge in threnodial dirges together.

Big hugs,

Becs xxx

From: Margaret Hayton
[margarethayton@yahoo.co.uk]
Sent: 27/6/05 22:50
To: Rebecca Prichard [becs444@btinternet.com]

Dear Becs,

Sorry, I've been at Gran's. I only got back late last night, and to be honest I haven't been able to face turning my mobile on. I just wanted to be out of circulation for a bit. Damn right, too – the first thing I got when I switched it back on was an earful from Mum about embarrassing Dad, and having a position to keep up in the parish, and the rest of the familiar sermon. I thought she was going to ask me what I thought I looked like, going out dressed like that, as though I was fifteen. I think Dad saw the funny side, though – he was always fond of Roald Dahl.

Richard had to go somewhere to lie low, out of the way of the newspapers and TV, and he knew that he couldn't hope to dodge them for long in either London or Ipswich. The phone was already ringing non-stop by Saturday mid-morning. I asked him where his parents live, suggested he go there, but he said that he only has a mother, and they are not in close touch. I just said I was sorry in a non-specific sort of way, because his tone didn't invite either sympathy or further inquiry. Then I thought of Gran. East Markhurst is the back of nowhere, and there would be no way of linking him to Hampshire. He drove us straight there, more or less as soon as we'd read the article. All he did first was dash off a letter of apology to the Prime Minister (whom he refers to as 'Tim'. I find it utterly surreal that I should know anybody who writes to the Prime Minister as Tim). He has offered to resign if necessary, which would be just awful. I desperately hope it won't come to that. I assumed he would want to sleep on the decision before saying anything to the PM, maybe take the weekend to think about it, and I was on the brink of saying so, but didn't quite dare, because he was in this really focused mood, almost manic, like I've never seen him before. I wanted to write to the Prime Minister, too, to help to convince him of the truth, but Richard said it wouldn't help, and I suppose he knows best – but it was horribly frustrating not being able to do anything about it at all. Richard posted his letter, and we just grabbed his duvet and some sheets, got in the car and set off. He drove north a little way first, instead of heading straight for Chelsea and the A3, and then doubled back, and he kept looking in the driving mirror to see if we were being followed. It was just like a cop movie, and it gave me the giggles, and then he started giggling too, and all that feverish tension began to ebb away. By the time we were out on the M3 he had relaxed completely, and we had the windows wide open and the music up full blast so we couldn't hear ourselves think, which I guess was the idea.

It was easy enough down in Hampshire to pretend nothing had happened, but it had to come to an end. I had school today and he had to go back and face the music at Westminster. And now . . . well, of course I need to stay out of his way. What he needs is to just let it die down, and if the press saw me anywhere near him it would kick everything off again. But it's bloody difficult, knowing he's down in London fighting for his job, with the vultures probably camping outside his flat, and me here unable to do anything to help. And you are right, I know, Becs – why would he want any more 'help' from me, anyway, when I've lost him his good name and quite possibly his career? But I've got far too much time to think. To think about the people who would print those poisonous slanders, with no regard for Richard's feelings, still less for the truth. Apparently they did try to ring him for a comment before they went to press, but having only got his voicemail they decided in line with proud Docklands tradition to go ahead and print it regardless.

Tonight, just to complete my cheerful day, I went to visit Helen, who has finally caved in and gone into hospital full-time for a spell. She is in a ward with five other beds, and although it's meant to be an acute ward, not the chronic long-stay patients, some of the others looked pretty far gone, to be honest. God, those places are depressing – I think being in psychiatric hospital might be my worst nightmare.

Helen looked different, somehow, even after just these few days. More detached. Maybe in less actual mental pain, but still, more . . . hopeless, though I would have found that hard to believe possible. I suppose they have increased her levels of medication, though she didn't seem to know exactly. The patients don't have responsibility for their own medication, the staff just come round with it twice a day, and it's little cups of liquid, not tablets. I suppose it's so no one can secrete them away to avoid taking them, or else stockpile them with a view to sale, trade or overdose. They must have to tell people exactly what they are on, if they ask, but I expect not many of them do. Helen is in no state to care about it. I might ask for her, but I expect they would refuse to tell me anything, since I'm not next of kin.

I'm sorry about Gil/Bill/Will. 'Threnodial dirges' are worth a 6.5, but you could have had bonus points if you'd thrown in a coronach or a jeremiad. They would all suit my present mood perfectly.

Love,

Margaret xxx

Flat 6
14 Charterhouse Square
London EC1 9BL

28 June 2005

Dear Mum,

I have been picking up the phone and putting it down again all morning, wanting to call you, and in the end I have chickened out, and am writing this letter instead. I know we haven't spoken in a while, but I needed you to know it isn't true, what it said in the paper. I know it doesn't look good, but she isn't a prostitute, in fact she's a primary school teacher, and her name is Margaret, and I haven't even kissed her yet, and I don't know if I ever will. But I do know that she would want me to tell you, so that you don't go on believing the press stories.

I know it was hard for you after Dad died, but it was hard for me too, and if you could have talked to me, tried to explain why I had to go to Aunty Sylvia's, I might have understood. I wasn't a little kid any more, I was fourteen. It was never the same after that; I was never sure when I came back home if it really was home any more. And I do think that somehow we could have found a way to keep Napoleon. But I love you, Mum, even if I never say it.

Richard.

From: Richard Slater [richard.slater@btopenworld.com]
Sent: 29/6/05 22:55
To: Michael Carragan [mikecarragan@yahoo.com]

Hi Michael,
Sorry I haven't been in touch sooner, but I've just

been keeping my head down completely for a while. I've had my phone off the hook, and the tabloid militia have been encamped outside both the flat and the office. Every time I open my door it's like that scene out of *Notting Hill* where Hugh Grant is in his boxers and gets blinded by all the flash bulbs. (Or was it the Welsh room-mate? And a towel? I forget.) I did escape briefly on Monday to go and be mauled by the Rottweiler. It wasn't an experience I'd wish to repeat. You were quite right – where bad press is concerned he doesn't distinguish much between the deserved and the undeserved. He made it quite plain that being caught in a clinch with a girl – any girl – in spike heels and feathers on a notorious pick-up strip is not behaviour conducive to winning favour and influence with him. But, against all the odds, he is letting me keep my job at CM&S – at least for the moment. My penance is an Our Father and three Hail Marys, to be offered up to my constituency chairman next week. Nothing to the press except that simple statement of denial that went out yesterday, which his office drafted for me, and then heads down and try to ride out the storm. No explanations, no details, and definitely no interviews – he was quite emphatic on that last point, clearly doesn't trust me within half a bar's length of a journalist. The dirt might stick to me for a while, but that is evidently of no great concern (I can always be quietly reshuffled back into the outer darkness at a convenient later date), and seemingly

it's better than the messier and more long-lived furore
that would surround either my resignation or any
attempt to tell the real story publicly. At least it means
I don't have to drag Margaret into it – she can be
spared that. Characteristically, she of course wanted
to take up pen and paper at once (this being her
answer to everything) in order to clear my name in
the eyes of the world in general, beginning with the
ROTW and working methodically downwards. I
managed to convince her that it would be a waste
both of her time and (more important, in her view) of
paper, since at No. 10 the appearance of sin in the
national print media is viewed as no less reprehensible
than the sin itself. It clearly sits most uneasily with
Margaret's scorching sense of justice, but in the end I
persuaded her that the best thing is for us both to
keep quiet and lie low for a while. Anyway, I'd love to
take you up on that drink, Mike, but at the moment
we'd be like goldfish in a bowl, and I'm not sure I
want to be branded with dipsomania on top of my
other vices.

When the article first came out, Margaret and I
sought temporary asylum at her gran's near
Winchester, just until Sunday night. She's sweet, the
gran, but she doesn't miss a trick. And the pair of
them are great together. There's a real warmth – I
could have settled into it very comfortably, stayed all
week and pretended everything was all right. Margaret
had nothing to wear, so I lent her some jeans of mine

and a belt. Why is it so unbearably sexy when a girl wears your clothes? Then on Sunday we dug out some old clothes of her gran's, and she chose a 1960s summer dress, blue rosebuds on a creamy white background, and because she's taller than her gran it showed a curved sweep of calf. It's funny – when she had it on she suddenly struck me differently. Fresh and lovely and wholesome, like something from a more innocent age – Elizabeth Montgomery in 'Bewitched', or Jackie Kennedy in those home movies of her with the kids, before the assassination. And I thought how much Margaret is all of those things all of the time, actually. I told her the dress suited her, and then felt how inadequate that was to express what I really meant.

Then of course she had to go back to school on Monday. I know she'll have had some explaining to do, though she laughs and plays it down – how can I have got her into this mess? And now of course I can't see her, can't go to Ipswich and meet her after school, and risk leading the wolf pack to her door. I've called her a few times, but I never know what to say. God, Mike, this is absolute torture!

Richard.

From: Rebecca Prichard [becs444@btinternet.com]
Sent: 30/6/05 21:53
To: Margaret Hayton [margarethayton@yahoo.com]

I've been thinking about it, Margaret, and looking at the pictures again, and whichever way you look at it, it's hard to avoid one conclusion. Men (and news editors in particular) are just plain peculiar.

Feathers, well OK, just maybe. But even at telephoto range, and reproduced in grainy newsprint, I can make out distinct traces of chicken wire and papier mâché.

Love and hugs,

Becs xx

From: Margaret Hayton [margarethayton@yahoo.co.uk]
Sent: 30/6/05 22:19
To: Rebecca Prichard [becs444@btinternet.com]

Dear Becs,

Sadly, I fear it may not be that implausible. Remember that girl at college, Nicole, the one doing the M.Sc. in sedimentology? She was once waiting for a taxi in the city centre after coming back late from doing fieldwork, measuring silt deposits over at the reservoir. Half of it was still adhering to her oilskins and waders, but some chancer pulled over and asked her if she was doing business. Clearly mistook her for a specialist of some sort. And it's only a short step from rubber to bird-fancying, I'd say.

Love,

Margaret x

42 Gledhill Street
Ipswich
Suffolk IP3 2DA

The Today Programme
BBC Radio 4
Television Centre
Wood Lane
London W12 7RJ

1 July 2005

Dear Sir or Madam,

I am writing to complain about the way in which tabloid news stories are occasionally taken up and discussed on the Today programme as if they were established fact.

Repeating unsubstantiated allegations which have been made in tabloid newspapers, under the guise of reporting upon the political fall-out from those stories, is poor journalism, and unworthy of a public service broadcaster with the (usually deserved) reputation of the BBC. You are only encouraging the printing of these scurrilous and ill-researched pieces, by giving the papers concerned extra publicity. These people do not care whose lives they ruin – and you are making yourselves complicit in the damage they cause.

Yours faithfully,

Margaret Hayton.

PS. I still think that John Humphrys does a marvellous job.

From: Rebecca Prichard [becs444@btinternet.com]
Sent: 4/7/05 21:40
To: Margaret Hayton [margarethayton@yahoo.co.uk]

Jeez, what a day, Margaret! In a misguided moment of
cultural head-rush a couple of weeks ago, the head
declared today to be Music Monday, and all the kids
were invited to bring in musical instruments from
home. Now, if this were Chorlton-cum-Hardy, we'd
have had guitars, a smattering of assorted woodwind,
and perhaps even an ABIE mum who's a concert
violinist showing up with a Stradivarius under her arm
in lieu of egg-boxes. All very nice and civilised. But
not so at Brunswick Road, oh no.

We did get a sitar and a pair of clay ghatams, and
luckily I had laid in a more indigenously British supply
of combs and greaseproof paper, and some rice and
empty Pringles tubes for making impromptu shakers.
But it appears that the main recourse for infant music-
makers in the homes of Moss Side is a distinctive
form of battery-operated plastic keyboard. Between
them my class brought in nine of them. Approximately
fifty centimetres in length, they are preprogrammed to
play a medley of the first lines of various well-known
nursery rhymes and cheesy pop classics, at a
frequency precisely calculated to fry the cortex of the
human brain, particularly when deployed in an
enclosed space, such as a classroom. I suspect that
the technology is directly descended from that used by

the Kremlin to beam destructive rays at the US embassy in Moscow during the height of the Cold War. To say that I now have a headache is a bit like saying that Joan of Arc felt a mild burning sensation. It is a miracle that I am not yet bleeding from the eyes or ears.

Rather weak and sickly hugs,

Becs x

From: Margaret Hayton
[margarethayton@yahoo.co.uk]
Sent: 4/7/05 22:06
To: Rebecca Prichard [becs444@btinternet.com]

Dear Becs,

Poor you – and that on top of the rigours of your self-imposed abstinence. I must say, my lot's music sessions are surprisingly melodious: I really have nothing to complain about. Except, oddly enough, Jack Caulfield. I mean, you somehow expect blind people's other senses to be compensatingly finely tuned, don't you? Like the way impeded sight seems to be *de rigueur* for piano tuners – it's practically a requirement of the job, I've always thought. But in this case, nature has dealt Jack another set of sensorily challenged organs, in the shape of the most solid-rubber of unmusical ears. He's tone deaf, and has the singing voice of a laryngitic herring gull.

Cora and Persephone are downstairs concocting something that would probably have helped with your head. Apparently Professor Sprout, their herbology teacher, has set them an assignment involving the blending of infusions with supposedly analgesic properties. (OK, so her name is actually Spreight, and anyway, the allusion is lost on Cora. I have yet to set her on to reading Harry Potter.)

Persephone turned up with some lemon verbena which her niece had brought over from Jamaica for her. The niece is nursing in a specialist neonatal unit in London, and Persephone is immensely proud of her, you can tell. She knows that Persephone is fond of Jamaican verbena tea, so she brought some back for her after a recent trip over there. Apparently she just waltzed straight through customs clutching this large polythene bag full of suspicious-looking dried leaves. Persephone says they are so busy treating as putative mass killers anyone with unbarbered facial hair and a Muslim name on their passport that they no longer give a second glance to a black kid with a bag of weed. She admits to quite missing the old familiar days of the tail end of the last century, when even institutional racism seemed to take a simpler and more innocent form!

Meanwhile, I am still keeping away from London and Richard. I stayed here at the weekend, did nothing more about looking for Nas, and nothing to support Richard through his press nightmare. He says they are still hassling him. He plays it down, of course, because he doesn't want me to feel more guilty than I do already, but I can tell that he's upset. And I so want to be there with him, even though I know it's impossible, and would make everything ten times worse. It's not the same at all to talk on the phone. I get tongue-tied and never seem able to say the things I want to. It's really killing me!

   Love,

   Margaret xx

WITCH

Women of Ipswich Together Combating Homelessness

<u>Extract from minutes of meeting</u> at Della's house, 7th July 2005, 8 p.m.

News of residents

We were devastated to learn yesterday of Helen's death. She hanged herself with her dressing-gown belt in the hospital bathroom at 9.30 a.m., while all the staff were in a ward meeting. The hospital manager informed Helen's parents immediately, but did not ring Witch House. Emily found out the news when she went to visit Helen in the afternoon. She returned at once to tell the other residents, and she and Pat T. phoned members of the collective to let them know.

From: Richard Slater
[richard.slater@btopenworld.com]
Sent: 7/7/05 22:16
To: Michael Carragan [mikecarragan@yahoo.com]

Hi Michael,

Yesterday afternoon at four o'clock Margaret
phoned me, and I knew at once something was
terribly wrong – her voice was fugged with tears. One
of the women in the hostel has committed suicide. Or
rather *not* in the hostel, that is the sickening irony of
it. This girl – Helen, her name was – had recently
gone into psychiatric hospital because she was
depressed and suicidal and it was felt that the levels
of cover in Witch House were insufficient. Then, after
all the care and support she has had from that ill-
assorted bunch of untrained and largely unpaid
women, she goes into hospital, where the
professionals turn their backs for a moment and let
her die. Of course it is a sickener for the nurses, too –
what a bloody awful job they have – it's no good
feeling anger towards them. But I do feel anger, Mike
– I feel absolutely churning with it. But mainly (and
probably quite illogically) I feel, poor Margaret, this is
so unfair!

After I'd put down the receiver all I could think
about was getting to her. There were ample
opportunities, had the press posse been able to see
my tail-lights for the smoke from the burning rubber,

243

for 'Minister in Road Rage' stories all the way up through north-east London, and when I reached the open tarmac of the A12 I just sank my right foot to the floor and held it there. I don't know if the speed cameras caught me, and it probably makes little difference, because the needle reached 140 mph and proceeded to get stuck there, so that there is indelible evidence of my insanity. I didn't care – I don't care. I can lose my licence, go to prison – I just needed to be with Margaret.

When I reached the house, she opened the door and she was in my arms at once. I really didn't plan any of it. She was crying freely now, and I was rubbing her tears away with my thumb, and then (why am I telling you this, Mike?) kissing them away, and suddenly she had turned her head a fraction and her mouth was underneath mine, and I was tasting the salt of her tears on her lips, and then on her tongue . . . But into my spiralling consciousness there then obtruded an unexpected scrabbling at my hip, gentle but insistent. Hang on, this doesn't feel quite right, I thought. Looking down, I encountered two accusing, liquid brown eyes. We broke apart, and Margaret effected a formal introduction to W. G. Snuffy Walden. This was the spaniel, the disposal of whose bodily wastes, you may recall, featured large in our early correspondence. She doesn't permit any public demonstrations of affection from which she herself is excluded, Margaret explained.

Snuffy and I were just getting acquainted when

Cora the pale green landlady emerged from the kitchen, trailing plumes of malodorous steam. She was displaying more normal skin tones this time – except immediately round her eyes, where livid red weals were beginning to delineate themselves with alarming rapidity as we watched. 'It's the nettles!' she cried, brandishing aloft half a hedgeful of greenstuff in her gloved hands, rather in the manner of Ophelia clutching the fantastic garlands of crow-flowers. (What *are* crow-flowers, anyway?) It seems she had made the mistake of rubbing her eyes in the middle of a tricky leaf-stripping operation. Margaret escorted her to the bathroom to apply Optrex, Savlon, and copious amounts of cold water, leaving me alone with W. G. Snuffy Walden, who produced a red plastic hedgehog with a surprised expression on its face, and proposed that she and I might engage in a little light throwing and fetching to pass the time.

After this, there seemed little hope of any reprise of the earlier interrupted and all too brief amorous explorations. Margaret made us all cocoa and toast, and Snuffy squeezed jealously between Margaret and me on the settee. But when we talked a bit about Helen, Margaret's fingers crept silently into my hand under the long, silky fringed cover of Snuffy's outspread ears.

When the cocoa was all drunk and the toast eaten, I came back to my Ipswich flat. Geoff Howard and his cohorts at the *Town Crier* seem to have stopped picketing it, and I got in undetected. This meant that it was safe to come and go tonight, too, with caution. I saw her after school, but not for very long, because it was the WITCH meeting at eight o'clock. Cora had invited me to eat with them, and we had shepherd's pie, which was odd, because I could have sworn Margaret said she's a vegetarian. The meeting was in the same street as the hostel, at the house of a new member. I drove her there with one hand, holding hers pressed tightly to my thigh with the other. I drove slowly – partly to make the drive last longer, and partly in order to keep to the 30 limit without any functioning means of gauging my speed. I pulled up, and at the last moment, just as she was about to get out of the car, I managed to blurt out 'Come back to mine tonight?' and she just said 'Yes' quietly, and was gone. Now I am sitting here waiting for her like an over-excited schoolkid before his first date, and feeling guilty for thinking far too little about poor Helen and far too much about Margaret.

   Richard.

From: Margaret Hayton
[margarethayton@yahoo.co.uk]
Sent: 8/7/05 07:03
To: Rebecca Prichard [becs444@btinternet.com]

Dear Becs,
   Well, I think I am about to be stripped of my habit

and wimple. My vow of chastity has effectively been breached, at least in thought and word if not technically in deed. But I haven't told you yet how it all started.

Helen is dead. Writing it down like that doesn't make it any more real, but it is true. She hanged herself in hospital while the nurses were in a meeting. We were so sure that hospital was the safest place for her to be – I even tried to persuade her to go in, several times, and I'm sure the others did too. Now I can't help feeling as if we just passed the buck, abdicated responsibility for her. To be honest, my mind still just blanks off if I even try to think about what I feel about it.

As soon as Pat T. rang off after telling me about Helen, I dialled Richard's number. I didn't even think about it. Cora wasn't home from the bank yet, and I needed to hear his voice. He said, 'Wait there, I'm coming over,' although I've no idea where he thought I might go. Cora came in, and I told her, and she gave me a big hug and tried to feed me toad in the hole, which she claimed has comforting properties, but on this occasion I couldn't even pretend to want it, however kindly it was meant. She then produced a large bin-liner full of nettles (I've no idea where she got these after a day working in a bank in central Ipswich), donned an enormous pair of gauntlets which she said were Pete's old motorcycle gloves, and went back into the kitchen to start on what she described as her 'herbalism homework'.

Considerably before the earliest time at which I had calculated it to be possible that he might make it here from central London, there was a ring at the front door. I flew to open it and straight into Richard's arms. Suddenly the tears that I had been holding back started to flow in earnest, all over the front of his shirt, and he was murmuring soothing words and wiping the tears away with his thumb, and then catching them with his lips on my cheek. I wasn't aware of making any decision, Becs, it was just the most natural thing in the world to turn my head towards him, and then he was kissing me and I was kissing him, I don't know which, both at once, all together. It didn't go on long – not nearly long enough! – because Snuffy came and got in the way, and then Cora had a crisis with her nettles that needed sorting out. But my pulse didn't go back to normal all evening, and that night the fearful images of Helen that were keeping away sleep were confusingly interwoven with the memory of how his mouth had felt against mine.

Anyway, last night he came over for supper, and later on, after the Witch meeting (which passed in a sort of collective daze – no pun intended – with almost everyone red-eyed and shaky), I came back to his flat. I haven't been here before, though he told me the address ages ago. I knew it was in an old converted warehouse down at the docks, but I hadn't realised it was right on the waterfront, with a view out to the estuary. You can sit at his desk, where I am writing this now, and watch the shipping come and go. Well, I climbed the stairs – he's right near the top – and rang the bell, and we were soon kissing again, his hands were in my hair, and it was wonderful, Becs . . . But I had this feeling that he was holding back somehow, that something was wrong, when all I wanted was just to carry on sliding down the glorious slope that was leading into bed. After more hesitancy, he finally extracted himself completely, and picked himself up off the floor (where we somehow found ourselves), taking my hand and pulling me up too. There was quite a bit of panting going on by now on both sides, and there had been a certain amount of disarrangement of clothing, but he stood his ground, and told me what was on his mind. Apparently he thought he mustn't take advantage of my grief and shock over Helen, and my resultant putative need for comfort. (Bloody hell, Becs – why did I have to find the only male in East Anglia with such an over-developed conscience? Maybe it's my vicar's daughter sonar.) I knew what I needed, and comfort may have been a part of it, but isn't it always? And what is wrong with a bit of mutual physical comfort between consenting adults, anyway? But he was not to be swayed (and it didn't seem fair to try *too* hard, when the poor man was attempting to be noble), and we ended up sleeping curled up together in his bed as chaste as two babes in the wood. In some ways it was an agony, all that touching-but-not-touching, but in the end it *was* a comfort just to have his reassuring warmth round me, and I slept much better than the night before.

Oh, God – school today, and I haven't given a thought to my lesson plan. I'm going to be dragging myself in wearing yesterday's shirt and no knickers under my trousers because I don't have a clean pair. Maybe I am the slut that half the parents believe I am after all!

And you – still celibate? Must be getting on for a fortnight now . . . something of a record!

Love and hugs,

Margaret xx

From: Rebecca Prichard [becs444@btinternet.com]
Sent: 8/7/05 22:08
To: Margaret Hayton [margarethayton@yahoo.co.uk]

Hi Margaret,

Blimey! I needed a cold shower after just reading your e-mail – I don't know how you managed to be so restrained. As for him . . . you should have picked a Tory MP. They have any vestiges of conscience surgically removed by the Party chairman when they accept the candidacy.

And yes, my nunnish lifestyle here continues unstained. Men are right off my menu.

But it is just horrible about your friend Helen.

Big hugs,

Becs xx

From: Margaret Hayton [margarethayton@yahoo.co.uk]
Sent: 11/7/05 21:43
To: Rebecca Prichard [becs444@btinternet.com]

Dear Becs,

Well, life goes on . . . in the shape of the St Edith's sports day this afternoon. We have separate events for boys and girls, to mask differences which are, I suspect, due not so much to their pre-pubertal musculature as to socialisation. In the practice sessions, the girls always win the skipping, with even the tubbiest and most knock-kneed rotating the rope in smooth synchronism to their stride, while the boys (those that do not end in a tangled heap) either lollop along awkwardly or else simply sprint, half-halting to put in a token turn of the rope every few metres. All, that is, except David Phillips in Year 4, the sole brother among four sisters, and a veritable wizard with the rope. At running, the boys excel almost uniformly, but I wonder whether this is also more down to nurture than nature. They just spend a higher percentage of their lives careering at full tilt – and a correspondingly lower percentage talking to one another.

Also, if you ask me, the peculiar Britishness of all those skipping ropes and hoops and bean bags and eggs-and-spoons is not preserved out of any respect for quaint tradition. Nor is it merely, in these egalitarian days, intended to introduce a random element in order to disguise the innately competitive ethos of the whole event, sparing the blushes of the wheezy, the overweight and the uncoordinated. I'm sure I'm not allowed to say this, but my observations suggest that it is primarily to stop the black children from winning everything, and to leave the weedy white and Asian kids in with a fighting chance.

The biggest excitement of the afternoon came when the hot favourite for the infant girls' egg-and-spoon race (a leggy, high-stepping Year 2 with a flowing pale chestnut mane) was dramatically brought down by toddler with a pushalong tractor, straying out from the crowd at the rails in a manner reminiscent of Emily Davison at Epsom in 1913. Sniffling and lame, she subsequently pulled out of the sack race without coming under starter's orders, causing major readjustments in the trackside prices, and confounding those who had laid large sums upon her ante post.

Richard has gone back to London and out of the way of temptation (i.e. me), but he has promised to come back for Helen's funeral.

Love,

Margaret x

From: Richard Slater [rpslater@hc.parliament.uk]
Sent: 12/7/05 10:55
To: Michael Carragan [mmcarragan@hc.parliament.uk]

Mike,

Thanks for the drink and the listening ear last night, and sorry if I was bleating on even more than usual. The weekend with Margaret was wonderful, but seventy-two solid hours of keeping my hands off her did take quite a toll. And then back to the office again on Monday, where you could still ignite the air of disapproval with a match, it's so volatile. A month into my new post, and the holy grail I've been pursuing all these years is yielding a pretty bitter draught so far. I'm still at the stage of needing to be briefed from page one on everything, so that I already feel like a schoolboy receiving remedial tuition in the lunch-hours, and now I also have to face silent, unswerving hostility from all the staff (especially the female ones). One of the junior assistants looked at me with such distaste just now that I had to stop myself from ducking into the gents to check that I don't have 'Abductor of Young Women' branded across my forehead. Can't exactly see myself having the loyal backing of my team here if I come under pressure to resign again, or if there are soundings from On High about how I'm shaping up. Half of them clearly see me as an extremely temporary hindrance to getting on with their jobs.

This morning the team from the 2012 London Olympic bid did leave behind some good merchandise. I've got a nifty desk jotter featuring a different British gold medallist on every page (OK, yes, it's quite a slim jotter). But even this seems to have lost some of its former glitter for me at the moment.

I may be in need of a second dose of beer and sympathy tonight – do you think you can stand it?

Richard.

Richard Slater (Labour)
Member of Parliament for Ipswich

From: Michael Carragan
[mmcarragan@hc.parliament.uk]
Sent: 12/7/05 11:17
To: Richard Slater [rpslater@hc.parliament.uk]

'Bleating' doesn't really do justice to it. Sheep are far too mellow an image for the state you were in. More like an over-agitated spider monkey on the way to its first ulcer. You knocked over two perfectly good pints. What's the matter with you? You've got the job (for the moment, at least), you've got the girl . . . What you need, in my opinion, is to get laid, mate, and soon.

Meanwhile, the whisper on the Corridor of Power (which, OK, I pass through occasionally on the way to the water cooler from my own humble boxroom) is that you are under surveillance. The Stasi from the Private Office are watching your every move – so you'd better come up with some pretty smart ones, if you want to convince them to keep you in post much beyond the start of the next session. It's not just about your performance at CM&S – it's the all-round Slater brand that's under scrutiny. Every constituency issue that arises, you need to pedal the Party line, and pedal it visibly and with conviction. Show them that you can handle the press: seize the whip hand, after being the tabloids' whipping boy.

And yes, I'll stand you another round or two of liquid solace tonight – just so long as you promise not to mention Margaret's breasts.

Michael.

Michael Carragan (Labour)
Member of Parliament for West Bromwich West

WITCH
Women of Ipswich Together Combating Homelessness

Extract from minutes of meeting at Alison's house, 14 July 2005, 8 p.m.

Witch House: current occupancy
Room 1: Carole
Room 2: Lauren
Room 3: [held for Nasreen]
Room 4: Joyce
Room 5: [void]

Referrals for Helen's old room (room 5) were considered.

The possibilities were (i) Rosemary, aged 56, who has recently had to give up a long-term live-in job as house-keeper at a private nursing home, due to worsening arthritis (she is currently awaiting a hip operation); and (ii) Rrezja, a 19-year-old Kosovo Albanian whom Margaret met in London. There was some discussion about the problems of housing someone from out of area, but Margaret pointed out that the borough council funding does not give them any referral rights, and there is no actual obligation to accommodate only local women. It might be very beneficial, moreover, to get Rrezja away from London. There are potential problems about Rrezja's immigration status (at present she is an illegal over-stayer) but it may be possible to resolve this situation once she is in Witch House. In the end it was agreed, regretfully, that the time has come to stop holding Nasreen's room for her. Therefore Rosemary would be offered room 3 (it being on the ground floor), and Rrezja would be offered room 5.

Any other business

Helen's mother phoned Witch House on Monday and asked Pat T. and Emily to pack up Helen's things, and to bring them over to her house. She did not wish to come to the hostel herself to collect them. The family have arranged Helen's funeral for 11 a.m. tomorrow (Friday), at the crematorium.

42 Gledhill Street
Ipswich

15 July 2005

My darling Pete

I'm on my own tonight, writing this in Aunt Alice's armchair, and Snuffy is on my knee which is why the handwriting is a bit bumpy. It's been a dreadful couple of weeks. Nasreen is still missing, and then there was this nasty story in the papers about poor Margaret and Richard (Mr Slater, you know). They had photos of them together having a hug, and they were making out that Margaret was a prostitute, and poor Richard nearly had to give up his job – well, not his seat in Parliament, I don't mean, just his new job in the government – but he managed to persuade the Prime Minister to let him stay. Only they aren't allowed to tell everyone the truth; Richard has just had to ignore all the lies that have been printed. And then last week we had the real bombshell. Helen – the young girl from the hostel whose father abused her, you remember, and she has been so depressed – well, she killed herself while she was in hospital.

It was the funeral today. Of course, the family organised it, even though she hardly saw them any more, but we all went along. The other residents from the hostel were there, and the staff and all the support group. Richard drove Margaret and me there in his car. He'd just got it back from the garage, having the speedo fixed or something. It was the first time I had been back to the crem since . . . well, you know, so it felt a bit peculiar, but everyone was so upset

257

anyway about Helen that I don't think anyone noticed. Apart from all of us, there were just Helen's parents there, and an elderly couple and another older lady who looked like the grandparents, but very few friends – just two girls of about Helen's age that I didn't recognise from the hostel. It was the usual sort of thing. They played that song 'The Wind Beneath My Wings' at the beginning when we were walking in, and that set me off crying, and Margaret was sniffing, too. I noticed Richard take hold of her hand, and she held mine with her other one. The vicar lady made a little speech. I don't suppose she knew much about Helen or who she was – it was just a fairly general thing about what a sad event it was, and Helen being with God now, and at peace. But it did strike a chord of sorts – I thought how little peace the poor thing had had in her short life, and how her being at rest was maybe something we could be thankful for.

And then the father stood up and read out this poem. I really don't know how he can have had the gall. This is the man who messed about with Helen from when she was a little girl of eight, the man who is the reason for all that misery – misery so unbearable that in the end she couldn't stand it any more and took her own life. As he began to read, I could feel Margaret stiffen beside me. Her fingers in mine went all rigid – they actually seemed to get suddenly colder, if that's possible. They'd printed the poem that he read on the Order of Service, so I can tell you exactly how it went:

You were my foundation in all things.
Your arms first encircled me, circumference of my world;
your hand guided my infant steps
and held me up from falling.
You were my moon, the rudder of my tides;
my sun, warming me along my way;
my stars, guiding my path in darkness;
my harbour, you held me safe against the wind's rage;
my rock, my earth — my growing was rooted in your love.

Now that I have passed into another realm
and have no need for anchorage
do not mourn my going.
I shall still shimmer in your moonlight,
dance in your sunshine, walk tall under your stars
and whisper through the growing grass
that I love you still.

'Held her safe', indeed! I don't think I have ever seen
Margaret angrier. She was even whiter than usual, her face
looked sort of tense and pinched, and she didn't speak at
all until we got home. There was another reading, too,
from one of the grandmothers, and it was also completely
inappropriate. It was about dying young, but it was all
sickly sweet, about how Helen had walked only in the
golden morning and never known the shadows, when of
course her life was almost nothing but shadow, poor thing.

Persephone came back to our house, and two other
women called Alison and Ding (I think I heard that right),

only Ding couldn't stay more than half an hour because she had to get back to check on her mother. Apparently she can't be left too long on her own – last week Ding went shopping and came back to find her mother halfway up the street in her nightie. Richard produced a bottle of whisky and we all had a tot, and Alison asked me whether I might plant up a little patch in the garden of Witch House in Helen's memory. Margaret said maybe we could get a tree, and Richard started to say that there isn't space and its roots would get into the foundations, but then stopped and just said maybe a fruit tree on the fence. I said we could espalier it, but then I felt embarrassed because I've never been quite sure how to say that word, I've just read it in my gardening book, but it was OK because Margaret smiled and gave me a hug. Persephone said a peach would be nice, because when the blossom comes you can use the petals in healing, and she and I went to Margaret's room to look it up. You would tease me about this I know, Pete, but Margaret has been teaching me to use the internet, and there are some really good websites about herbs and herbalism. It's silly that I've never tried it before, the internet I mean. I use the computer all the time at work, but only the bank's internal system, I've never been in chat rooms or done internet shopping or anything, like Sarah does. I might even do a beginner's computer course. We were talking about it, and Alison said they do some good courses over the summer at Suffolk College.

Well, I'd better stop now. Isn't it odd, I have just realised what a long time it is since I last wrote to you, Petey. I can't even remember, but it must be more than a month. But that is a good thing, isn't it? I hope that you think so too.

With all my love, sweetheart,

Cora xxx

From: Margaret Hayton
[margarethayton@yahoo.co.uk]
Sent: 16/7/05 08:25
To: Rebecca Prichard [becs444@btinternet.com]

Dear Becs,

Yesterday was Helen's funeral, up at the crematorium. Richard came up from London, which meant a lot to me – just him being there with me when I was saying goodbye to Helen. I still can't believe it, really. All that she was – all her pain, all her courage in breaking away from that cloying hell of abuse and smug denial – all reduced to a powdery nothing. Just a puff of smoke drifting over those over-trimmed lawns, and the clumps of clinically optimistic French marigolds.

Everyone from WITCH was there, and Cora came along too, which was nice, because actually I realised she had never met Helen, because whenever Cora was at the hostel doing the garden it was the weekend and Helen was in hospital. But of course she had heard all about her from me, and she said she felt as if she knew her. Probably a sign that I do go on a bit too much sometimes – though Cora is so sweet, she would never say so.

It felt odd to be outsiders at the funeral, there as guests of the family, whom most of us have never met. It made me angry to think of them taking over Helen's life again, right at the end – claiming her back somehow. It's hard to explain. And carrying on with that blind charade of theirs, pretending to be a normal family, suffering a normal bereavement. There was no mention of suicide, or of Helen's overwhelming pain – even the vicar just made a brief euphemistic allusion to her 'illness' as if she had died of cancer or something – let alone the whole big unmentionable subject of what had caused it all. I kept looking at Helen's father, and he looked so *ordinary*, Becs – like someone whose newspaper you might borrow if you were sitting next to him on a train. And then he read out this poem. I hardly know how to tell you. It was meant to be Helen's voice, saying how much she had loved him, and how he had been her harbour and kept her safe – when really the storm that battered her was him. And he didn't read it in a falsely syrupy voice or anything, he just sounded like a dad really, choked up but brave, like any father would sound if he'd lost his little girl.

I couldn't wait to get away. We had a stiff drink back at Cora's, a bottle of single malt that Richard had brought, and Alison, Ding and Persephone came too. I asked Alison how her family are, and she said the middle one, Edward, has been a bit better recently, not so many angry outbursts. She didn't mention what's-his-name, Derek, but the clear unspoken message was 'no regrets'. I love all those women dearly, but I must admit I was relieved when Richard suggested we go back to his flat, because I wanted to be on our own. Not for the reason you think, although I must admit the idea did suggest itself to me quite strongly later, after we'd had something to eat and were cuddled up on the sofa. He kissed me then, but ever so gently, as if I were something fragile that might shatter into pieces if he applied any pressure, and when I tried being a little more . . . direct (shall we say), he went all noble on me again, talking about the strain of the funeral and me still being emotionally vulnerable. So it was another night in bed together but not together, and now I'm watching the cargo ships from his desk again, while he sleeps the sleep of the too damned virtuous.

But sorry to go on about me – how's your dad?

Love,

Margaret xxx

From: Rebecca Prichard [becs444@btinternet.com]
Sent: 16/7/05 09:26
To: Margaret Hayton [margarethayton@yahoo.co.uk]

For goodness' sake, Margaret, either tell him how you feel, or just jump him. But don't tantalise me with your tales of unrequited lust. I am still confined to the convent here, don't forget.

If you ask me, that Mr Rochester of yours at college has a lot to answer for. Where would Jane Eyre have been, after all, had it not been for a convenient house fire? Incapable of getting into the missionary position with that Apollo, St John Rivers. Mark may have been a green and vigorous chestnut tree, jetty brows and all – but, reader, he fucked you up!

Dad is halfway through his course of chemo, and the specialist declares himself pleased with how he's responding. They've also got him some different anti-nausea tablets which seem to help. Last night I took them over a fish supper and he ate half of his chips and nearly a whole portion of haddock. Mum finished off his chips. In fact I suspect that she may have been eating up a lot of his food for him these last few weeks. While he gets thinner, she seems to be doing her best to maintain the household's overall aggregate weight.

Love and hugs,
Becs xxx

IPSWICH TOWN CRIER   MONDAY 18TH JULY 2005

HOSPITAL DEATH SPARKS INQUIRY CALLS

MP BACKS PARENTS' PLEA

BY GEOFFREY HOWARD
POLITICAL CORRESPONDENT

The suicide of a teenager in the psychiatric wing of Ipswich General Hospital on 6 July has triggered calls for an investigation. Helen Adamson (19) hanged herself in a bathroom using an item of clothing at a time when the acute psychiatric ward on which she was staying as a voluntary patient was temporarily unstaffed. Her father, Mr Keith Adamson, backed by Ipswich MP Mr Richard Slater, has called for a public inquiry into the events leading up to his daughter's death.

'Both the individual hospital staff and the management structures which allowed this to happen must be called to account,' said a visibly drawn and angry Mr Adamson, his distraught wife at his side, speaking yesterday from his Ipswich home, from which he also practises as an orthodontist. Mr Slater echoed the call for an inquiry, saying, 'Clearly the circumstances of a tragic incident such as this must always be investigated in full.'

The MP went on to link Miss Adamson's suicide to the need for wholesale changes in the structure of the country's mental health services. 'The government is already spending £300 million more per year on adult psychiatric provision than it was in 2000/01,' pointed out Mr Slater. 'However, we need greater powers to identify and treat those patients who constitute the greatest risk to themselves or others, if further deaths like Miss Adamson's are to be prevented,' he continued. 'We also need more rigorous procedures for inspection of mental health providers and their services. These and other important and timely reforms are contained in the Government's Mental Health Bill, which is currently before Parliament, but which has unfortunately encountered some opposition from misguided health professionals.'

Mr Adamson is pictured below, comforting a tearful and distressed Mrs Adamson, as they attended their daughter's funeral, which took place at Ipswich Crematorium on Friday.

From: Margaret Hayton [margarethayton@yahoo.co.uk]
Sent: 18/7/05 17:14
To: Rebecca Prichard [becs444@btinternet.com]

Oh, Becs, my hands are shaking so badly I can scarcely hit the keys, and I hardly know what to write anyway, where to begin . . . I've just come off the phone to Richard – well, to his answering machine, in fact – telling him exactly what I think of him. Someone at school showed me today's *Town Crier* at break time, and there was this article about Richard, or about Helen, I mean. Here's the link, so you can see it for yourself. I can't begin to convey it to you.

www.ipswichtowncrier.co.uk/news/hospitalinquiry/0,2 16443.html

It's just so appalling, such a . . . betrayal, or that's what it feels like.

Doesn't he care at all about Helen, or about her friends' feelings? How can he even contemplate *using* her death like this, treating it as merely a handy opportunity, to make self-serving political points about some bloody Bill that his precious Tim is trying to get through? A Bill which, I might add, from everything I've read, seems to have more to do with social control than with patients' rights or any improvements in patient care. I very much doubt whether he has any great belief in the wretched thing himself, which just seems to make the whole business even more distasteful. Why was I ever so crazy as to trust a career politician in the first place? Especially one whose heart has had nearly two decades of hardening since he was our age and may have had ideals.

He obviously actually *invited* his chums from the press along to the funeral, for God's sake! I remember now, there was a man there who said hi to Richard, and he said 'Hello, Geoff' but didn't introduce us, and I didn't think anything of it, but now I know why! Richard has talked about his friend Geoff at the *Crier*, but I didn't put two and two together, I suppose I wasn't in any state to do so, and anyway it would never have crossed my mind that he could be so brazen. And there was another man who must have been the photographer (though I didn't notice a camera – he must have been keeping it hidden). It wasn't the man who came to take the photographs when Richard visited my class; this one was older and kind of stoopier. But of course, it wouldn't be the same one, would it, or he might have risked my recognising him! Oh yes, he certainly went to some lengths to make sure I didn't know what was going on – there's almost no skulduggery or subterfuge I would put past him just now. Maybe, at least, it shows he still has some traces of shame left – but not nearly enough, not by a very long way! Lord knows, I shouldn't want to waste any sympathy on Helen's sodding parents. But I still feel violated by the press being there – on behalf of Helen, and of all of us who were really fond of Helen, and wanted to say our goodbyes. Richard, more than most people at the moment, surely ought to be aware of what damage and hurt the press can cause, trampling roughshod all over people's private lives and feelings.

But it isn't the shameless arse-licking that gets me

the most, the unprincipled politicking to further his own
worthless career on the back of others' suffering. Nor
is it even the callousness, the crass insensitivity of
inviting the press to a funeral, to take intrusive pictures
of the bereaved. It's my own stupid naive blindness.
Fool that I was, I genuinely believed that he'd come
down for the funeral to support me, because he cared
about Helen's death (Helen, whom he'd never even
met!), because he cared about me . . . When all the
time it was just another twist in his careerist political
manoeuvres.

Anyway, I told all this and a lot more besides to his
answering machine, as soon as I got home from school.
I said some pretty nasty things – but he deserves them
all! I really didn't know what I was saying, half the time,
once I'd started, and I only stopped when the tape ran
out. I fear much of it may have been rather incoherent.
But the message will have been clear enough. One
thing is certain: after what he's done, and what I've said
about it, there can be no going back.

What I didn't mention – the thing that is almost too
painful to articulate even now – is my outrage that
he should be sharing a platform with Helen's father.
Backing his calls for an inquiry, when Richard knows
perfectly well that it's not those poor nurses, nor the
hospital management, that are really to blame for
Helen's death, but the man standing there in his
neatly pressed suit playing the grief-stricken parent.
How can he even go near that man, even speak to

him, let alone support his cause in public like this?
After the funeral, there was Richard, sharing his
whisky and his consolation with all the WITCH crew
in Cora's sitting room, seeming so much one of us,
and now it feels as though he has changed sides
completely, gone over to the other camp somehow.
Of course there was no mention of Witch House in
the newspaper. Why would I expect Richard to have
mentioned us? It's just like at the funeral, the way
we were all sidelined, invalidated somehow, as if that
part of Helen's life had never existed. All the connec-
tions she made, all our efforts to keep her safe, all
reduced to nothing. I feel let down, deceived . . .
Betrayed, as I said before – it's the only word for it.
All weekend Richard was pretending to be the big
liberal with the bleeding-heart conscience, listening
oh-so-tenderly while I told him how I felt about
Helen, playing the saint who wouldn't even sleep
with me because I was so upset, and all the time
he's in bed with the enemy!

Sorry, Becs, I'm so sorry – none of this is anything
to do with you – I just don't know where to turn.

Margaret xxxx

From: Rebecca Prichard [becs444@btinternet.com]
Sent: 18/7/05 19:30
To: Margaret Hayton [margarethayton@yahoo.co.uk]

Don't be sorry, Margaret honey. But I really have no idea what to say.

Except, what a bastard. And big, big hugs,

Becs xxxx

From: Richard Slater [richard.slater@btopenworld.com]
Sent: 18/7/05 21:57
To: Michael Carragan [mikecarragan@yahoo.com]

So, Michael . . . Well done, mate! Why on earth did I ever listen to you? Damage limitation, you said. Must use all the chances that present themselves, you said. The Mental Health Bill, you said, one of the Rottweiler's favourite pet projects. Never mind that it was none of my business – that the bloody Bill had nothing to do with my patch, not with culture or media or sport, nor actually with the real reasons for Helen's death. Start repairing your image at every opportunity (and this is a golden one) you said, or you'll be out in the wilderness at the next reshuffle. Well, maybe – just maybe – the political wilderness might have been preferable to the comfortless desert in which your damned stupid advice has landed me this time.

Just take a look on the *Town Crier's* website and see how the story appeared! I'm afraid poor Geoff Howard caught the sharp end of my frustration on the phone this morning, though in fairness I suppose it isn't really his fault. He didn't write anything that wasn't true, he didn't misquote me. And how was he to know I wouldn't exactly relish the public association with that man Adamson? Though I still think he could have run the story by me first.

Well, quite naturally Margaret is furious. You can hardly blame her! How could I not have realised the way she would perceive it? I should have spoken to her about it before I talked to Geoff. But of course then I wouldn't have talked to Geoff at all, would I? And this whole nightmare would never have happened. I've been calling and calling all evening. Cora picked up once and said that Margaret didn't want to speak to me, but after that they stopped answering at all, and they don't have an answering machine on their land line. Her mobile is switched off, and there's a limit to the number of times you can say sorry into the electronic emptiness of a person's voicemail. I'm sure she's deleting it all without listening to it anyway. I'd go down there, but I know there's no point; she'd never see me.

Oh God, Mike, I've wrecked everything – and for what? Did I really imagine that an article in the Ipswich local rag would ever make it anywhere near the PM's desk? And it was never going to be a story with national media appeal, even with the summer season of news famine on the horizon. Who cares about the sodding Mental Health Bill anyway?

Aaaaaaggghhh!

Richard.

More Than Love Letters

From: Michael Carragan [mikecarragan@yahoo.com]
Sent: 18/7/05 22:17
To: Richard Slater [richard.slater@btopenworld.com]

Seemed like a good idea at the time, Richard. But I am truly sorry, the way it's worked out – I know how she had got under your skin. Would you accept a few penitent pints in recompense? Tomorrow lunchtime, perhaps? Give me a ring in the morning.

Michael.

INBOX

| Reply | Delete | Expunge | Display: | All | Sent |

From:/To:	Date Sent:	Thread:
1 ✉ ← Richard Slater	18/7/05	Sorry
2 ✉ ← Richard Slater	18/7/05	Sorry
3 ✉ ← Richard Slater	18/7/05	Sorry again
4 ✉ ← Richard Slater	19/7/05	Really really sorry
5 ✉ ← Richard Slater	19/7/05	Please open this
6 ✉ ← Richard Slater	20/7/05	Please, Margaret, at least just open this!
7 ✉ ← Richard Slater	21/7/05	PLEASE!!

Unopened ✉: 7

From: Richard Slater
[richard.slater@btopenworld.com]
Sent: 22/7/05 00:26
To: Michael Carragan [mikecarragan@yahoo.com]

Michael, I'm wretched, I'm wrecked.

Margaret won't answer my e-mails. The arts budget to your constituency coffee morning takings that she's deleting them without even opening them. Her mobile is still off, and Cora is fielding phone calls to the house like the most fearsomely dragonish of Victorian chaperons. And there's so much I want to say to her, so much to try to explain . . .

I keep going over and over in my head all the things she said on my answerphone that day. I've taken out the tape (her tirade had filled it up, and somehow I couldn't bring myself to press rewind and wipe it all away), and it lurks accusingly in the bottom of my briefcase. I don't need to listen to it again, even if I could bear to. I can remember every word – and, worse, every wounded inflection of her voice.

She said I've never really cared about people as individuals, not *really* cared, that I've only ever been interested in using their problems to make larger policy points. It should be the other way round, she said, with policies only mattering because of how they can help individuals. Well, it may have been true of my cosmetically engineered surgeries – hell, Mike, it definitely *was* true – and I'll admit that making an issue out of Helen's death in the way that I did was a huge mistake. I knew how high Margaret's feelings were running about poor Helen, and about our respected colleagues in the Great British press. So yes, that was crassness of the highest order. But what about Nasreen? I never even met the girl, any more than I met Helen, but I was genuinely concerned about her. Didn't I tread half the pavements north of the river fly-posting her photo on every prominent object? That hare-brained wild goose chase (if you'll forgive the zoologically mixed metaphor) nearly cost me the promotion for which I've worked and waited (not to mention swallowed my principles and crawled on my belly) for eight long years. And what is getting into government, getting into a position of power and influence, all about, after all? It's so I can help more of those all-important individuals about whom Margaret is so concerned!

She said I only took up the issues she raised (the sanitary towels, the wheelie bins, and the inevitable blasted dog poo) to impress her, and not because I ever believed that any of it mattered. Well, too damned right, actually! None of it would have merited a second glance if it hadn't been for her – if I hadn't seen how much she cared about those things. But she's so indiscriminate in her passions. She's got no sense of perspective – no comprehension that yes, actually, some causes simply *are* bigger and more worth spending time on than others. Wasn't securing a change in national asylum policy bigger than finding Nasreen? Though I'm not sure Margaret would agree. She always takes up with equal gusto the cause of every waif and stray that crosses her path, however undeserving, however unhinged. She'd call it being 'non-judgemental'. But one woman's non-judgemental is the next man's blindly undiscerning. Sometimes you *have* to make a judgement. In politics, judgements matter, judgements are everything. Otherwise, nothing would ever get done.

But I can't argue with her about it, can't tell her how she's so right but also so wrong, because she won't talk to me. I can't see any way out of it, but nor can I seem to accept that it's all over. God, I want her back – but I don't think it's fixable.

I'd ask your advice, mate, but I would probably end up sacked, arrested, evicted, deselected and/or bankrupt.

Richard.

From: Michael Carragan [mikecarragan@yahoo.com]
Sent: 22/7/05 09:16
To: Richard Slater [richard.slater@btopenworld.com]

Good grief, Richard! All this introspective soul-searching is most unnatural in a red-blooded male – bad for the liver, you know. Speaking of which . . . want to try that new Bavarian Bierkeller off Birdcage Walk, over near the park?

Michael.

From: Rebecca Prichard [becs444@btinternet.com]
Sent: 22/7/05 17:43
To: Margaret Hayton [margarethayton@yahoo.co.uk]

Hi Margaret,

Still feeling delicate around the Richard issue? Have you spoken to him at all? Or is it beyond that? Even if the whole thing is over, it sometimes helps to clear the air, I always think. And I don't mean just on to a tape going round and round in a machine.

Broken heart apart, how was your end of term, chuck? The usual orgy of stock-taking and recorder concerts and dismantling of displays and mini Mars bar distribution and deciding who takes home the hamster? I think I would probably have been better giving Hammy his freedom and letting him take his chances on the estate than entrusting him to any of mine, but in the end I took a risk on Chitra Prabhu because at least her family are veggies so he won't end up on toast.

It's funny saying goodbye to your very first ever proper class, isn't it? And I discovered there were some things I was finding it even harder to let go of than others. Specifically, the thought of Declan outside my classroom door at three o'clock. But we ursulines must fight fleshly temptation, through immersion in prayer and the study of improving texts. Or in this case, weather permitting, five weeks on a rug on the patch of grass behind our flats (the latter being the exact size of the former), with the Ambre Solaire and some Louise Bagshawe. Interspersed with one week of much the same in Gran Canaria with Paula. Plus the usual amount of time spent jollying Mum and Dad along.

And you? You know, you really ought to do something to take your mind off men. Other than your witchy support group stuff, I mean. You could come and see me – you know you're welcome any time.

Great big hugs,

Becs xxx

From: Margaret Hayton
[margarethayton@yahoo.co.uk]
Sent: 22/7/05 18:55
To: Rebecca Prichard [becs444@btinternet.com]

Dear Becs,

Well, until Monday, my closely nursed plan had been to spend a large part of the summer holidays in Richard's flat. In fact, to be brutally frank, in Richard's bedroom, in the approximate vicinity of the bed. So now, nothing particular in prospect. Might go to Mum

and Dad's for a bit. I've definitely promised Gran a
visit – I had intended to take Richard down there, too.
She'll be disappointed, because they got along really
well.

We've finally decided, after another month gone
by with no word, to report Nasreen to the police as
a missing person. Mind you, I don't exactly expect
the Met to pull out all the stops looking for just
another young runaway – a foreigner at that, and
not even underage. Alison says that once last year
Marianne went on a bender and didn't turn up for
three days, so on the third evening they reported
her missing at Ipswich police station. The desk
sergeant solemnly took note of all the details and
circulated her description, but it later transpired that
they'd actually had her belowstairs all day, floating
slowly back down to reality in their own cells. I feel I
ought to go back to London and continue the search
for Nasreen myself, but I'm pretty sure it would be
fruitless, and somehow, on my own, I don't have the
heart for it.

I was watching the six o'clock news just now,
downstairs with Cora, when Snuffy came in from the
garden with half a rosemary bush forming an
extension to her imperviously wagging tail. She
flopped down against the settee to watch the rest of
the bulletin with us, apparently blithely unaware of
the mass of spiky vegetation adhering to her nether
end. By chance, the next item concerned the ever-

mounting stakes in the War on Terror. Heightened airport security, Aunty Beeb reassured us, is the latest plank in the nation's defence against terrorist atrocity – this bracing news accompanied by footage of two officious-looking spaniels, one black and white and one liver and white, applying enthusiastic noses to the contents of a litter bin. So, on the one hand, ranged against us we have the uncompromising and unknowable might of Al-Qaeda. On the other, lined up in defiant opposition, we have, er . . . a few extra springer spaniels. I must say, it is not a thought to make me sleep any easier in my bed at nights.

Anyway, I'm very grateful for the invitation to come and experience for myself the glories of Moss Side – I might well take you up on it.

Much love,

Margaret x

From: Rebecca Prichard [becs444@btinternet.com]
Sent: 1/8/05 18:33
To: Margaret Hayton [margarethayton@yahoo.co.uk]

Well, Margaret, I have abandoned my uncharacteristic cloistered ways. There was a medieval fair this weekend, out of town on the Cheshire side, and I went along on a reconnaissance mission for school. Useful, too. I think the kids would enjoy a visit from this shoemaker I came across. He not only shrinks his end product to the size and shape of his feet by soaking them in his own urine and wearing them in that state overnight, but also prepares his shoe leather himself, straight from the abattoir it appears, and swears by dog faeces as being an unrivalled caustic agent for use in the tanning process. Believe me, that man brings a whole new dimension to the concept of smelly feet!

But where was I? Oh yes, my abduction from the convent, which was effected by a gentil knight in shining armour, resplendent upon a white charger. Fate willed that his name is Hugh, which seemed suitably seignorial. Or that's what I thought it was at first, but it turns out to be Huw (he's from the Rhondda valley), which if not positively Arthurian is at least redolent of the Celtic fringe. Of which he possesses rather an attractive specimen, shading mystic jade-green eyes. And actually the horse was brown (so, also the wrong hue). Anyway, he is a telephone engineer during the week and a historical reconstructionist at the weekends, with a nifty line in jousting. (We'll take as read the jokes about how he handles his lance, shall we?)

It all happened when I was watching the grand tourney. At the entrance to the lists, Huw's refractory steed decided to take a dislike to all the fluttering flags, and began cavorting and tittuping in a theatrical style, rolling its eyes melodramatically, and moving in any direction but forward, like a

temperamental supermarket trolley. Huw applied his
homemade spurs with a little too much vigour,
the horse kicked up its heels in protest, and one
horseshoe flew off and caught me a far from lucky
blow across the right instep. (It had been shod, I
afterwards learned, by an anthropology student named
Henry, a callow and implausibly unsinewy youth, who
had only lately turned his hand to costume
blacksmithery. The horse itself, fortuitously also called
Henry, was moonlighting from its day job at the local
riding school.) Huw dismounted at once, and my flow
of muttered expletives was arrested in midstream by
the blaze of concerned green eyes, rendered strangely
disembodied by the interjacent visor of his helmet.
Paying no heed to my protests, he picked me up
bodily and carried me over to Henry (the equine one),
who was standing nearby on three and a half legs,
nonchalantly browsing the clover and trying to look
uninvolved. Huw lifted me into the saddle, managing
to redouble the pain in my foot as he did so, with an
unscheduled bash against the pommel (or it might
equally have been a pastern, a poll or a pelham, for
all I know the difference).

Once inside his tent, the deftness with which Huw
removed my Timberland and slid his finger down into my
sock captured my attention immediately, and my outrage
began to be tempered with warmer feelings. These
increased when he doffed his helmet, and unbuckled his
breastplate to reveal a buttonless shirt and an expanse

of well-muscled knightly torso. (Though, given his ancestry, probably in reality more collier than warrier.) I offered to help him off with the rest of his armour, and found myself coming over like Sir Thomas Tom of Appledore ('at times like these the bravest knight may find his armour much too tight'). It turned out that Huw had also been brought up on *Now We Are Six*, and we were soon both giggling like schoolgirls on a sugar high. But later, when he was reclining armourless and open-shirted on a pile of sheepskins by the flickering firelight, I can tell you, kid, Huw looked all man. In fact he was every damsel's dream come true. I was lost – and all for want of a horseshoe nail.

You see how I live only to divert and entertain you with my amorous exploits, and take your mind off Richard? How is the trying-to-forget-him-and-move-on coming along, by the way?

Love and hugs,

Becs xx

From: Margaret Hayton
[margarethayton@yahoo.co.uk]
Sent: 7/8/05 23:51
To: Rebecca Prichard [becs444@btinternet.com]

Dear Becs,

Dear oh dear. Following your exploits with the pornographic plumber, I fear you have now strayed into the pages of a trashy historical bodice-ripper. I'm not sure that the carrying off and ravishment of nuns is exactly consistent with the ideals of the age of chivalry – though I expect a lot of it did go on. If you twist my arm I could give you 4.5 for 'seignorial', I suppose, and a 3 for 'refractory', which I always mistake for a kind of dining room. And OK, no lance jokes, but what about his sword? I bet he can hew away pretty smartly with that, too!

You have cheered me up no end, thanks, Becs – and boy, did I need it! It's not proving so easy to put Richard, and Helen, and the whole awful business out of my mind. Her father has been banging on in the paper again about an inquiry, though I must say Richard seems to have backed off a bit now. He hasn't been quoted talking about it again, so maybe he has rediscovered some remnants of conscience. But there's something else. Helen left a diary. Pat T. and Emily at the hostel found it when they packed up her things. They wanted to give it back to Helen's mother with the rest of her possessions, but I said that then it would never be read, would probably just end up thrown away, and I couldn't bear that to happen. So I kept it myself. It has taken me until now to bring myself to open it at all, but once I'd started I haven't been able to stop. It's incredibly painful, but I feel this horrible compulsion to read every word (so far I'm up to midway through 2003). In a funny kind of way, I feel that I owe it to Helen.

I remember Richard saying that they used to call one of the Labour Party's 1980s election manifestos the 'longest suicide note in history'. But it wasn't – this is. It's agony, reading about her life in that family – what that man did to her, and how it made her feel. And then I get even more knotted up inside, remembering that Richard was prepared to meet him, to fight his corner, to lend his support to the public pretence that Helen's depression and suicide were just bad luck, just one of those things that can happen, even in the nicest families. However much I miss him, and whatever else he's done, that's the one thing for which I can never forgive him.

But, this visit? Would it still be OK for me to come up? (That is, if you aren't engaged full-time in the lists . . .) Are you doing anything later in the week? I'll call you tomorrow.

Love,

Margaret xxx

Extract from Helen's diary

Tonight I was suddenly remembering when I was fourteen, and Danny Mercer asked me to dance at the school disco. He was cute, and kind, and his hand holding mine was soft, not like Dad's at all. But the thought of Danny touching me sent me into a flat panic – he would know! As soon as he touched

*me he would know the truth, they all would. I found it
difficult to believe that they couldn't all tell already, just by
looking at me. Look at Helen, look what she lets her dad do
to her.*

*We did dance, uncomfortably, just one song. I held him
at a safe distance, stiff-armed, and Danny was either too
sweet or too inexperienced to try to soften my hold and
draw me in closer. The next day, at break, he asked me to
go to a film with him at the weekend. I almost said yes,
before I remembered that the cinema meant darkness. How
could a person of fourteen explain being afraid of the dark?
Worse still, it would have meant that ever-present
nightmare, a pressing darkness heavy with the fear of unseen
invading hands . . .*

From: Rebecca Prichard [becs444@btinternet.com]
Sent: 14/8/05 22:04
To: Margaret Hayton [margarethayton@yahoo.co.uk]

Hi Margaret,

It was great to see you last week, hon. I'm really
glad you came. We shouldn't leave it so long next
time.

But I am worried about you. You've got even less
colour than normal (if that's possible), and I couldn't
fail to notice you not eating anything. You can wear
baggy jeans all you like, babe, but your wrists are like
sticks – remember, it was always how we used to

spot the anorexics at college? And that accursed diary! Don't imagine I didn't see it there, pushed discreetly under the futon, when we were folding it back up. You've got to stop torturing yourself. It can't help Helen now, and it's certainly doing you no good at all.

I know you are badly in need of something to smile about, so please excuse the rather lumpy segue from tragedy into farce . . . but you might like to know that Sir Huw has receded back into the mists of history whence he came. I spent the weekend at his place. He is an asthmatic, and his condition is brought on specifically by certain plant allergens released by rain during the summer months. Moving away from South Wales was, in the circumstances, a wise decision, but the choice of Greater Manchester as a destination somewhat less so. Huw harbours the belief that sleeping in a room with the windows sealed tightly shut will prove a deterrent to airborne pollen particles. With Saturday's thunderstorm sending clouds of the offending motes into the atmosphere (thereby transforming Huw's lungs into a pair of bagpipes), and with temperatures over the weekend soaring to 30 degrees even in Lancashire, conditions in his bedroom last night resembled those endured by troops engaged in desert warfare wearing full chemical protection gear.

He has a fan, which besides emitting a constant,

sleep-preventing, clattery whirr, serves only to move around the same indecently hot air, which thus plays over your skin like a hairdryer. Fans also have a tendency to make me wake up in the morning with a stiff neck, so I was obliged as a precautionary measure to make my attempt at sleep clad in a pair of his fleecy pyjamas, with the collar turned up against the tropical sirocco. (I considered and rejected the extra protection of a woollen scarf.) Add to this, if you will, the auditory assault of Sir Huffsalot's laboured breathing: each breath in a quick, tight, gravelly gasp, and each breath out a series of softly modulating musical whistles. (*This* Sir Hugh, take my word for it, certainly did not 'make a nicer sound than other knights who lived around'!) At first his wheezing exhalations sounded to my overtired and overheated brain like his name, Huw, repeated over and over. Then the whole thing started to remind me, in its endlessly repetitive variations, of a Mike Oldfield track which my mother used to put on while she was ironing. I nearly had to get up and phone her to put an end to the jaw-grinding frustration of not remembering what it was called, and would surely have done so if it had not by then been 3.47 a.m.

I might also say that Huw's breathing gets even more noisy and desperate during any physical exertion. Luckily any such activity on his part tends to be short-lived. (Or unluckily, depending on whose side of the bed you look at it from.)

Perhaps the whole thing was an elaborate ruse on his part to discover whether he really was more dear to me than breathing. Well, he wasn't, so I've left him to it.

Big hugs,

Becs xxx

(Huw probably begins with a W or a Y in Welsh, anyway.)

Extract from Helen's diary

Maybe he won't come. That's what I used to say to myself, the words repeating over and over, hammering in my skull like a mantra into the silence: perhaps tonight he won't come.

I used to bargain with the fates, there in the almost darkness. I'll give Joanne Miller my new strappy top with the sequinned butterfly on the front, only don't let him come. So many nights: howling November blackness, frost-stilled Januaries, creeping April dawns. But memory, playing false, casts me always in the sticky heat of high summer, the sweat prickling along my back and thighs, as I lie stifled, unbreathing, but afraid to throw aside the make-believe protection of the quilt. Between my prison-bar fingers I can see the digital display floating in the darker patch above the bookcase which I know to be my Scooby Doo alarm clock. 2:23, 2:24, 2:25. If it reaches 2:30, he won't come, I plead. 2:26, 2:27. If I get ten out of ten for spellings on Friday, he won't come.

Even when I've heard, along the landing, the soft click of
their bedroom door, the rush and gurgle of the flushed toilet
which will be his alibi should she wake at his departure – the
same flimsy, mechanical gesture to be repeated on his return.
Even then . . . If it reaches 2:45, he won't come. My eyes sting
from staring at the luminous disembodied numbers, willing
each flicked change. 2:41, 2:42, 2:43.

And now every night, still, my brain pounds out the
endless, unclosed deal. I'll be good, I'll be good, I'll be good –
only please don't let him come.

From: Margaret Hayton
[margarethayton@yahoo.co.uk]
Sent: 15/8/05 20:51
To: Rebecca Prichard [becs444@btinternet.com]

Dear Becs,

Too bad about the puffing cavalier. And look out,
the Ians of Manchester!

I did some serious thinking over the weekend. I
had, in fact, put Helen's diary on one side while I was
staying with you. I admit it was under the futon, but I
had stopped reading it. But when I came home I
plucked up the courage to read on to the end, and it
was pretty harrowing stuff, as you can imagine. Poor
Cora had to mop me up a few times, while I was
getting through it. But one thing that is clear is how
much it helped Helen, when we were all coming round

to sit with her in the evenings. And it occurred to me that a lot of young people with mental health problems are probably very isolated, like Helen was. They might not always want to talk to their family, or the family might be too close to the problem. And off-loading on their friends might be too risky; they might not want to risk driving them away. You could be scared that your GP might try to section you if you said too much. There are the Samaritans, of course, but for that you have to feel able to talk. Somebody on the end of a telephone line can't put her arm round you, or play Scrabble with you, or sit with you while you fall asleep. So my idea is a voluntary befriending scheme for teenagers who are depressed and vulnerable. Giving them someone to be there and listen, someone who won't be scared off by their pain, because that's why they're there.

I really needed to ask someone if it was just a crazy notion or not, and I must admit that it was Richard I thought of first, but of course he's no longer here to ask, and anyway, what did he ever care about Helen or other people like her? So I phoned the ever-sensible Alison (from WITCH) and she says she thinks it sounds feasible, and Cora, somewhat to my surprise, is also really keen. I think perhaps Helen's funeral really affected her. She is going to see if she can get some seedcorn funding from the Charitable Donations Fund at her bank.

Somehow, having something practical to think about

seems to help. Anyway, I'd be really pleased to see you here any time for a return visit before the end of the holidays, I'm sure you know that without my saying. I'm quite safe, now that the thing with Richard is over (as I'm sure it is over, it *has* to be over, despite the gnawing ache of his absence) – even if in the meantime you work your way through I to Q in double-quick time.

Much love,

Margaret xx

Extract from Helen's diary

I keep thinking about Mum's bridge nights, back when I was nine or ten. Every Monday night it was. She used to change and put on powder and lipstick, and she never came back until after eleven. Did she know?

I used to beg her not to go out, crying and wheedling like a toddler. She would always stand there in the hall, smelling of scent, with her arms folded defensively over her chest, and demand, 'Why not?' It was a challenge thrown down, we both knew it. And every time I didn't answer, every time I just sobbed louder and shuffled my slippers without speaking, it underlined the illusory, comfortable untruth, the unvoiced, perfidious, safe certainty that there could be no reason for her not to go . . .

42 Gledhill Street
Ipswich

18 August 2005

Dearest Pete,

Oh dear, love, I'm ever so worried about Margaret! First, as you know, there was all that business in the papers, and then Helen's death and the funeral, and the next thing, she's split up with Richard over something he said in the *Town Crier*. It all just seemed like a lot of politics to me, but what really got to Margaret, I think, was that he was running a campaign with that horrible man, Helen's father, the one that abused her.

Then, next thing, Margaret gets hold of this diary that Helen kept, right since she was a little girl, writing down all the dreadful things that she went through. Margaret being Margaret, of course she insisted on reading it from cover to cover. Poring over the blessed thing in every spare moment, she was, in tears more often than not. I could see it tearing her up, and it was awful to watch, since obviously nothing I could say would make it any different. We have had a good idea, though (well, it was Margaret's idea), about setting up a support scheme for other youngsters like Helen, you know, with depression – arranging for people to go and sit with them and so on. I'm going to see if they might have any money for it at work.

Anyway, on top of all this, this afternoon at about six o'clock Margaret had a call from her mum, to say that her gran has had another stroke, poor thing. She's in hospital and it doesn't sound too good. Of course, Margaret packed a quick bag and went straight off to get the train – down Hampshire way, it is, where the old lady lives. She promised to phone me before bedtime and let me know how things were, but she hasn't yet. It will have taken her a while to get there, of course, and then she'll want to be with her gran, and the family. It's getting late for me to be up, what with work in the morning, but I don't want to go to bed and miss her call.

I'm sorry it's just a short note this time, Petey – but it has really helped me to write this all down.

With my best love, as always,

Cora xxxx

From: Margaret Hayton
[margarethayton@yahoo.co.uk]
Sent: 19/8/05 19:54
To: Rebecca Prichard [becs444@btinternet.com]

Dear Becs,

Sorry to bend your ear from the train yesterday like that, but I just had to talk to someone, and you did a great job of calming me down. You were quite right, I'd have been no earthly use to Gran or anybody else in the state I was in when I called!

I said I'd give you a progress report today, so here it is, from an otherwise eerily deserted internet café near the hospital in Winchester. Well, things don't look quite so bleak as they did when I arrived last night. She has at least regained consciousness now, and seems to have some hazy idea of where she is and who we are, though she's not able to speak at all, not for the moment at least, so it's hard to be sure exactly how much she is aware of. Her right arm and hand are completely useless, like they were at the beginning last time, but this time she doesn't seem able to move either of her legs – nothing below the waist at all yet – so of course she's incontinent, too. One good thing is they've disconnected her drip and said that she's OK to take food by mouth now. There was some macaroni cheese with peas tonight, which was do-able because it didn't need much chewing, and she can just about manage a fork with her left hand (you know she's a lefty like me). But the whole right-hand side of her face is frozen, and her coordination seems to be all haywire, so just finding her mouth took every ounce of her concentration. Then swallowing was another whole challenge – she seems to be having to relearn all the things which are normally more or less a reflex. An hour and five minutes it took her, but she finished the whole plate with a real sense of achievement. I wouldn't have stepped in and fed it to her for the world.

She looked so frail, Becs, lying propped partway up in that metal bed. Hospital always seems to diminish people, somehow (probably a combination of the disempowerment and the high ceilings). I couldn't help being reminded of Helen, that last time I saw her. Gran seemed about half the size she did when I saw her last, when I came down with Richard . . . but everything was different then. What I care about most, though, the thing that scares me so much I hardly dare write it, is whether she'll have lost any of her mental faculties. I'd happily watch her eat soup through a tube, wheel her around in a chair, anything – but I need my gran to come back to me as the person she is. What would I do without her?

It looks likely that Gran will be in hospital for quite some time, and it's not at all clear whether she'll be able to go home to The Hollies even when they are ready to discharge her. I'm going to stay at the house for the time being, so I can sit with her in the daytime – it's only a half-hour bus journey from East Markhurst into Winchester. Mum and Dad were both here last night – none of us really went to bed at all – but they had to get back today. Apparently it's the annual round-the-parishes sponsored bike ride, and St Mary's is hosting the grand finish this year, and Dad has to award medals to those that make it all the way round. As Mum points out, vicars – much less vicars' wives – don't get those lovely long holidays that we teachers do!

Will phone or e-mail tomorrow with further update.

Love and hugs,

Margaret xxx

From: Rebecca Prichard [becs444@btinternet.com]
Sent: 19/8/05 20:19
To: Margaret Hayton [margarethayton@yahoo.co.uk]

Thanks so much for letting me know how it's going.
I've been worrying about you all day. Are you sure you
are going to be OK in your gran's house all by
yourself down there with no one about? It might go on
for a while, if what you say is right. Though if she
needs to find a place in a nursing home when she
comes out, I suppose you'll need to be there to sort
that out for her. (I'm usually careful not to say
anything, but quite honestly, it sounds like your
parents are pretty useless.) I would come down and
keep you company if I could, chuck, but I'm at Mum
and Dad's at the moment. Mum's got the flu, and
whatever they might say, neither of them is up to
looking after the other just now.
   Love, and an even bigger hug than usual,
   Becs xx

From: Rebecca Prichard [becs444@btinternet.com]
Sent: 19/8/05 20:50
To: Richard Slater [rpslater@hc.parliament.uk]

Dear Mr Slater,
   You don't know me, but I am a friend of Margaret
Hayton. I thought you would wish to know that

Margaret's grandmother has had another stroke.
Margaret is down there with her now. Whatever you've
done, I think you need to get your arse down there
PDQ. Go and fix things. Margaret needs you.
   Yours sincerely,
   Rebecca Prichard.

From: Margaret Hayton
[margarethayton@yahoo.co.uk]
Sent: 20/8/05 18:11
To: Rebecca Prichard [becs444@btinternet.com]

Dear Becs,

   You will think I am overtired and suffering delusions,
this is all so weird, but you are going to just have to
take my word for it all, because it's true.

   Gran seemed a little better today. She is getting
some feeling back in her left leg, and she is starting
to speak a little, though it is still very slurry and
costs her an enormous amount of energy. Much of
what she has been saying is indistinct, so it's hard
to be absolutely certain yet about what she's
understanding and what she isn't. But the way she
smiled at me when I came in this morning, with the
functioning half of her face and both her eyes, made
me feel convinced that the old gran is still in there
and fighting her way back. I stayed all morning,
watched her defeat a plate of scrambled eggs

through sheer willpower, and then headed back to
The Hollies because the nurse said Gran could do
with some more nightclothes. (The incontinence is
still taking its toll.) By the time I arrived back on the
ward it was after four o'clock. I came in and saw
Gran in a full sitting position, with extra pillows
behind her, bending over something. I thought at
first it was one of the little aluminium trays that they
bring the meals on, but when I got close I could see
that it was in fact, of all things, a laptop! Gran saw
me and nodded an acknowledging smile, but didn't
try to say anything. I came round beside her and
looked at the screen – and she was playing chess!
Some kind of computer chess game. Well, Gran
used to play quite a bit of chess with Grandad
before he died (she used to oblige him endlessly,
though he always beat her), but I'm pretty certain
she has never touched a computer in her life, let
alone played a computer game! But she could work
the keys quite steadily with her left forefinger, and
she seemed to be getting along fine. I was so
overwhelmed, Becs. Gran, not only sitting up, but
apparently totally compos mentis, sufficiently so to
be picking up keyboard skills and playing chess
against a computer! I was so happy I could have
cried. I assumed that one of the nurses, or maybe
another patient's visitor, had lent her it – though as
to how such an unlikely thing would have come
about, I was somewhat at a loss.

Then Gran started trying to say something, so I bent close to her, and with a great effort she managed to croak a couple of words. I was frustrated at first that I couldn't make out her meaning – worse, I feared that she might not have regained all of her marbles after all – because what it sounded like, more than anything, was 'Richard' and 'here'. But then suddenly it hit me, with a lurch of recognition – it was his laptop! His old one, the one he used to use all the time before he got his state-of-the-art new one from Culture, Media and Sport, and still takes when he's going anywhere by train, and uses when he's in Ipswich. I could tell by the dent on the lid. I remember he mentioned once that it was sustained playing an ill-advised smash during an improvised game of desktop table tennis with the MP he used to share an office with, using laptops and an old squash ball.

How could Richard possibly have been here? It just didn't make any sense. But how could Gran have got his laptop, otherwise? He certainly didn't leave it behind after we were down here in June, because I remember him having it on the day of Helen's funeral. I wanted to quiz Gran about it, but of course that was impossible; she could barely get out a few single, strangled words. All I could do was to sit in bewilderment, and take her hand – the left one, the one with the feeling in it – and give it a squeeze. And to relish the joy of feeling her returning my pressure, faintly but perceptibly.

A while later, still mulling over her next chess
move, Gran nodded off, so I made her as
comfortable as I could against the pillows and then
gently slid the laptop from out of her slackening
grasp in order to get it out of her way. I thought I'd
close it down, so I exited the chess game, but
underneath that there was another window which
also needed closing. It was Richard's hard disc,
containing the chess-game icon, and also all his
other stored files displayed. I really didn't look on
purpose, Becs, honestly, I just couldn't help it – but
one of the filenames caught my eye. 'Adamson', it
was called. It had to be something about Helen and
her family! Well, I know that what I did next is utterly
unforgivable and not a thing I would ever remotely
contemplate doing normally, but all the fury and the
hurt suddenly came surging back up, hardening into
a tight ball in my throat like something gristly you
can't swallow. And in my defence I might plead being
still shell-shocked following the discovery of Richard's
laptop and Gran's unexpected penchant for electronic
games. The whole afternoon was beginning to take
on a dream-like quality, in any case. And I am only
human. So I opened the file.

It consisted of just one short letter. I suppose he
must have written it in Ipswich, since it was on his old
laptop. I am still struggling to take in the implications,
so I am copying it to you so you can read it for
yourself. (OK, so when I say I opened the file, it may

also have found its way on to my memory stick. But I
really did need more time to digest it.)

>   House of Commons
>   London
>   SW1A 0AA
>
>   13 July 2005
> Dear Mr Adamson,
>   Thank you for your letter of 10 July. I am sorry,
> but I am not prepared to meet you, or to speak
> to you on the telephone about the circumstances
> of your daughter's death. I believe you know why.
>   Yours sincerely,
>   Richard Slater, MP.

     I just don't get it. The *Town Crier* said that Richard
was backing Helen's father's calls for an inquiry – they
were actually quoted in the paper together, saying the
same things. Campaigning together – or that's how it
sounded, anyway. But now it looks like Richard never
spoke to the man after all! I don't understand – what
does it all mean?

     I'm at the same café again – still just as empty. The
guy at the counter, who has a most unfortunate wispy
beard which looks like the result of a shaving blind
spot, welcomed me like a long-lost friend when I came
in. At least his americano has a passing acquaintance

with the coffee bean – the muck in the machine at the
hospital tastes of nothing at all. Then I'm going to get
off home to East Markhurst. But I'll be back in the
morning, and see if any of it makes any more sense
then.

Love,

Margaret xx

From: Rebecca Prichard [becs444@btinternet.com]
Sent: 20/8/05 18:21
To: Margaret Hayton [margarethayton@yahoo.co.uk]

What it means, I suspect (and you of all people ought
to know this by now, Margaret my dear), is that you
can't always believe everything you read in the
newspapers.

Hugs,

Becs xxx

From: Richard Slater
[richard.slater@btopenworld.com]
Sent: 20/8/05 21:26
To: Michael Carragan [mikecarragan@yahoo.com]

Hi Michael,

The reason that you and I are not at this moment
sitting outside the Black Boar on Carteret Street

together, contemplatively skimming the froth from the top of our second pint, is that I am currently at an internet booth in the lobby of a small hotel on the outskirts of Winchester. Sorry I didn't ring you as promised, but it has been quite a day.

It began when I switched on my computer in the office this morning and opened up my e-mail, to find a message from somebody called Rebecca. Whom, through the matutinal haze which always clouds my brain while the hour is yet in single figures, I only later identified with Margaret's much-spoken-of friend Becs. (For some reason it had never occurred to me that Becs was short for anything. I'd always vaguely pictured it as Becks, like the lager.) What she had to impart was bad news – Margaret's gran has had a second stroke and is in hospital. But her e-mail also suggested to me in no uncertain terms that I ought to be at Margaret's side.

Now, as you know, Mike, I am not normally given to flights of unbridled optimism, but it did occur to me that this Becs must be to some extent at least in Margaret's confidence. It was apparent that this SOS call was made on compassionate grounds, and almost certainly without Margaret's knowledge or approval. But would Becs have felt that my presence was required if she didn't have some cause, however insubstantial or misguided, to believe that Margaret might welcome my appearance at the bedside? It was a possibility, and that was enough for me.

First, however, there was the obstacle of discovering the grandmother's whereabouts. The relative in question is Margaret's maternal antecedent, so not herself a Hayton, and it took several hours, and flagrant misuse of my House of Commons credentials, to find amongst all the hospital wards in Hampshire someone known to me only as Gran.

I must admit to feeling a little self-conscious when I finally located the correct elderly relative, around mid-afternoon. I mean, I am well aware that the mercy dash to the sickbed is something of a mawkish cliché, the staple stuff of romantic fiction (though, admittedly, I believe that by tradition it should be the heroine herself lying pale and interesting in the bed, and not her 81-year-old grandmother). On the threshold of the ward, I all of a sudden lacked the courage to go in, and decided to fortify myself first with a cup of coffee from the machine in the corridor outside. However, the insipid brew, deposited in the white polystyrene foam cup in a half-hearted dribble followed by a damply flaccid hiss, was a transparent light tan in colour, incongruously pétillant, and clearly contained insufficient caffeine to pep up a drowsy woodlouse. I experimented with sugar, breaking out the tea-stained spoon from the surface crust in the hospital-issue metal sugar bowl, and ladling in a heaped measure, but already the temperature of the watery liquid had fallen too far to have any hope of dissolving the forged-together granules. There was nothing left for it but to quell both my embarrassment and my desperate hope, and to go in.

Both emotions proved unnecessary. Margaret wasn't there. Gran seemed to recognise me, though – and, even more encouragingly, did not immediately summon hospital security to seek my summary removal. Indeed, she actually seemed quite pleased to see me, and took hold of my hand, even though her facial muscles couldn't be induced to form much of a smile. I suddenly realised with a nasty stab of guilt that I had hardly thought about Gran at all, all day, so consumed had I been with the prospect of seeing Margaret, and what I should say to her, and how she might react. But to see her there in the bed was a real shock. She's such a positive, feisty person – we had great fun that weekend when Margaret and I went to hide out with her (in spite of the reason we were there), so witnessing her suddenly reduced in that way gave me a real jolt. She couldn't really speak, so I sat and chatted for a bit, but, well, you know, men and hospital bedsides . . . And it isn't easy to keep your end up for too long in a completely one-sided conversation, especially when you daren't mention the one thing you have in common (Margaret). So quite soon I lapsed into silence.

Looking idly around, my eye lighted upon a white polystyrene cup on the bedside table, a twin to the still-full one in my hand. It contained less than an inch of cold, brownish liquid. Somebody (it could surely only be Margaret – sweet, indomitable Margaret!) had made valiant efforts to drink the undrinkable. The image of her sipping the abominable beverage without wincing, determined to appear cheerful and uncomplaining in front of Gran, I found inexplicably moving, and I had to pull my hand back from caressing the extruded polystyrene foam.

Anyhow, Gran still seemed to be quite glad to have me there, even unspeaking, so after a bit I asked if she minded me opening up my laptop, and I picked up a game of computer chess where I'd left off in the train. I had just got out of check, but had lost both rooks and a bishop and was still in a tricky corner. I was sitting in a chair beside her head, and presently I noticed that she was watching me, so I showed her how I was doing, and when I was check-mated five minutes later I set up a new game, put it on her lap, and explained to her how to work it . . . and she was soon well away. Not a highly strategic player, I'd say, but certainly a competent one.

Time wore on, and still no sign of Margaret, but the ward sister told me that she's staying at her gran's house and comes every day. So I decided to cut my losses for today, get a hotel room, and try my luck again tomorrow. I left the computer with Gran, as she was just beginning to mount what looked like a pretty solid defensive rearguard action in the face of a two-pronged onslaught by the computer's queen and bishop.

I wonder if Margaret plays. And if so, whether I'll
ever get the chance to take her on.
　Richard.

42 Gledhill Street

Ipswich

23 August 2005

Dear WITCH committee members,

　I'm writing to you with some suggestions for plants that
we might get for the patch of garden we are creating at
Witch House in memory of Helen. As you know, we
decided against a tree, as the space is very limited, and
Margaret tells me that you would like me to suggest some
smaller things we might put in instead. I have been looking
in my gardening books and on the internet, and have had
quite a few ideas, which I thought I'd put down on paper
for you.

　For a start, I do think some herbs would be a good
plan, because it's nice to have plants that are useful, as well
as looking and smelling good. As Persephone says, healing
herbs to remember someone in sore need of healing. A
couple of suitable ones might be self-heal and comfrey,
both of which are used in balms for the binding of
wounds. I'd also love to get hold of some elecampane, a
less common medicinal herb. Its proper name is *Inula
helenium*, so it seems rather appropriate. Mrs Spreight, our
herbalism teacher, says it is called after Helen of Troy. The

Chinese used to plant it outside their windows because of the sound the leaves make when it rains, like tears, but the Romans made candied sweets out of the roots and reckoned that it causes mirth, and I'm sure you'd like to remember Helen with a smile. It's also meant to be good for eczema.

Then I thought we should have some ordinary flowers, too, to make a bit of colour. The ones I've always known as heleniums are very cheerful – they have orangey daisy heads, and they come out in the mid to late summer, so you would always have a bright splash in the garden each year around the time of Helen's death. And what about some heartsease? They are sweet little things, like three-coloured violets, and make excellent ground cover. And it's such a perfect name, isn't it? It's the thing we all hope Helen has found at last.

I've already got the bed dug over, with the kind help of Lauren and Rrezja, so as soon as you decide what you would like, I can go ahead. All the plants I've mentioned, I've checked, and I can get hold of locally. As Margaret is away at the moment, down in Hampshire with her gran, I will drop this into the Witch House office, so you can see what you think.

With best wishes,
Cora.

From: Margaret Hayton
[margarethayton@yahoo.co.uk]
Sent: 26/8/05 18:31
To: Rebecca Prichard [becs444@btinternet.com]

Dear Becs,

Well, I'm back in the internet café but this time
Richard is here, too, doubling the clientele – and
holding my hand across the table so I have to type
one-handed. I also think it might be my last visit
here – leaving poor straggle-beard with no reason
to remain in business at all. Because Gran is
decidedly improved, so much so that they are
discharging her from hospital tomorrow. Not home
to The Hollies, it's still too soon for that, but we've
arranged a room in a residential care home a
couple of miles from East Markhurst, and on the
bus route. She can form her words with less
difficulty now, and the speech therapist (a very nice
woman) is going to be able to carry on seeing her
in the new place. She's working with some other
recuperating patients there, and visits every
Tuesday and Friday. The function in Gran's right
side is returning gradually, though there is still a
long way to go before she'll be walking or starting
to look after herself again.

But what you'll be wanting to know about is Richard,
of course. Well, I agonised half the night on Saturday,
after I'd e-mailed you and gone back to Gran's. About

whether he might come back, and what I should say to him if he did. Going back and forth over it all in my head. What I kept coming back to was a sick feeling of shame, that I had believed him capable of campaigning for that rat Adamson. How to confess what I'd thought, and how I'd found out that it wasn't true. But in the end none of it ended up mattering. He just walked into the ward, with flowers for Gran and a book entitled *Thinking Ahead in Chess*, and suddenly it was so easy, it didn't seem necessary to say anything at all.

Later on, when we were back at The Hollies, we did talk, and once we'd started we couldn't stop, until finally the talking turned into kissing . . . But then I was encountering reticence again, like before, and we were right back where we left off after Helen's funeral. Sleeping together in Gran's spare bed, but with his T-shirt and boxers still resolutely in place, and only an incorruptible arm curled round me, his hand carefully resting somewhere in the safe zone between navel and ribs. This time it's because I'm so anxious about Gran, apparently, that I am regarded as untouchable.

And it was much the same the next night, before he had to go back to London on Tuesday. He just came down again this afternoon, bringing the car this time, to help get Gran moved tomorrow. Then he's said he'll take me home to Ipswich, after we've settled her in. In fact 'to Cora's' is what he said, and I fear he might actually mean it. Not that I won't be very glad to see Cora, but . . . well, you know.

Hope your mum is over her flu. We could probably both do with a break from being Florence Nightingale.
Love,
Margaret xx

From: Margaret Hayton [margarethayton@yahoo.co.uk]
Sent: 29/8/05 19:09
To: Richard Slater [richard.slater@btopenworld.com]

Dear Richard,

Thank you so much for all you've done for Gran this last week or so. She really likes you – I don't think people normally tease elderly stroke patients nearly enough! – and I really don't know how I would have coped without you. Thank you for a lovely bank holiday weekend, too. This afternoon was so beautiful, walking along the foreshore down at Pin Mill, before you had to leave and go back to London. When I took my trainers off just now they were still half full of sand from walking barefoot. You expect mud along an estuary somehow, not that fine powdery sand, and I never thought we'd find shells (the pockets of Gran's rosebud dress are still jangling). I thought you were joking about that, until you said about the east coast oyster – and then I felt silly, because of course we'd been sitting outside the Butt and Oyster drinking our beer and looking at the boats.

Every time you kissed me this weekend it felt great, it felt blissful, but I wanted more. I wanted *you*. There, I've said it now, after not quite being brave enough to say it all weekend when I was actually with you.

I'm sure if I was your age we'd have been in bed together that first time I came to London. But I'm not a child, Richard. I am twenty-four. I bet you knew your own mind well enough when you were twenty-four. That month thinking that you had gone from my life has only shown me what I want even more clearly. I know that you think that I am out of kilter somehow, that you mustn't let me do anything while my feet are less than firmly on the ground which I might regret later. And it is true, I do seem to be in a state of dizzying disequilibrium. I've felt off balance nearly every time I've been with you. But it has had nothing to do with Nas, or with Helen's death, or worrying about Gran. It's because I love you.

Margaret xx

From: Richard Slater [richard.slater@btopenworld.com]
Sent: 29/8/05 20:42
To: Margaret Hayton [margarethayton@yahoo.co.uk]

M – Just got in and read your message. Don't move. I'm coming straight back.

R.

NEWTON'S GARAGE

SPECIALISTS IN RENAULT AND PEUGEOT

188, Station Road, Ipswich IP1 6DZ

30 August 2005

Dear Mr Slater,

I have pleasure in enclosing our invoice for the replacement of the speedometer on your Renault Mégane, carried out today to your instructions.

We are slightly puzzled as to why this second speedometer should have malfunctioned so soon after being fitted by ourselves on 14 July 2005. If you have any further problems with the unit, please let us know immediately, and we will take it up with the manufacturer.

With respectful thanks for your continuing esteemed custom,

Yours sincerely,

Arthur Newton (Manager).

WITCH

Women of Ipswich Together Combating Homelessness

Extract from minutes of meeting at Pat and Pat's house, 1 September 2005, 8 p.m.

News of residents

It was noted that Rrezja needs to put in train her application for permanent leave to remain. Margaret agreed to talk to Richard Slater about possible assistance with this.

Rosemary has heard that she can expect to be admitted to hospital for her hip replacement towards the end of October, which is great news. Persephone is starting Rosemary upon a course of moxabustion, which will help prepare her body to cope with the effects of the general anaesthetic. In future they are going to have the sessions at Persephone's house, as the Witch House fire-detection and sprinkler system seems to be rather sensitive to the burning moxa.

Alison has had to have a stiff word with Carole. The laboratory are very strict about not allowing apparatus to be taken off the premises, even to be brought home overnight for an extra polish.

Any other business

Margaret outlined her idea for a befriending scheme for young people in the community with psychiatric illnesses, particularly depression. The Volunteer Centre would probably provide the person-power, and the Young People's Psychiatric Unit the referrals of those needing support. What would be needed would be funding to cover the task of matching befriender to befriended, as well as the initial training and ongoing supervision of the volunteers, the maintaining of records, etc. It was agreed that WITCH's name should be used to lend weight to any grant applications, although if funding is secured the scheme would be fully independent, and would accept referrals of men as well as women. (Pat W. pointed out, however, that statistically speaking most of the likely users would probably be young women, nevertheless.)

From: Rebecca Prichard [becs444@btinternet.com]
Sent: 7/9/05 19:15
To: Margaret Hayton [margarethayton@yahoo.co.uk]

So Margaret, hi. A new term, a new class. In my case just six of the little darlings on Monday, followed by three further cohorts of six, to start at half-weekly intervals. Even six seems like a classroomful at this stage, when just getting them all to sit cross-legged on the Quiet Room carpet at once and facing in the same direction can be a whole morning's undertaking. I am reminded of a cardboard boxful of puppies my friend Sasha's Staffordshire bull terrier had when we were nine. There is a similar level of squirming and wrestling, and only marginally less untimely urination.

The opening of the school year has, of course, also brought back Declan, now adorning the courtyard outside the Year 1 classrooms at 3 p.m., with a summer's deeper bronzing in his face, and over his shoulder a brand new silver scooter for Zoe's journey home. The way I see it is, he's not a parent any more. Or rather, not a parent of anyone in my class. So I asked him what he and Zoe have planned for the new term, and it turned out not much, except cooking me lunch on Saturday. Zoe is going to help, so experience suggests that the menu will include grated cheese, which is her speciality. It goes right against the alphabetical grain, of course, but this time I find I'm struggling to care.

Love and hugs,

Becs xx

From: Margaret Hayton [margarethayton@yahoo.co.uk]
Sent: 7/9/05 21:05
To: Rebecca Prichard [becs444@btinternet.com]

Dear Becs,

You mean, you might go back to square D? But can you really step twice in the same lexicographical river?

We started on Monday, same as you, and my class seem lively and full of beans. I have no fewer than four Emilys, beating even Mrs Martin's personal best. I do so love the feeling of new beginnings that you get when the school year opens. All that fresh hope and ambition, all those newly sharpened pencils and brand new exercise books as yet unblotted: everything in front of you, everything possible. I don't know about you, but it always makes me think of that paragon of a teacher, Miss Stacy, who reminded Anne Shirley of the exciting truth that 'tomorrow is always fresh with no mistakes in it'.

Meanwhile, from what I can make out, the Westminster summer recess appears to go on until shortly before Christmas. Of course, with his ministerial position, Richard is supposed to be hard at work on behalf of the nation whether Parliament is in session or not, but when I ask him whether he ought not to be at the department rather more often, he gets that hunted look which I have witnessed in colleagues' eyes (no doubt mirroring my own) when the head mentions the reworking of next year's lesson plans. In fact, I have noticed that he generally tries to distract me, often by the use of underhand means, such as the unbuttoning of his shirt, or mine, or both.

But if he insists on abandoning his desk occasionally in order to spend time here with me, then I intend to find things to keep him busy over the next few weeks, never fear. There is Rrezja's leave to remain to be obtained, with which she might well need the assistance of her constituency MP. Richard isn't the Home Secretary (yet!), and Rrezja isn't my nanny, so a little spot of fast-tracking shouldn't cost him his job. (I've already nearly done that once, so I'm being extra careful.) Nothing is happening yet about those raised gratings in bike lanes. And I have been reading a lot recently about the need to improve Africa's access to the markets of the developed world. It's not just a case of dismantling trade barriers and reducing tariffs, we also have to eliminate trade-distorting support to western commodities, which make it impossible for poorer countries to compete. I may find that I need to lobby my parliamentary representative about that too. Mind you, since European beet sugar is one of the subsidised commodities in question, I may have to tread softly. I think I'll get him focused on cotton to start off with – there's not a lot of that growing along the banks of the river Orwell.

I'm going to see Gran on Saturday, just for the day. Richard has gone away for a few days – to Minsk, of all places, on some sort of cultural exchange or link-forging visit or something, although he has been very vague about the details. Gran has invited me to go again at half term, and stay with her for a few days (they have guest rooms in the care home, if she's still not back home by then). I think I'll ask her if Richard can come too that time. I know he'd enjoy that. I expect I'll bite the bullet and take him to Mum and Dad's some time this term, too. He's already dutifully spoken to them both on the phone. He won an immediate place in Dad's heart by informing him, in the words of John Thornton, that he very much wanted 'to see the place where Margaret grew to what she is'. I was touched, too, because Richard had never even mentioned that he knew the book, when I told him where my name came from. I'd very much like to meet Richard's mother, too, but I rather gather it's

been a long time . . . I don't want to push my luck all
at once right at the beginning.

   With love, and best wishes to your parents,

   Margaret xxx

42 Gledhill Street

Ipswich

8 September 2005

Dear Richard,

   I know there is no point in posting this to Minsk.
Goodness knows what the Belarusian postal service is like,
and you have only gone for five days – you would certainly
be back again before it arrived. So I am sending it to
Charterhouse Square. I can imagine you reading it when
you arrive back at the flat on Sunday, before you head
home to Ipswich. I dare say you will think me crazy – I'll
be seeing you just a few hours after that. And yes, there is
the telephone, and e-mail (even in Minsk). I'm sure we'll
be doing that as well, but I wanted to write you a letter. A
proper old-fashioned love letter. To tell you how hard it
was seeing you off at the station this morning, having to
break our embrace when the London train pulled in,
having to relinquish your lips. And how long five days is
going to seem – and five nights without being able to reach
out and touch you whenever I wake up, or even stir in my
sleep.

   Don't you think it would be sad if nobody ever wrote

each other love letters any more? I was just sitting here, thinking about all those letters which were written from the trenches to wives and sweethearts. About loyal, hare-shotten Prue Sarn, pouring into the letters she wrote to Jancis for Gideon all her tenderness for Kester Woodseaves, the weaver. And about Héloïse writing to her Abelard, and dear Captain Wentworth dropping his pen in his flurry to scribble to Anne Elliot the words of agony and hope that he dared not voice. I would love it if you would write to me next time we are apart, Richard. It is partly about having the letter to go over again (like Gran always says, you can't re-read a phone call). But it isn't just that, because you can save an e-mail and open it up again whenever you want, or even print it out and keep it. It's also the idea of having the paper that you touched, that you looked at while you thought of the words – and then the writing itself, telling me how you were feeling by whether the words are flowing along smoothly, or scrawled in a great rush, or uneven and halting.

I've e-mailed it to you once, and I've whispered it against your chest, but you've never seen it in my hand-writing before: I love you.

Margaret x

From: Margaret Hayton [margarethayton@yahoo.co.uk]
Sent: 11/9/05 23:55
To: Rebecca Prichard [becs444@btinternet.com]

Dear Becs,

What's new? Still alphabetically back-sliding into another dalliance with Declan?

Scenes of carnage here on Saturday morning. Snuffy has recently developed an inconvenient habit, never previously displayed, of intercepting the post. A set of model dinosaurs arrived, which I had ordered for use in some work on prehistory later in the term, and Snuffy was through the parcel tape and bubble wrap before Cora heard the joyful snarling and interrupted her. I think she smelt the seductive new plastic aroma, and mistook the contents of the package for new chew toys. By the time I came upon the scene Stegosaurus and Velociraptor had been buried under the forsythia, Pteranodon was in a condition making it well-nigh impossible that it would ever have heralded the evolution of birdkind by leaving the earth in flight, while Triceratops had suffered considerable ravages, and will now have to be passed off as its little known and lopsided cousin, Uniceratops (which probably died out long before the onset of cataclysmic climate change, due to its peculiar vulnerability to any predator approaching from the right). Even the mighty Tyrannosaurus Rex is a shadow of its former self, with its neck now bent into a submissive position somewhere around its knees, its head hanging low in slack-jawed servitude.

Richard arrived back from Minsk this evening. His

suitcase was crammed with mysterious objects
wrapped in newspaper, including a thickset cast-iron
ballerina with a body builder's muscles under her
tights, and what looked like a ceramic sugar-beet, very
similar to the one he used to have on his desk at
work. It's funny, though, he seemed a little ashamed
of it all, and he says he's going to take the lot to the
Oxfam shop (but in London, not the Ipswich one). I
went over to his flat and cooked him my very best
River Café *ribollita*. I even peeled the outside skin off
the broad beans, you know, the papery bit – an
occupation which I would normally rank, as a
constructive use of time, somewhere alongside picking
oakum or darning laddered tights. Oh, Becs, I know
it's quite shockingly drippy of me, but it is wonderful to
have him back!
  Love,
  Margaret xx

From: Rebecca Prichard [becs444@btinternet.com]
Sent: 12/9/05 08:05
To: Margaret Hayton [margarethayton@yahoo.co.uk]

You should be grateful that he has apparently been
converted to your own herbivorous persuasion.
(T Rex, that is, not Richard.)
  Hugs,
  Becs xxx

42 Gledhill Street

Ipswich

14 September 2005

Dear Gran,

The enclosed parcel is just a few more books for you to
borrow, plus another pot of Cora's herbal ointment for your
ankle. She says that even if the stroke has taken some of
the feeling away, you still need to keep on treating the
sprain. I told her that the inflammation was pretty much
gone by now, but she said to tell you that her stuff also
works for any general rheumatic pain, and even headaches,
if you rub it on your temples. If you are prepared to put
the stuff that near to your eyes, you are a braver woman
than I am, Gran!

How have you been, anyway, since I saw you on
Saturday? You seemed so much brighter, and it was great to
see you getting to the bathroom now, on the frame. I'm
determined we'll have you back home in The Hollies before
I come at half term.

Things have been busy at the hostel this week, with the
two new residents I told you about. Emily and I have been
helping Rosemary to sort out her disability benefit – we
both went on a course about it in the spring, which
helped. And Rrezja, the Kosovo Albanian girl from
London, has made her formal application for leave to
remain in Britain. My lawyer friend, Caroline, came up on
Monday evening to help with it. Richard and I took Caro
for a drink afterwards to say thank you, before she caught

the last train back to London. Rrezja is already as thick as
thieves with Lauren. Pat T. and Emily have had to read
them the Riot Act a couple of times about boyfriends
hanging about outside, but Della is brilliant at going out
and getting rid of any rowdy or unwanted ones.

Oh, and about Richard and me . . . You were too polite
to enquire on Saturday, and I was too embarrassed to say
anything. But to quote Lizzy Bennet back to your Aunt
Gardiner, you may now suppose as much as you choose.
Give a loose to your fancy – unless you believe me actually
married, you cannot greatly err.

Lots of love,
Margaret xx

Flat 6
14 Charterhouse Square
London EC1 9BL

20 September 2005

Dear Margaret,
You are right, of course, about love letters. Not only am I
a bloke, but a middle-class white bloke from the southern
half of England into the bargain, and as such there are
things that if we live to be an old married couple of eighty I
could never say to you face to face. (Though of course you
would only be sixty-three, and still full of queenly beauty.)
So I shall write them down instead, and you can read them
tomorrow at Cora's (if the first class post can be relied
upon), and you'll have to laugh off, as best you can over the

breakfast table, the possessiveness of a madman who writes to you when he's just sleeping back in London for two nights in an attempt to get some much-neglected work done.

Such as how much I miss the taste of your mouth, which eleven weeks ago had never touched mine, and which only five weeks ago I thought I might never kiss, or see, again. That the shifting colour of your eyes, so difficult to describe or discern, has always enthralled me, and does so all the more now, when gazed at from too close for focus. How, when I first slipped open the buttons of your rosebud dress, my fingertips could not believe the impossible pale softness of your skin. And that you were – you are – literally the most beautiful thing I have ever seen. How the delicate fragility of the secret places of your body is all of a piece with you, with who you are, your tender-heartedness, your precious untainted zeal. And how when we are lying together, with your body gloving mine, the little sounds you make, of pleasure and need, are not only the most erotic, but also the most deeply moving thing I have ever experienced, concussing me with an overwhelming heady sweetness I did not know existed.

And above all how much I love you, my Margaret.

Richard x

From: Richard Slater
[richard.slater@btopenworld.com]
Sent: 20/9/05 22:48
To: Michael Carragan [mikecarragan@yahoo.com]

Michael, hi, and terribly sorry for the long air silence, not to mention the unforgivable failure to join you on the crowded pavement outside the Grapevine for a few long cool ones to toast the lingering autumn haze of the tail end of the parliamentary recess.

But life is sweet. Last Thursday I was called into the Inner Sanctum, shaking with trepidation as to what delphic pronouncement would be uttered by The Oracle. Against all the odds, the Rottweiler told me (in a short breather between phone calls) that I 'feature in his plans' – words which were dulcet music to my ears. Upon hearing them, I would willingly have offered to have his babies. Though (probably wisely) I did not.

That apart, events seem to have conspired, somehow, to keep me away from London more than is good for me, visible-presence-in-the-office-wise. What events would these be, you ask? Well, the return leg of the Ipswich-Minsk sugar factory twinning for one thing. I managed to wangle a departmental jaunt beneath which to cloak it. A visit to mark the official merger of the State Ballet of Belarus with its long-standing rival, the Belarus State Ballet. The history and repertoire of neither illustrious corps (nor indeed of any other ballet company) exactly forms a central part of my mental furniture. In fact, I'm not at all sure I could spot a *pas de chat* if it waltzed in through the cat flap. Hence, although the impediment of translation may have masked my ineptitude to some extent from our hosts, the trip provided limitless opportunities for me to look inadequate in front of my staff.

And for another thing – well, to be honest, Mike, Margaret. Putting in the shade even the splendours of the rolling beetfields of Belarus, and reducing me (even more in the fruition than in the heated imagination) to a state of love-crazed incapacity. And no, not *that* kind of incapacity, in case you were wondering; in fact in that arena I seem to have rediscovered hidden reserves of youthful stamina. Frankly, it has proved quite tough to tear myself away from her. So, all in all, when I have been here in London I have had my head buried eyebrow deep in CM&S briefings, like a guilt-ridden student behind schedule with his exam revisions – in the vain hope of sounding as though I know what I'm talking about when my staff occasionally allow me to open my mouth in public. I actually don't care, though. Let them think what they wish – nothing can touch me. I feature in Tim's plans – and seemingly, for the moment, in Margaret's too. I stand impervious to their scorn.

Does the Home Office keep your shoulder to the creaking wagon right through the recess, or are you taking the chance to get away and spend some time in West Brom before the madhouse reopens? We must converge soon for that drink. Maybe I'll bring Margaret, so that you can join me in paeans of praise to her beauty.

Richard.

PS. Margaret, in her unflagging campaign to convince me that the small stuff matters as much as the big, today played what she clearly regards as her trump card, in response to some throwaway remark of mine about dog poo. Jack Caulfield (you know, the blind kid in her class) turns out to be living in his own personal darkness because of toxocariasis, following exposure to roundworm eggs in dog faeces. It's a chance in a million! Well, two cases per million per year, to be precise. I'm still sure that she's wrong, but I just couldn't argue in the face of odds like that.

Appartamento 7
Via San Giuliano 84
20146 Milano
Italia

3 October 2005

Dear Margaret and every one,

I am very sorry that I am not writing to you before, to tell you where I go. It is being very long time, I know. Gjergj is phoning me when I am in Ipswich, to say he is OK and he is escaping in Italia. I am not wanting to tell you then, because I am frightened to tell anyone that he is speaking to me. I get out to Italia too, so now we are being safe here together.

In Italia we both are being decided as refugees, so we

can stay here, and never going back. Gjergj is already having his work permission. He is doing a job building a factory. There are three other Albanian boys building it, with Italian boys also. Gjergj is asking me to marry him. In Italia we are having both Muslim and Christian wedding. In Milano they have some mosques, and we are also finding an Albanian Orthodox priest, the friend of one of the builder boys.

I am wanting to say thank you again for every thing you are doing for me in England. Gjergj and me are just getting a flat, the address is writing on this letter. So if Margaret or Lauren or any one wants to come and visiting us, we are being very happy to be seeing our good friends.

Nasreen xx

From: Rebecca Prichard [becs444@btinternet.com]
Sent: 11/10/05 19:15
To: Margaret Hayton [margarethayton@yahoo.co.uk]

Hi, Margaret,
  I've found out something about Declan.
  It was Zoe who let it slip, actually, because last year I noticed she kept transposing the letters of her name, and I was keeping an eye out (thinking about possible dyslexia, you know), but it was the only word she ever did it with. And it was striking, because usually of course their own name is very strongly

imprinted from early on. Well, yesterday she had drawn an alarmingly maculose pink-and-purple self-portrait (I'll spare you the trouble, hon: 'maculose' is a 7.5). She came up to show me it in the playground at lunchtime, and her name, on the bottom, was misspelt again. I happened to say, 'Your name's not Zeo, is it?' and she laughed and said, 'No, that's my daddy!' It's his middle name. It seems his parents just liked it – and in some respects were therefore unlucky, since their choice predated both the Power Rangers' crystal and the hangover prevention pills. Zoe's subsequent naming was a rather sweetly anagrammatic gesture. So you see, it seems he may just be my Zorba after all!

Of course it does mean that at family gatherings – Christmas and Easter – I'll always risk running into a brother I've snogged in a lift. But maybe the minions of Mephistopheles aren't that big on the major Christian festivals anyway.

Big hugs,

Becs xx

From: Ellen Reed [gran-reed@ntlworld.com]
Sent: 26/10/05 19:24
To: Margaret Hayton [margarethayton@yahoo.co.uk]

Dear Margaret,

This seems like the most appropriate way to say

thank you properly to you both for the wonderful gift of the portable computer. (What is it you call it, dear, a laptop, isn't it? I think I heard Richard referring to it as his notebook, too, though to me that's something with spiral binding that you keep by the phone or write your shopping list in.) I know you said that it is only Richard's old one, and that he doesn't use it very often, but still, it is so generous of him to think of me. I must admit, it's still easier for me to hit the keys than to grip a pen and write without wobbling. And then you went to all that trouble to set up the e-mail connection for me while you were here, too. First it was the mobile phone, and now this – you are certainly turning me into a very twenty-first-century grandmother! Maybe your mum will have time to e-mail me sometimes – I've given her the address. It does seem to be so much quicker to dash off than a letter – or I feel certain it will be once I've got the hang of it. And you can tell Richard I've been practising my chess, against the machine. I shall be able to give him a much better game next time he comes to visit!

I also want to say again how much I enjoyed having you and Richard to stay these last few days. Wasn't it funny, Richard insisting upon going back to the New Forest to play Pooh sticks? I'm not sure I am supposed to tell you this, but he whispered to me that it was because last time he had been longing to take hold of your hand while you leaned over the railing, so he wanted to go again, so that he could hold hands with you this time. And what a lovely dinner Richard cooked for us on Sunday! Your grandad always used to expect a roast dinner on a Sunday, beef or lamb or chicken with roast potatoes and two or three different vegetables. I sometimes felt as though I spent all morning on a Sunday, after church, peeling and chopping and basting. What Richard produced took half the time, and was just as tasty. I didn't even notice there was no meat in it until you pointed it out. I must ask Kirsty if she can get some of that balsamic vinegar for me, next time she goes into Winchester. Really, Richard is as good as one of those television chefs – and a lot less bossy and rude than some of them seem to be!

Well, I shall press the 'send' button now, like you showed me, and hope that I've got it right!

With love from Gran xx

From: Margaret Hayton
[margarethayton@yahoo.co.uk]
Sent: 26/10/05 20:20
To: Ellen Reed [gran-reed@ntlworld.com]

Dear Gran,

I'm so glad that you are using the computer! I wasn't sure that you would want it really – I wondered if you were just being polite, earlier, when you said how pleased you were. And we both had a lovely time with you, so 'thank you for having us', as Mum always taught me to say when I was a little girl.

It was just so satisfying to see you back in your own home again, Gran. With Kirsty coming on Sundays as well for a while, I'm sure you'll be able to cope. I thought you were getting about better than I've seen you for ages, since before you sprained your ankle, in fact. Did you manage to make it to the post office on the frame by yourself to get your pension today, like you said you might?

And don't worry, Gran, I shall still keep writing you proper letters as well as sending you e-mails.

Lots of love,

Margaret xx

42 Gledhill Street
Ipswich

27 October 2005

Darling Pete,

Margaret is staying over at Richard's flat again tonight after her hostel meeting. The two of them seem to be very much an item now. They are at his place most nights when he is in Ipswich, which is where he mainly seems to be in the evenings at present while Parliament is still on holiday (or 'not sitting', I think they say, don't they?). Although they do come round here a lot, and even take me out for drinks, which is nice. Last night Richard cooked a lovely pasta dinner for us all, with these Italian wild mushrooms. At first I wasn't keen on the texture, they were a bit rubbery, but when you got used to the chewiness they were certainly very tasty. Margaret tells me she is thinking of becoming a vegetarian. She is probably very sensible – Persephone has lent me a book all about factory farming and it is enough to turn you right off meat. But I don't think I could do without my chops, and a nice steak once in a while.

It is quieter again here, what with Margaret always being either busy with school, or visiting her gran, and out so often in the evenings, leaving me and Snuffs by ourselves. But I find I don't mind it any longer. I quite like the extra space, and Margaret has kindly let me bring her computer down to the kitchen, and says I can use it whenever I like. I'm quite the expert, you know, since my course at the college in the summer! A few Sunday afternoons ago, Margaret and Richard came round and we drafted an application to the charities fund at work, and I did all the typing in, and when they'd gone I made it look really professional, with fancy typefaces and everything. We want to get some money to set up that support scheme I mentioned to you, the one to give a helping hand to people like poor Helen. Margaret was talking about the plan as 'Friends for Helen', and I said, you should really call it that, so that her name will be remembered.

Summer really seems to be stretching on late into the

autumn this year. September was blazing, and it's stayed very dry even these past few weeks, and there's not been a single frost to speak of so far. I've hardly had to put on a cardy yet, in the house. The only green bits left in the lawn are the clover and the moss. It makes me glad I haven't treated it with weedkiller – which Persephone says is death to all sorts of wildlife, anyway. Snuffy spent most of her time in the really hot weather at the back of the flower bed, in a cool spot under the forsythia. She seems finally to have worked out what to do in the heat. Do you remember when she was a pup, how she was always wanting to chase her ball in the garden in the full sun, even though it made her pant fit to burst? And how she used to whimper when we took the ball away and told her to lie down?

Pete, I think this is the last letter I am going to write to you. I shall pop it in the envelope now, and then in the morning on the way to work I shall go round by the park, and put it with all the others in the old cashbox in the hollow tree. Do you remember, sweetheart, how we used to leave little messages for each other there, when we were first going out? That's where I scattered your ashes – two years ago now – in the park, there by the hollow tree. It will always be our special place.

You know that I will always love you, Petey, that hasn't changed, and I don't think I shall ever stop missing you, either. But I don't want to lie to Margaret any more. I told her you were working on the oil rigs! At first it was just to give me a way of carrying on writing letters to you without Margaret thinking it odd, but after a while it came to help me, too, to be able to imagine that you were just away somewhere, and coming back in a few weeks or months. I thought you might have rather liked your glamorous new job. If you were going to live on in my imagination I decided it might as well be doing something with a little excitement to it, and the wind in your hair, after twenty-five years behind a desk at the Inland Revenue, and then that last horrible one, in and out of hospital.

Anyway, I don't think I need to keep writing to you any more. They have been more than just letters for me, Pete – even more than love letters. They have been my refuge. It has really helped, feeling that I could still tell you about what I was doing, even just the little things that nobody else would care about. But I think that now I am ready to get on with being on my own and living my life without you.

Goodbye, love,

Cora xxx

IPSWICH TOWN CRIER WEDNESDAY 21 DECEMBER 2005

MP ATTENDS TOWN'S FIRST GAY 'WEDDING'

Ipswich MP Mr Richard Slater today attended the first ever civil partnership ceremony to be held at the town's register office. This is the first day upon which the formation of legal unions between gay and lesbian couples is permitted under the Civil Partnerships Act 2004. Such partnerships will give those concerned certain mutual legal rights and duties akin to those enjoyed by heterosexual married couples. Ipswich Borough Council is among a number of progressive local authorities choosing to exercise a discretion in the legislation to offer a formal ceremony to gay couples entering into a partnership agreement.

Pat Westley and Pat Turner, who tied the knot today, have been together for eight years, and both said how delighted they are to have this chance to formalise their relationship publicly in front of family and friends. Following a party this evening, the two Pats will be honeymooning in the Greek islands, although they refused to confirm whether or not their itinerary is to include Lesbos.

Asked whether his attendance at today's ceremony may be taken as an indication of his support for the further extension of gay rights, Mr Richard Slater said, 'It indicates, first and foremost, my affection and support for Pat and Pat.'

Mr Slater, who this summer came close to forfeiting his front bench post in a scandal involving a prostitute, was seen to arrive at the register office arm in arm with a mystery dark-haired woman. It seems that Mr Slater's days of loose living may be over. Asked whether the people of Ipswich might be hearing wedding bells ringing for him in the near future, he merely smiled enigmatically as he commented, 'Anything is possible.'

CAROLE MATTHEWS

You Drive Me Crazy

The last place Anna Terry expects to fall in love is in the waiting room of her divorce lawyer's office. But that's where she meets Nick Diamond and Cupid's arrow strikes . . .

Anna's had more than her fair share of heartache. Her first marriage ended before her pregnancy was over, and her second husband has disappeared, leaving her with two children and not a penny to her name. Nick's luck hasn't been any better: his wife has run off with the local butcher and his second-hand car dealership is in chaos.

When Anna gets a job as Nick's secretary, what starts as a mild flirtation soon accelerates into overdrive – but that's before their ex-partners show up and they're all in for a bumpy ride.

Praise for Carole Matthews' previous bestsellers:

'Carole Matthews writes of the travails of romance, relationships and motherhood with hilarity, tenderness and despair . . . a story loaded with laughter, tears and hope' Adriana Trigiani

'Touching. Feelgood. Funny' *Heat*

'Matthews is one of the few writers who can rival Marian Keyes' gift for telling heart-warming tales with buckets of charm and laughs' *Daily Record*

'Hilarious . . . Saucy, but nice' *Daily Express*

0 7553 3210 5

headline
<u>review</u>

PAULINE MCLYNN

Summer In The City

Lucy White can't quite believe what's happened to her happy, ordinary life. Ending up homeless – not to mention husbandless – has come as an almighty shock. All she wants to do is lie low for a while, but when she arrives in a quiet street in South London she's in for a surprise.

The residents of Farewell Square are anything but quiet. There's a housewife with a secret that needs to be shared, a publicist whose behaviour outside office hours would shock his clients and an artist who can't seem to control her lodgers. They're as intrigued by Lucy as she is by them, and as she's drawn into their midst, she realises that life can be kind as well as cruel. And that no one has to be lonely if they don't want to be.

'Pauline McLynn is still fondly remembered for her role as Mrs Doyle in the Channel 4 sitcom Father Ted but her career as an author may yet prove her most memorable move' *Scotland on Sunday*

'Mrs Doyle may be gone, but long live Pauline McLynn' *Irish World*

'She is a gifted storyteller as well as an exceptional comic actress' *Sunday Express*

0 7553 2635 0

headline
review

You can buy any of these other **Headline Review** titles from your bookshop or *direct from the publisher.*

FREE P&P AND UK DELIVERY
(Overseas and Ireland £3.50 per book)

My Fabulous Divorce	Clare Dowling	£6.99
Amazing Grace	Clare Dowling	£7.99
Welcome to the Real World	Carole Matthews	£6.99
You Drive Me Crazy	Carole Matthews	£6.99
Summer in the City	Pauline McLynn	£6.99
Wives of Bath	Wendy Holden	£7.99
Azur Like It	Wendy Holden	£7.99
The Wedding Day	Catherine Alliot	£7.99
Not That Kind of Girl	Catherine Alliot	£6.99
Sparkles	Louise Bagshawe	£6.99
The One You Really Want	Jill Mansell	£7.99
Falling For You	Jill Mansell	£7.99

TO ORDER SIMPLY CALL THIS NUMBER

01235 400 414

or visit our website: www.madaboutbooks.com

Prices and availability subject to change without notice.